JEANNE OF
THE MARSHES

MORE WILDSIDE CLASSICS

JEANNE OF THE MARSHES

E. PHILLIPS OPPENHEIM

WILDSIDE PRESS

JEANNE OF THE MARSHES

This edition published 2005 by Wildside Press, LLC.
www.wildsidepress.com

BOOK I

CHAPTER I

The Princess opened her eyes at the sound of her maid's approach. She turned her head impatiently toward the door.

"Annette," she said coldly, "did you misunderstand me? Did I not say that I was on no account to be disturbed this afternoon?"

Annette was the picture of despair. Eyebrows and hands betrayed alike both her agitation of mind and her nationality.

"Madame," she said, "did I not say so to monsieur? I begged him to call again. I told him that madame was lying down with a bad headache, and that it was as much as my place was worth to disturb her. What did he answer? Only this. That it would be as much as my place was worth if I did not come up and tell you that he was here to see you on a very urgent matter. Indeed, madame, he was very, very impatient with me."

"Of whom are you talking?" the Princess asked.

"But of Major Forrest, madame," Annette declared. "It is he who waits below."

The Princess closed her eyes for a moment and then slowly opened them. She stretched out her hand, and from a table by her side took up a small gilt mirror.

"Turn on the lights, Annette," she commanded.

The maid illuminated the darkened room. The Princess gazed at herself in the mirror, and reaching out again took a small powder-puff from its case and gently dabbed her face. Then she laid both mirror and powder-puff back in their places.

"You will tell monsieur," she said, "that I am very unwell indeed, but that since he is here and his business is urgent I will see him. Turn out the lights, Annette. I am not fit to be seen. And move my couch a little, so."

"Madame is only a little pale," the maid said reassuringly. "That makes nothing. These Englishwomen have all too much colour. I go to tell monsieur."

She disappeared, and the Princess lay still upon her couch, thinking. Soon she heard steps outside, and with a little sigh she turned her head toward the door. The man who entered was tall, and of the ordinary type of well-born Englishmen. He was carefully dressed, and his somewhat scanty hair was arranged to the best advantage. His features were hard and lifeless. His eyes were just a shade too close together. The maid ushered him in and withdrew at once.

"Come and sit by my side, Nigel, if you want to talk to me," the Princess said. "Walk softly, please. I really have a headache."

"No wonder, in this close room," the man muttered, a little ungraciously. "It smells as though you had been burning incense here."

"It suits me," the Princess answered calmly, "and it happens to be my room. Bring that chair up here and say what you have to say."

The man obeyed in silence. When he had made himself quite comfortable, he raised her hand, the one which was nearest to him, to his lips, and afterwards retained it in his own.

"Forgive me if I seem unsympathetic, Ena," he said. "The fact is, everything has been getting on my nerves for the last few days, and my luck seems dead out."

She looked at him curiously. She was past middle age, and her face showed signs of the wear and tear of life. But she still had fine eyes, and the rejuvenating arts of Bond Street had done their best for her.

"What is the matter, Nigel?" she asked. "Have the cards been going against you?"

He frowned and hesitated for a moment before replying.

"Ena," he said, "between us two there is an ancient bargain, and that is that we should tell the truth to one another. I will tell you what it is that is worrying me most. I have suspected it for some time, but this afternoon it was absolutely obvious. There is a sort of feeling at the club. I can't exactly describe it, but I am conscious of it directly I come into the room. For several days I have scarcely been able to get a rubber. This afternoon, when I cut in with Harewood and Mildmay and another fellow, two of them made some sort of an excuse and went off. I pretended not to notice it, of course, but there it was. The thing was apparent, and it is the very devil!"

Again she looked at him closely.

"There is nothing tangible?" she asked. "No complaint, or scandal, or anything of that sort?"

He rejected the suggestion with scorn.

"No!" he said. "I am not such an idiot as that. All the same there is the feeling. They don't care to play bridge with me. There is only young Engleton who takes my part, and so far as playing bridge for money is concerned, he would be worth the whole lot put together if only I could get him away from them — make up a little party somewhere, and have him to myself for a week or two."

The Princess was thoughtful.

"To go abroad at this time of the year," she remarked, "is almost impossible. Besides, you have only just come back."

"Absolutely impossible," he answered. "Besides, I shouldn't care to do it just now. It looks like running away. A week or so ago you were talking of taking a villa down the river. I wondered whether you had thought any more of it."

The Princess shook her head.

"I dare not," she answered. "I have gone already further than I meant to. This house and the servants and carriages are costing me a small fortune. I dare not even look at my bills. Another house is not to be thought of."

Major Forrest looked gloomily at the shining tip of his patent boot.

"It's jolly hard luck," he muttered. "A quiet place somewhere in the country, with Engleton and you and myself, and another one or two, and I should be able to pull through. As it is, I feel inclined to chuck it all."

The Princess looked at him curiously. He was certainly more than ordinarily pale, and the hand which rested upon the side of his chair was twitching a little nervously.

"My dear Nigel," she said, "do go to the chiffonier there and help yourself to a drink. I hate to see you white to the lips, and trembling as though death itself were at your elbow. Borrow a little false courage, if you lack the real thing."

The man obeyed her suggestion with scarcely a protest.

"I had hoped, Ena," he remarked a little peevishly, "to have found you more sympathetic."

"You are so sorry for yourself," she answered, "that you seem scarcely to need my sympathy. However, sit down and talk to me reasonably."

"I talk reasonably enough," he answered, "but I really am hard up against it. Don't think I have come begging. I know you've done all you can, and it's a matter with me now of more than a few hundreds. My only hope is Engleton. Can't you suggest anything?"

The Princess rested her head slightly upon the long slender fingers of her right hand. Bond Street had taken care of her complexion, but the veins in her hand were blue, and art had no means of concealing a certain sharpness of features and the thin lines about the eyes, nameless suggestions of middle age. Yet she was still a handsome woman. She knew how to dress, and how to make the best of herself. She had the foreigner's instinct for clothes, and her figure was still irreproachable. She sat and looked with a sort of calculating interest at the man who for years had come as near touching her heart as any of his sex. Curiously enough she knew that this new aspect in which he now presented himself, this incipient cowardice — the first-fruits of weakening nerves — did not and could not affect her feelings for him. She saw him now almost for the first time with the mask dropped, no longer cold, cynical and calculating, but a man moved to his shallow depths by what might well seem to him, a dweller in the narrow ways of life, as a tragedy. It looked at her out of his grey eyes. It showed itself in the twitching of his lips. For many years he had lived upon a little less than nothing a year. Now for the first time his means of livelihood were threatened. His long-suffering acquaintances had left him alone at the card-table.

"You disappoint me, Nigel," she said. "I hate to see a man weaken. There is nothing against you. Don't act as though there could be. As to this little house-party you were speaking of, I only wish I could think of something to help you. By the by, what are you doing tonight?"

"Nothing," he answered, "except that Engleton is expecting me to dine with him."

"I have an idea," the Princess said slowly. "It may not come to anything, but it is worth trying. Have you met my new admirer, Mr. Cecil de la Borne?"

Forrest shook his head.

"Do you mean a dandified-looking boy whom you were driving with in the Park yesterday?"

The Princess nodded.

"We met him a week or so ago," she answered, "and he has been very attentive. He has a country place down in Norfolk, which from his description is, I should think, like a castle in Hermitland. Jeanne and I are dining with him tonight at the Savoy. You and Engleton must come, too. I can arrange it. It is just possible that we may be able to manage something. He told me yesterday that he was going back to Norfolk very soon. I fancy that he has a brother who keeps rather a strict watch over him, and he is not allowed to stay up in town very long at a time."

"I know the name," Forrest remarked. "They are a very old Roman Catholic family. We'll come and dine, if you say that you can arrange it. But I don't see how we can all hope to get an invitation out of him on such a short acquaintance."

The Princess was looking thoughtful.

"Leave it to me," she said. "I have an idea. Be at the Savoy at a quarter past eight, and bring Lord Ronald."

Forrest took up his hat. He looked at the Princess with something very much like admiration in his face. For years he had dominated this woman. Today, for the first time, she had had the upper hand.

"We will be there all right," he said. "Engleton will only be too glad to be where Jeanne is. I suppose young De la Borne is the same way."

The Princess sighed.

"Every one," she remarked, "is so shockingly mercenary!"

CHAPTER II

The Princess helped herself to a salted almond and took her first sip of champagne. The almonds were crisp and the champagne dry. She was wearing a new and most successful dinner-gown of black velvet, and she was quite sure that in the subdued light no one could tell that the pearls in the collar around her neck were imitation. Her afternoon's indisposition was quite forgotten. She nodded at her host approvingly.

"Cecil," she said, "it is really very good of you to take in my two friends like this. Major Forrest has just arrived from Ostend, and I was very anxious to hear about the people I know there, and the frocks, and all the rest of it. Lord Ronald always amuses me, too. I suppose most people would call him foolish, but to me he only seems very, very young."

The young man who was host raised his glass and bowed towards the Princess.

"I can assure you," he said, "that it has given me a great deal of pleasure to make the acquaintance of Major Forrest and Lord Ronald, but it has given me more pleasure still to be able to do anything for you. You know that."

She looked at him quickly, and down at her plate. Such glances had become almost a habit with her, but they were still effectual. Cecil de la Borne leaned across towards Forrest.

"I hear that you have been to Ostend lately, Major Forrest," he said. "I thought of going over myself a little later in the season for a few days."

"I wouldn't if I were you," Forrest answered. "It is overrun just now with the wrong sort of people. There is nothing to do but gamble, which doesn't interest me particularly; or dress in a ridiculous costume and paddle about in a few feet of water, which appeals to me even less."

"You were there a little early in the season," the Princess reminded him.

Major Forrest assented.

"A little later," he admitted, "it may be tolerable. On the whole, however, I was disappointed."

Lord Ronald spoke for the first time. He was very thin, very long, and very tall. He wore a somewhat unusually high collar, but he was very carefully, not to say exactly, dressed. His studs and links and waistcoat buttons were obviously fresh from the Rue de la Paix. The set of his tie was perfection. His features were not unintelligent, but his mouth was weak.

"One thing I noticed about Ostend," he remarked, "they charge you a frightful price for everything. We never got a glass of champagne there like this."

"I am glad you like it," their host said. "From what you say I don't imagine that I should care for Ostend. I am not rich enough to gamble, and as I have lived by the sea all my days, bathing does not attract me particularly. I think I shall stay at home." "By the by, where is your home, Mr. De la Borne?" the Princess asked. "You told me once, but I have forgotten. Some of your English names are so queer that I cannot even pronounce them, much more remember them."

"I live in a very small village in Norfolk, called Salthouse," Cecil de la Borne answered. "It is quite close to a small market-town called Wells, if you know where that is. I don't suppose you do, though," he added. "It is an out-of-the-way corner of the world."

The Princess shook her head.

"I never heard of it," she said. "I am going to motor through Norfolk soon, though, and I think that I shall call upon you."

Cecil de la Borne looked up eagerly.

"I wish you would," he begged, "and bring your step-daughter. You can't imagine," he added, with a glance at the girl who was sitting at his left hand, "how much pleasure it would give me. The roads are really not bad, and every one admits that the country is delightful."

"You had better be careful," the Princess said, "or we may take you at your word. I warn you, though, that it would be a regular invasion. Major Forrest and Lord Ronald are talking about coming with us."

"It's just an idea," Forrest remarked carelessly. "I wouldn't mind it myself, but I don't fancy we should get Engleton away from town before Goodwood."

"Well, I like that," Engleton remarked. "Forrest's a lot keener on these social functions than I am. As a matter of fact I am for the tour, on one condition."

"And that?" the Princess asked.

"That you come in my car," Lord Ronald answered. "I haven't really had a chance to try it yet, but it's a sixty horse Mercedes, and it's fitted up for touring. Take the lot of us easy, luggage and everything."

"I think it would be perfectly delightful," the Princess declared. "Do you really mean it?"

"Of course I do," Lord Ronald answered. "It's too hot for

town, and I'm rather great on rusticating, myself."

"I think this is charming," the Princess declared. "Here we have one of our friends with a car and another with a house. But seriously, Cecil, we mustn't think of coming to you. There would be too many of us."

"The more the better," Cecil said eagerly. "If you really want to attempt anything in the shape of a rest-cure, I can recommend my home thoroughly. I am afraid," he added, with a shrug of the shoulders, "that I cannot recommend it for anything else."

"A rest," the Princess declared, "is exactly what we want. Life here is becoming altogether too strenuous. We started the season a little early. I am perfectly certain that we could not possibly last till the end. Until I arrived in London with an heiress under my charge, I had no idea that I was such a popular person."

The girl who was sitting on the other side of their host spoke almost for the first time. She was evidently quite young, and her pale cheeks, dark full eyes, and occasional gestures, indicated clearly enough something foreign in her nationality. She addressed no one in particular, but she looked toward Forrest.

"That is one of the things," she said, "which puzzles me. I do not understand it at all. It seems as though every one is liked or disliked, here in London at any rate, according to the amount of money they have."

"Upon my word, Miss Jeanne, it isn't so with every one," Lord Ronald interposed hastily.

She glanced at him indifferently.

"There may be exceptions," she said. "I am speaking of the great number."

"For Heaven's sake, child, don't be cynical!" the Princess remarked. "There is no worse pose for a child of your age."

"It is not a pose at all," Jeanne answered calmly. "I do not want to be cynical, and I do not want to have unkind thoughts. But tell me, Lord Ronald, honestly, do you think that every one would have been as kind to a girl just out of boarding-school as they have been to me if it were not that I have so much money?"

"I cannot tell about others," Lord Ronald answered. "I can only answer for myself."

His last words were almost whispered in the girl's ears, but she only shrugged her shoulders and did not return his gaze. Their host, who had been watching them, frowned slightly. He was beginning to think that Engleton was scarcely as pleasant a fellow as he had thought him.

"Well," he said, "Miss Le Mesurier will find out in time who are really her friends."

"It is a safe plan," Major Forrest remarked, "and a pleasant one, to believe in everybody until they want something from you. Then is the time for distrust."

Jeanne sighed.

"And by that time, perhaps," she said, "one's affections are hopelessly engaged. I think that it is a very difficult world."

The Princess shrugged her shoulders.

"Three months," she remarked, "is not a long time. Wait, my dear child, until you have at least lived through a single season before you commit yourself to any final opinions."

Their host intervened. He was beginning to find the conversation dull. He was far more interested in another matter.

"Let us talk about that visit," he said to the Princess. "I do wish that you could make up your mind to come. Of course, I haven't any amusements to offer you, but you could rest as thoroughly as you like. They say that the air is the finest in England. There is always bridge, you know, for the evenings, and if Miss Jeanne likes bathing, my gardens go down to the beach."

"It sounds delightful," the Princess said, "and exactly what we want. We have a good many invitations, but I have not cared to accept any of them, for I do not think that Jeanne would care much for the life at an ordinary country house. I myself," she continued, with perfect truth, "am not squeamish, but the last house-party I was at was certainly not the place for a very young girl."

"Make up your mind, then, and say yes," Cecil de la Borne pleaded.

"You shall hear from us within the next few days," the Princess answered. "I really believe that we shall come."

The little party left the restaurant a few minutes later on their way into the foyer for coffee. The Princess contrived to pass out with Forrest as her companion.

"I think," she said under her breath, "that this is the best opportunity you could possibly have. We shall be quite alone down there, and perhaps it would be as well that you were out of London for a few weeks. If it does not come to anything we can easily make an excuse to get away."

Forrest nodded.

"But who is this young man, De la Borne?" he asked. "I don't mean that. I know who he is, of course, but why should he invite perfect strangers to stay with him?"

The Princess smiled faintly.

"Can't you see," she answered, "that he is simply a silly boy?

He is only twenty-four years old, and I think that he cannot have seen much of the world. He told me that he had just been abroad for the first time. He fancies that he is a little in love with me, and he is dazzled, of course, by the idea of Jeanne's fortune. He wants to play the host to us. Let him. I should be glad enough to get away for a few weeks, if only to escape from these pestering letters. I do think that one's tradespeople might let one alone until the end of the season."

Forrest, who was feeling a good deal braver since dinner, on the whole favoured the idea.

"I do not see," he remarked, "why it should not work out very well indeed. There will be nothing to do in the evenings except to play bridge, and no one to interfere."

"Besides which," the Princess remarked, "you will be out of London for a few weeks, and I dare say that if you keep away from the clubs for a time and lose a few rubbers when you get back your little trouble may blow over."

"I suppose," Forrest remarked thoughtfully, "this young De la Borne has no people living with him, guardians, or that sort of thing?"

"No one of any account," the Princess answered. "His father and mother are both dead. I am afraid, though, he will not be of any use to you, for from what I can hear he is quite poor. However, Engleton ought to be quite enough if we can keep him in the humour for playing."

"Ask him a few more questions about the place," Forrest said. "If it seems all right, I should like to start as soon as possible."

They had their coffee at a little table in the foyer, which was already crowded with people. Their conversation was often interrupted by the salutations of passing acquaintances. Jeanne alone looked about her with any interest. To the others, this sort of thing — the music of the red-coated band, the flowers, and the passing throngs of people, the handsomest and the weariest crowd in the world — were only part of the treadmill of life.

"By the by, Mr. De la Borne," the Princess asked, "how much longer are you going to stay in London?"

"I must go back tomorrow or the next day," the young man answered, a little gloomily. "I sha'n't mind it half so much if you people only make up your minds to pay me that visit."

The Princess motioned to him to draw his chair a little nearer to hers.

"If we take this tour at all," she remarked, "I should like to start the day after tomorrow. There is a perfectly hideous function on Thursday which I should so like to miss, and the stupidest dinner-party on earth at night. Should you be home by then, do you think?"

"If there were any chance of your coming at all," the young man answered eagerly, "I should leave by the first train tomorrow morning."

"I think," the Princess declared softly, "that we will come. Don't think me rude if I say that we could not possibly be more bored than we are in London. I do not want to take Jeanne to any of the country house-parties we have been invited to. You know why. She really is such a child, and I am afraid that if she gets any wrong ideas about things she may want to go back to the convent. She has hinted at it more than once already."

"There will be nothing of that sort at Salt-house," Cecil de la Borne declared eagerly. "You see, I sha'n't have any guests at all except just yourselves. Don't you think that would be best?"

"I do, indeed," the Princess assented, "and mind, you are not to make any special preparations for us. For my part, I simply want a little rest before we go abroad again, and we really want to come to you feeling the same way that one leaves one's home for lodgings in a farmhouse. You will understand this, won't you, Cecil?" she added earnestly, laying her fingers upon his arm, "or we shall not come."

"It shall be just as you say," he answered. "As a matter of fact the Red Hall is little more than a large farmhouse, and there is very little preparation which I could make for you in a day or a day and a half. You shall come and see how a poor English countryman lives, whose lands and income have shrivelled up together. If you are dull you will not blame me, I know, for all that you have to do is to go away."

The Princess rose and put out her hand.

"It is settled, then," she declared. "Thank you, dear Mr. Host, for your very delightful dinner. Jeanne and I have to go on to Harlingham House for an hour or two, the last of these terrible entertainments, I am glad to say. Do send me a note round in the morning, with the exact name of your house, and some idea of the road we must follow, so that we do not get lost. I suppose you two," she added, turning to Forrest and Lord Ronald, "will not mind starting a day or two before we had planned?"

"Not in the least," they assured her.

"And Miss Le Mesurier?" Cecil de la Borne asked. "Will she really not mind giving up some of these wonderful entertainments?"

Jeanne smiled upon him brilliantly. It was a smile which came so seldom, and which, when it did come, transformed her face so utterly, that she seemed like a different person.

"I shall be very glad, indeed," she said, "to leave London. I am looking forward so much to seeing what the English country is like."

"It will make me very happy," Cecil de la Borne said, bowing over her hand, "to try and show you."

Her eyes seemed to pass through him, to look out of the crowded room, as though indeed they had found their way into some corner of the world where the things which make life lie. It was a lapse from which she recovered almost immediately, but when she looked at him, and with a little farewell nod withdrew her hand, the transforming gleam had passed away.

"And there is the sea, too," she remarked, looking backwards as they passed out. "I am longing to see that again."

CHAPTER III

Perhaps there was never a moment in the lives of these two men when their utter and radical dissimilarity, physically as well as in the larger ways, was more strikingly and absolutely manifest. Like a great sea animal, huge, black-bearded, bronzed, magnificent, but uncouth, Andrew de la Borne, in the oilskins and overalls of a village fisherman, stood in the great bare hall in front of the open fireplace, reckless of his drippings, at first only mildly amused by the half cynical, half angry survey of the very elegant young man who had just descended the splendid oak staircase, with its finely carved balustrade, black and worm-eaten, Cecil de la Borne stared at his brother with the angry disgust of one whose sense of all that is holiest stands outraged. Slim, of graceful though somewhat undersized figure, he was conscious of having attained perfection in matters which he reckoned of no small importance. His grey tweed suit fitted him like a glove, his tie was a perfect blend between the colour of his eyes and his clothes, his shoes were of immaculate shape and polish, his socks had been selected with care in the Rue de la Paix. His hair was brushed until it shone with the proper amount of polish, his nails were perfectly manicured, even his cigarette came from the dealer whose wares were the caprice of the moment. That his complexion was pallid and that underneath his eyes were faint blue lines, which were certainly not the hall-marks of robust health, disturbed him not at all. These things were correct. Health was by no means a desideratum in the set to which he was striving to belong. He looked through his eyeglass at his brother and groaned.

"Really, Andrew," he said calmly, but with an undernote of anger trembling in his tone, "I am surprised to see you like this! You might, I think, have had a little more consideration. Can't you realize what a sight you are, and what a mess you're making!"

Andrew took off his cap and shook it, so that a little shower of salt water splashed on to the polished floor.

"Never mind, Cecil," he said good-humouredly. "You've all the deportment that's necessary in this family. And salt water doesn't stain. These boards have been washed with it many a time."

The young man's face lost none of his irritation.

"But what on earth have you been doing?" he exclaimed. "Where have you been to get in a state like that?"

Andrew's face was suddenly overcast. It did not please him to think of those last few hours.

"I had to go out to bring a mad woman home," he said. "Kate Caynsard was out in her catboat a day like this. It was suicide if I hadn't reached her in time."

"You — did reach her in time?" the young man asked quickly.

Andrew turned to face the questioner, and the eyes of the brothers met. Again the differences between them seemed to be suddenly and marvellously accentuated. Andrew's cheeks, bronzed and hardened with a life spent wholly out of doors, were glistening still with the salt water which dripped down from his hair and hung in sparkling globules from his beard. Cecil was paler than ever; there was something almost furtive in that swift insistent look. Perhaps he recognized something of what was in the other's mind. At any rate the good-nature left his manner — his tone took to itself a sterner note.

"I came back," he said grimly. "I should not have come back alone. She was hard to save, too," he added, after a moment's pause.

"She is mad," Cecil muttered. "A queer lot, all the Caynsards."

"She is as sane as you or I," his brother answered. "She does rash things, and she chooses to treat her life as though it were a matter of no consequence. She took a fifty to one chance at the bar, and she nearly lost. But, by heaven, you should have seen her bring my little boat down the creek, with the tide swelling, and a squall right down on the top of us. It was magnificent. Cecil!"

"Well?"

"Why does Kate Caynsard treat her life as though it were of less value than the mackerel she lowers her line for? Do you know?"

The younger man dropped his eyeglass and shrugged his shoulders contemptuously.

"Since when," he demanded, "have I shown any inclination to play the village Lothario? Thick ankles and robust health have never appealed to me — I prefer the sicklier graces of civilization."

"Kate Caynsard," Andrew said thoughtfully, "is not of the villagers. She leads their life, but her birth is better on her father's side, at any rate, than our own."

"If I might be allowed to make the suggestion," Cecil said, regarding his brother with supercilious distaste, "don't you think it would be just as well to change your clothes before our guests arrive?"

"Why should I?" Andrea asked calmly.

"They are not my friends. I scarcely know even their names. I entertain them at your request. Why should I be ashamed of my oilskins? They are in accord with the life I live here. I make no pretence, you see, Cecil," he added, with a faintly amused smile, "at being an ornamental member of Society."

His brother regarded him with something very much like disgust.

"No!" he said sarcastically. "No one could accuse you of that."

Something in his tone seemed to suggest to Andrew a new idea. He looked down at the clothes he wore beneath his oilskins — the clothes almost of a working man. He glanced for a moment at his hands, hardened and blistered with the actual toil which he loved — and he looked his brother straight in the face.

"Cecil," he said, "I believe you're ashamed of me."

"Of course I am," the younger man answered brutally. "It's your own fault. You choose to make a fisherman or a labouring man of yourself. I haven't seen you in a decent suit of clothes for years. You won't dress for dinner. Your hands and skin are like a ploughboy's. And, damn it all, you're my elder brother! I've got to introduce you to my friends as the head of the De la Bornes, and practically their host. No wonder I don't like it!"

There was a moment's silence. If his words hurt, Andrew made no sign. With a shrug of the shoulders he turned towards the staircase.

"There is no reason," he remarked, carelessly enough, "why I should inflict the humiliation of my presence on you or on your friends. I am going down to the Island. You shall entertain your friends and play the host to your heart's content. It will be more comfortable for both of us."

Cecil prided himself upon a certain impassivity of features and manner which some fin de siecle oracle of the cities had pronounced good form, but he was not wholly able to conceal his relief. Such an arrangement was entirely to his liking. It solved the situation satisfactorily in more ways than one.

"It's a thundering good idea, Andrew, if you're sure you'll be comfortable there," he declared. "I don't believe you would get on with my friends a bit. They're not your sort. Seems like turning you out of your own house, though."

"It is of no consequence," Andrew said coldly. "I shall be perfectly comfortable."

"You see," Cecil continued, "they're not keen on sport at all, and you don't play bridge — "

Andrew had already disappeared. Cecil turned back into the hall and lit a cigarette.

"Phew! What a relief!" he muttered to himself. "If only he has the sense to keep away all the time!"

He rang the bell, which was answered by a butler newly imported from town.

"Clear away all this mess, James," Cecil ordered, pointing in disgust to the wet places upon the floor, and the still dripping southwester, "and serve tea here in an hour, or directly my friends arrive — tea, and whisky and soda, and liqueurs, you know, with sandwiches and things."

"I will do my best, sir," the man answered. "The kitchen arrangements are a little — behind the times, if I might venture to say so."

"I know, I know," Cecil answered irritably. "The place has been allowed to go on anyhow while I was away. Do what you can, and let them know outside that they must make room for one, or perhaps two automobiles. . . ."

Upstairs Andrew was rapidly throwing a few things together. With an odd little laugh he threw into the bottom of a wardrobe an unopened parcel of new clothes and a dress suit which had been carefully brushed. In less than twenty minutes he had left the house by the back way, with a small portmanteau poised easily upon his massive shoulders. As he turned from the long ill-kept avenue, with its straggling wind-smitten trees all exposed to the tearing ocean gales, into the high road, a great automobile swung round the corner and slackened speed. Major Forrest leaned out and addressed him.

"Can you tell me if this is the Red Hall, my man — Mr. De la Borne's place?" he asked.

Andrew nodded, without a glance at the veiled and shrouded women who were leaning forward to hear his answer.

"The next avenue is the front way," he said. "Mind how you turn in — the corner is rather sharp."

He spoke purposely in broad Norfolk, and passed on.

"What a Goliath!" Engleton remarked.

"I should like to sketch him," the Princess drawled. "His shoulders were magnificent."

But neither of them had any idea that they had spoken with the owner of the Red Hall.

CHAPTER IV

About halfway through dinner that night, Cecil de la Borne drew a long sigh of relief. At last his misgivings were set at rest. His party was going to be, was already, in fact, pronounced, a success. A glance at his fair neighbour, however, who was lighting her third or fourth Russian cigarette since the caviare, sent a shiver of thankfulness through his whole being. What a sensible fellow Andrew had been to clear out. This sort of thing would not have appealed to him at all.

"My dear Cecil," the Princess declared, "I call this perfectly delightful. Jeanne and I have wanted so much to see you in your own home. Jeanne, isn't this nicer, ever so much nicer, than anything you had imagined?"

Jeanne, who was sitting opposite, lifted her remarkable eyes and glanced around with interest.

"Yes," she admitted, "I think that it is! But then, any place that looks in the least like a home is a delightful change after all that rushing about in London."

"I agree with you entirely," Major Forrest declared. "If our friend has disappointed us at all, it is in the absence of that primitiveness which he led us to expect. One perceives that one is drinking Veuve Clicquot of a vintage year, and one suspects the nationality of our host's cook."

"You can have all the primitivism you want if you look out of the windows," Cecil remarked drily. "You will see nothing but a line of stunted trees, and behind, miles of marshes and the greyest sea which ever played upon the land. Listen! You don't hear a sound like that in the cities."

Even as he spoke they heard the dull roar of the north wind booming across the wild empty places which lay between the Red Hall and the sea. A storm of raindrops was flung against the window. The Princess shivered.

"It is an idyll, the last word in the refining of sensations," Major Forrest declared. "You give us sybaritic luxury, and in order that we shall realize it, you provide the background of savagery. In the Carlton one might dine like this and accept it as a matter of course. Appreciation is forced upon us by these suggestions of the wilderness without."

"Not all without, either," Cecil de la Borne remarked, raising his eyeglass and pointing to the walls. "See where my ancestors frown down upon us — you can only just distinguish their bare shapes. No De la Borne has had money enough to have them renovated or even preserved. They have eaten their way into the canvases, and the canvases into the very walls. You see the empty spaces, too. A Reynolds and a Gainsboro' have been cut out from there and sold. I can show you long empty galleries, pictureless, and without a scrap of furniture. We have ghosts like rats, rooms where the curtains and tapestries are falling to pieces from sheer decay. Oh! I can assure you that our primitivism is not wholly external."

He turned from the Princess, who was not greatly interested, to find that for once he had succeeded in riveting the attention of the girl, whose general attitude towards him and the whole world seemed to be one of barely tolerant indifference.

"I should like to see over your house, Mr. De la Borne," she said. "It all sounds very interesting."

"I am afraid," he answered, "that your interest would not survive very long. We have no treasures left, nor anything worth looking at. For generations the De la Bornes have stripped their house and sold their lands to hold their own in the world. I am the last of my race, and there is nothing left for me to sell," he declared, with a momentary bitterness.

"Hadn't you — a half brother?" the Princess asked.

Cecil hesitated for a moment. He had drifted so easily into the position of head of the house. It was so natural. He felt that he filled the place so perfectly.

"I have," he admitted, "but he counts, I am sorry to say, for very little. You are never likely to come across him — nor any other civilized person."

There was a subtle indication in his tone of a desire not to pursue the subject. His guests naturally respected it. There was a moment's silence. Then Cecil once more leaned forward. He hesitated for a moment, even after his lips had parted, as though for some reason he were inclined, after all, to remain silent, but the consciousness that every one was looking at him and expecting him to speak induced him to continue with what, after all, he had suddenly, and for no explicit reason, hesitated to say.

"You spoke, Miss Le Mesurier," he began, "of looking over the house, and, as I told you, there is very little in it worth seeing. And yet I can show you something, not in the house itself, but connected with it, which you might find interesting."

The Princess leaned forward in her chair.

"This sounds so interesting," she murmured. "What is it, Cecil? A haunted chamber?"

Their host shook his head.

"Something far more tangible," he answered, "although in its way quite as remarkable. Hundreds of years ago, smuggling on this coast was not only a means of livelihood for the poor, but the diversion of the rich. I had an ancestor who became very notorious. His name seems to have been a by-word, although he was never caught, or if he was caught, never punished. He built a subterranean way underneath the grounds, leading from the house right to the mouth of one of the creeks. The passage still exists, with great cellars for storing smuggled goods, and a room where the smugglers used to meet."

Jeanne looked at him with parted lips.

"You can show me this?" she asked, "the passage and the cellars?"

Cecil nodded.

"I can," he answered. "Quite a weird place it is, too. The walls are damp, and the cellars themselves are like the vaults of a cathedral. All the time at high tide you can hear the sea thundering over your head. Tomorrow, if you like, we will get torches and explore them."

"I should love to," Jeanne declared. "Can you get out now at the other end?"

Cecil nodded.

"The passage," he said, "starts from a room which was once the library, and ends halfway up the only little piece of cliff there is. It is about thirty feet from the ground, but they had a sort of apparatus for pulling up the barrels, and a rope ladder for the men. The preventive officers would see the boat come up the creek, and would march down from the village, only to find it empty. Of course, they suspected all the time where the things went, but they could not prove it, and as my ancestor was a magistrate and an important man they did not dare to search the house."

The Princess sighed gently.

"Those were the days," she murmured, "in which it must have been worth while to live. Things happened then. Today your ancestor would simply have been called a thief."

"As a matter of fact," Cecil remarked, "I do not think that he himself benefited a penny by any of his exploits. It was simply the love of adventure which led him into it."

"Even if he did," Major Forrest remarked, "that same predatory instinct is alive today in another guise. The whole world is preying upon one another. We are thieves, all of us, to the tips of our fingernails, only our roguery is conducted with due regard to the law."

The Princess smiled faintly as she glanced across the table at the speaker.

"I am afraid," she said, with a little sigh, "that you are right. I do not think that we have really improved with the centuries. My own ancestors sacked towns and held the inhabitants to ransom. Today I sit down to bridge opposite a man with a well-filled purse, and my one idea is to lighten it. Nothing, I am convinced, but the fear of being found out, keeps us reasonably moral."

"If we go on talking like this," Lord Ronald remarked, "we shall make Miss Le Mesurier nervous. She will feel that we, and the whole of the rest of the world, have our eyes upon her money-bags."

"I am absolutely safe," Jeanne answered smiling. "I do not play bridge, and even my signature would be of no use to any one yet."

"But you might imagine us," Lord Ronald continued, "waiting around breathlessly until the happy time arrived when you were of age, and we could pursue our diabolical schemes."

Jeanne shook her head.

"You cannot frighten me, Lord Ronald," she said. "I feel safe from every one. I am only longing for tomorrow, for a chance to explore this wonderful subterranean passage."

"I am afraid," their host remarked, "that you will be disappointed. With the passing of smuggling, the romance of the thing seems to have died. There is nothing now to look at but mouldy walls, a bare room, and any amount of the most hideous fungi. I can promise you that when you have been there for a few minutes your only desire will be to escape."

"I am not so sure," the girl answered. "I think that associations always have an effect on me. I can imagine how one might wait there, near the entrance, hear the soft swish of the oars, look down and see the smugglers, hear perhaps the muffled tramp of men marching from the village. Fancy how breathless it must have been, the excitement, the fear of being caught."

Cecil curled his slight moustache dubiously.

"If you can feel all that in my little bit of underground world," he said, "I shall think that you are even a more wonderful person — "

He dropped his voice and leaned toward her, but Jeanne laughed in his face and interrupted him.

"People who own things," she remarked, "never look upon them with proper reverence. Don't you see that my mother is dying for some bridge?"

CHAPTER V

The Princess was only obeying a faint sign from Forrest. She leaned forward and addressed her host.

"It isn't a bad idea," she declared. "Where are we going to play bridge, Cecil? In some smaller room, I hope. This one is really beginning to get on my nerves a little. There is an ancestor exactly opposite who has fixed me with a luminous and a disapproving eye. And the blank spaces on the wall! Ugh! I feel like a Goth. We are too modern for this place, Cecil."

Their host laughed as he rose and turned towards Jeanne.

"Your mother," he said, "is beginning to be conscious of her environment. I know exactly how she is feeling, for I myself am a constant sufferer. Are you, too, sighing for the gilded salons of civilization?"

"Not in the least," Jeanne answered frankly. "I am tired of mirrors and electric lights and babble. I prefer our present surroundings, and I should not mind at all if some of those disapproving ancestors of yours stepped out of their frames and took their places with us here."

Cecil laughed.

"If they have been listening to our conversation," he said, "I think that they will stay where they are. Like royalty," he continued, "we can boast an octagonal chamber. I fear that its glories are of the past, but it is at least small, and the wallpaper is modern. I have ordered coffee and the card-tables there. Shall we go?"

He led the way out of the gloomy room, chilly and bare, yet in a way magnificent still with its reminiscences of past splendour, across the hall, modernized with rugs and recent furnishing, into a smaller apartment, where cheerfulness reigned. A wood fire burnt in an open grate. Lamps and a fine candelabrum gave a sufficiency of light. The furniture, though old, was graceful, and of French design. It had been the sitting chamber of the ladies of the De la Borne family for generations, and it bore traces of its gentler occupation. One thing alone remained of primevalism to remind them of their closer contact with the great forces of nature. The chamber was built in the tower, which stood exposed to the sea, and the roar of the wind was ceaseless.

"Here at least we shall be comfortable, I think," Cecil remarked, as they all entered. "My frescoes are faded, but they represent flowers, not faces. There are no eyes to stare at you from out of the walls here, Princess."

The Princess laughed gaily as she seated herself before a Louis

Quinze card-table, and threw a pack of cards across the faded green baize cloth.

"It is charming, this," she declared. "Shall we challenge these two boys, Nigel? You are the only man who understands my leads, and who does not scold me for my declarations."

"I am perfectly willing," Forrest answered smoothly. "Shall we cut for deal?"

Cecil de la Borne leaned over and turned up a card.

"I am quite content," he remarked. "What do you say, Engleton?"

Engleton hesitated for a moment. The Princess turned and looked at him. He was standing upon the hearthrug smoking, his face as expressionless as ever.

"Let us cut for partners," he drawled. "I am afraid of the Princess and Forrest. The last time I found them a quite invincible couple."

There was a moment's silence. The Princess glanced toward Forrest, who only shrugged his shoulders.

"Just as you will," he answered.

He turned up an ace and the Princess a three.

"After all," he remarked, with a smile, "it seems as though fate were going to link us together."

"I am not so sure," Cecil de la Borne said, also throwing down an ace. "It depends now upon Engleton."

Engleton came to the table, and drew a card at random from the pack. Forrest's eyes seemed to narrow a little as he looked down at it. Engleton had drawn another ace.

"Forrest and I," he remarked. "Jolly low cutting, too. I have played against you often, Forrest, but I think this is our first rubber together. Here's good luck to us!"

He tossed off his liqueur and sat down. They cut again for deal, and the game proceeded.

Jeanne had moved across towards the window, and laid her fingers upon the heavy curtains. Cecil de la Borne, who was dummy, got up and stood by her side.

"Do you know," she said, "although your frescoes are flowers, I feel that there are eyes in this room, too, only that they are looking in from the night. Can one see the sea from here, Mr. De la Borne?"

"It is scarcely a hundred yards away," he answered. "This window looks straight across the German Ocean, and if you look long enough you will see the white of the breakers. Listen! You will hear, too, what my forefathers, and those who begat them, have heard, from the birth of the generations."

The girl, with strained face, stood looking out into the darkness. Outside, the wind and sea imposed their thunder upon the land. Within, there was no sound but the softer patter of the cards, the languid voices of the four who played bridge. A curious little company, on the whole. The Princess of Strurm, whose birth was as sure as her social standing was doubtful, the heroine of countless scandals, ignored by the great heads of her family, impoverished, living no one knew how, yet remaining the legal guardian of a stepdaughter, who was reputed to be one of the greatest heiresses in Europe. The courts had moved to have her set aside, and failed. A Cardinal of her late husband's faith, empowered to treat with her on behalf of his relations, offered a fortune for her cession of Jeanne, and was laughed at for his pains. Whatever her life had been, she remained custodian of the child of the great banker whom she had married late in life. She endured calmly the threats, the entreaties, the bribes, of Jeanne's own relations. Jeanne, she was determined, should enter life under her wing, and hers only. In the end she had her way. Jeanne was entering life now, not through the respectable but somewhat bourgeois avenue by which her great monied relatives would have led her, but under the auspices of her stepmother, whose position as chaperon to a great heiress had already thrown open a great many doors which would have been permanently closed to her in any other guise. The Princess herself was always consistent. She assumed to herself an arrogant right to do as she pleased and live as she pleased. She was of the House of Strurm, which had been noble for centuries, and had connections with royalty. That was enough. A few forgot her past and admitted her claim. Those who did not she ignored. . . .

Then there was Lord Ronald Engleton, an orphan brought up in Paris, a would-be decadent, a dabbler in all modern iniquities, redeemed from folly only by a certain not altogether wholesome cleverness, yet with a disposition which sometimes gained for him friends in most unlikely quarters. He had excellent qualities, which he did his best to conceal; impulses which he was continually stifling.

By his side sat Forrest, the Sphynx, more than middle-aged, a man who had wandered all over the world, who had tried many things without ever achieving prosperity, and who was searching always, with tired eyes, for some new method of clothing and feeding himself upon an income of less than nothing a year. He had met the Princess at Marienbad years ago, and silently took his place in her suite. Why, no one seemed to know, not even at first the Princess herself, who thought him chic, and adored what she could not understand. Curious flotsam and jetsam, these four, of society which had something of a Continental flavour; personages, every one of them, with claim to recognition, but without any noticeable hall-mark. . . .

There remained the girl, Jeanne herself, half behind the curtain now, her head thrust forward, her beautiful eyes contracted with the effort to penetrate that veil of darkness. One gift at least she seemed to have borrowed from the woman who gambled with life as easily and readily as with the cards which fell from her jewelled fingers. In her face, although it was still the face of a child, there was the same inscrutable expression, the same calm languor of one who takes and receives what life offers with the indifference of the cynic, or the imperturbability of the philosopher. There was little of the joy or the anticipation of youth there, and yet, behind the eyes, as they looked out into the darkness, there was something — some such effort, perhaps, as one seeking to penetrate the darkness of life must needs show. And as she looked, the white, living breakers gradually resolved them-selves out of the dark, thin filmy phosphorescence, and the roar of the lashed sea broke like thunder upon the pebbled beach. She leaned a little more forward, carried away with her fancy — that the shrill grinding of the pebbles was indeed the scream of human voices in pain!

CHAPTER VI

With the coming of dawn the storm passed away northwards, across a sea snow-flecked and still panting with its fury, and leaving behind many traces of its violence, even upon these waste and empty places. A lurid sunrise gave little promise of better weather, but by six o'clock the wind had fallen, and the full tide was swelling the creeks. On a sand-bank, far down amongst the marshes, Jeanne stood hatless, with her hair streaming in the breeze, her face turned seaward, her eyes full of an unexpected joy. Everywhere she saw traces of the havoc wrought in the night. The tall rushes lay broken and prostrate upon the ground; the beach was strewn with timber from the breaking up of an ancient wreck. Eyes more accustomed than hers to the outline of the country could have seen inland dismantled cottages and unroofed sheds, groups of still frightened and restive cattle, a snapped flagstaff, a fallen tree. But Jeanne knew none of these things. Her face was turned towards the ocean and the rising sun. She felt the sting of the sea wind upon her cheeks, all the nameless exhilaration of the early morning sweetness. Far out seaward the long breakers, snow-flecked and white crested, came rolling in with a long, monotonous murmur toward the land. Above, the grey sky was changing into blue. Almost directly over her head, rising higher and higher in little circles, a lark was singing. Jeanne half closed her eyes and stood still, engrossed by the unexpected beauty of her surroundings. Then suddenly a voice came travelling to her from across the marshes.

She turned round unwillingly, and with a vague feeling of irritation against this interruption, which seemed to her so inopportune, and in turning round she realized at once that her period of absorption must have lasted a good deal longer than she had had any idea of. She had walked straight across the marshes towards the little hillock on which she stood, but the way by which she had come was no longer visible. The swelling tide had circled round through some unseen channel, and was creeping now into the land by many creeks and narrow ways. She herself was upon an island, cut off from the dry land by a smoothly flowing tidal way more than twenty yards across. Along it a man in a flat-bottomed boat was punting his way towards her. She stood and waited for him, admiring his height, and the long powerful strokes with which he propelled his clumsy craft. He was very tall, and against the flat background his height seemed almost abnormal. As soon as he had attracted her attention he ceased to shout, and devoted all his attention to reaching her quickly. Nevertheless, the salt water was within a few feet of her when he drove his pole into the bottom, and brought the punt to a momentary standstill. She looked down at him, smiling.

"Shall I get in?" she asked.

"Unless you are thinking of swimming back," he answered drily, "it would be as well."

She lifted her skirts a little, and laughed at the inappropriateness of her thin shoes and open-work stockings. Andrew de la Borne held out his strong hand, and she sprang lightly on to the broad seat.

"It is very nice of you," she said, with her slight foreign accent, "to come and fetch me. Should I have been drowned?"

"No!" he answered. "As a matter of fact, the spot where you were standing is not often altogether submerged. You might have been a prisoner for a few hours. Perhaps as the tide is going to be high, your feet would have been wet. But there was no danger."

She settled down as comfortably as possible in the awkward seat.

"After all, then," she said, "this is not a real adventure. Where are you going to take me to?"

"I can only take you," he answered, "to the village. I suppose you came from the Hall?"

"Yes!" she answered. "I walked straight across from the gate. I never thought about the tide coming up here."

"You will have to walk back by the road," he answered. "It is a good deal further round, but there is no other way."

She hung her hand over the side, rejoicing in the touch of the cool soft water.

"That," she answered, "does not matter at all. It is very early still, and I do not fancy that any one will be up yet for several hours."

He made no further attempt at conversation, devoting himself entirely to the task of steering and propelling his clumsy craft along the narrow way. She found herself watching him with some curiosity. It had never occurred to her to doubt at first but that he was some fisherman from the village, for he wore a rough jersey and a pair of trousers tucked into sea-boots. His face was bronzed, and his hands were large and brown. Nevertheless she saw that his features were good, and his voice, though he spoke the dialect of the country, had about it some quality which she was not slow to recognize.

"Who are you?" she asked, a little curiously. "Do you live in the village?"

He looked down at her with a faint smile.

"I live in the village," he answered, "and my name is Andrew."

"Are you a fisherman?" she asked.

"Certainly," he answered gravely. "We are all fishermen here."

She was not altogether satisfied. He spoke to her easily, and without any sort of embarrassment. His words were civil enough, and yet he had more the air of one addressing an equal than a villager who is able to be of service to some one in an altogether different social sphere.

"It was very fortunate for me," she said, "that you saw me. Are you up at this hour every morning?"

"Generally," he answered. "I was thinking of fishing, higher up in the reaches there."

"I am sorry," she said, "that I spoiled your sport."

He did not answer at once. He, in his turn, was looking at her. In her tailor-made gown, short and fashionably cut, her silk stockings and high-heeled shoes, she certainly seemed far indeed removed from any of the women of those parts. Her dark hair was arranged after a fashion that was strange to him. Her delicately pale skin, her deep grey eyes, and unusually scarlet lips were all indications of her foreign extraction. He looked at her long and searchingly. This was the girl, then, whom his brother was hoping to marry.

"You are not English," he remarked, a little abruptly.

She shook her head.

"My father was a Portuguese," she said, "and my mother French. I was born in England, though. You, I suppose, have lived here all your life?"

"All my life," he repeated. "We villagers, you see, have not much opportunity for travel."

"But I am not sure," she said, looking at him a little doubtfully, "that you are a villager."

"I can assure you," he answered, "that there is no doubt whatever about it. Can you see out yonder a little house on the island there?"

She followed his outstretched finger.

"Of course I can," she answered. "Is that your home?"

He nodded.

"I am there most of my time," he answered.

"It looks charming," she said, a little doubtfully, "but isn't it lonely?"

He shrugged his shoulders.

"Perhaps," he answered. "I am only ten minutes' sail from the mainland, though."

She looked again at the house, long and low, with its plaster walls bare of any creeping thing.

"It must be rather fascinating," she admitted, "to live upon an island. Are you married?"

"No!" he answered.

"Do you mean that you live quite alone?" she asked.

He smiled down upon her as one might smile at an inquisitive child. "I have a ser — some one to look after me," he said. "Except for that I am quite alone. I am going to set you ashore here. You see those telegraph posts? That is the road which leads direct to the Hall."

She was still looking at the island, watching the waves break against a little stretch of pebbly beach.

"I should like very much," she said, "to see that house. Can you not take me out there?"

He shook his head.

"We could not get so far in this punt," he said, "and my sailing boat is up at the village quay, more than a mile away."

She frowned a little. She was not used to having any request of hers disregarded.

"Could we not go to the village," she asked, "and change into your boat?"

He shook his head.

"I am going fishing," he said, "in a different direction. Allow me."

He stepped on to land and lifted her out. She hesitated for a moment and felt for her purse.

"You must let me recompense you," she said coldly, "for the time you have lost in coming to my assistance."

He looked down at her, and again she had an uncomfortable sense that notwithstanding his rude clothes and country dialect, this man was no ordinary villager. He said nothing, however, until she produced her purse, and held out a little tentatively two half-crowns.

"You are very kind," he said. "I will take one if you will allow me. That is quite sufficient. You see the Hall behind the trees there. You cannot miss your way, I think, and if you will take my advice you will not wander about in the marshes here except at high tide. The sea comes in to the most unexpected places, and very quickly, too, sometimes. Good morning!"

"Good morning, and thank you very much," she answered,

turning away toward the road.

* * *

Cecil de la Borne was standing at the end of the drive when she appeared, a telescope in his hand. He came hastily down the road to meet her, a very slim and elegant figure in his well-cut flannel clothes, smoothly brushed hair, and irreproachable tie.

"My dear Miss Jeanne," he exclaimed, "I have only just heard that you were out. Do you generally get up in the middle of the night?"

She smiled a little half-heartedly. It was curious that she found herself contrasting for a moment this very elegant young man with her roughly dressed companion of a few minutes ago.

"To meet with an adventure such as I have had," she answered, "I would never go to bed at all. I have been nearly drowned, and rescued by a most marvellous person. He brought me back to safety in a flat-bottomed punt, and I am quite sure from the way he stared at them that he had never seen open-work stockings before."

"Are you in earnest?" Cecil asked doubtfully.

"Absolutely," she answered. "I was walking there among the marshes, and I suddenly found myself surrounded by the sea. The tide had come up behind me without my noticing. A most mysterious person came to my rescue. He wore the clothes of a fisherman, and he accepted half a crown, but I have my doubts about him even now. He said that his name was Mr. Andrew."

Cecil opened the gate and they walked up towards the house. A slight frown had appeared upon his forehead.

"Do you know him?" she asked.

"I know who he is," he answered. "He is a queer sort of fellow, lives all alone, and is a bit cranky, they say. Come in and have some breakfast. I don't suppose that any one else will be down for ages."

She shook her head.

"I will send my woman down for some coffee," she answered. "I am going upstairs to change. I am just a little wet, and I must try and find some thicker shoes."

Cecil sighed.

"One sees so little of you," he murmured, "and I was looking forward to a tete-a-tete breakfast."

She shook her head as she left him in the hall.

"I couldn't think of it," she declared. "I'll appear with the others later on. Please find out all you can about Mr. Andrew and tell me."

Cecil turned away, and his face grew darker as he crossed the hall.

"If Andrew interferes this time," he muttered, "there will be trouble!"

CHAPTER VII

The Princess appeared for luncheon and declared herself to be in a remarkably good humour.

"My dear Cecil," she said, helping herself to an ortolan in aspic, "I like your climate and I like your chef. I had my window open for at least ten minutes, and the sea air has given me quite an appetite. I have serious thoughts of embracing the simple life."

"You could scarcely," Cecil de la Borne answered, "come to a better place for your first essay. I will guarantee that life is sufficiently simple here for any one. I have no neighbours, no society to offer you, no distractions of any sort. Still, I warned you before you came."

"Don't be absurd," the Princess declared. "You have the sea almost at your front door, and I adore the sea. If you have a nice large boat I should like to go for a sail."

Cecil looked at her with upraised eyebrows.

"If you are serious," he said, "no doubt we can find the boat."

"I am absolutely serious," the Princess declared. "I feel that this is exactly what my system required. I should like to sit in a comfortable cushioned seat and sail somewhere. If possible, I should like you men to catch things from the side of the boat."

"You will get sunburnt," Lord Ronald remarked drily; "perhaps even freckled."

"Adorable!" the Princess declared. "A touch of sunburn would be quite becoming. It is such an excellent foundation to build a complexion upon. Jeanne is quite enchanted with the place. She's had adventures already, and been rescued from drowning by a marvellous person, who wore his trousers tucked into his boots and found fault with her shoes and stockings. She has promised to show me the place after luncheon, and I am going to stand there myself and see if anything happens."

"You will get your feet very wet," Cecil declared.

"And sand inside your shoes," Forrest remarked.

"These," the Princess declared, "are trifles compared with the delightful sensation of experiencing a real adventure. In any case we must sail one afternoon, Cecil. I insist upon it. We will not play bridge until after dinner. My luck last night was abominable. Oh, you needn't look at me like that," she added to Cecil. "I know I won, but that was an accident. I had bad cards all the time, and I only won because you others had worse. Please ring the bell, Mr. Host, and see about the boat."

"Really," Cecil remarked, as he called the butler and gave him some instructions, "I had no idea that I was going to entertain such enterprising guests."

"Oh, there are lots of things I mean to do!" the Princess declared. "I am seriously thinking of going shrimping. I suppose there are shrimps here, and I should love to tuck up my skirts and carry a big net, like somebody's picture."

"Perhaps," Cecil suggested, "you would like to try the golf links. I believe there are some quite decent ones not far away."

The Princess shook her head.

"No!" she answered. "Golf is too civilized a game. We will go out in a fishing boat with plenty of cushions, and we will try to catch fish. I know that Jeanne will love it, and that you others will hate it. Between the two of you it should be amusing."

"Very well," Cecil declared, with an air of resignation, "whatever happens will be upon your own shoulders. There is a boat in the village which we can have. I will have it brought up to our own quay in an hour's time. If the worst comes to the worst, and we are bored to death, we can play bridge on the way."

"There will be no cards upon the boat," the Princess declared decidedly. "I forbid them. We are going to lounge and look at the sea and get sunburnt. Jeanne can wear a veil if she likes. I shall not."

Cecil shrugged his shoulders.

"Very well," he said. "Whatever happens, don't blame me."

* * *

The Princess had her way and behaved like a schoolgirl. She sat in the most comfortable place, surrounded with a multitude of cushions, with her tiny Japanese spaniel in her arms, and a box of French bonbons by her side. Jeanne stood in the bows, bareheaded and happy. Lord Ronald, who was feeling a little sea-sick, sat at her feet.

"I had no idea," he remarked plaintively, "that your mother was capable of such crudities. If I had known, I certainly would not have trusted myself to such a party. This sea air is hateful. It has tarnished my cigarette-case already, and one's nails will not be fit to be seen. To be out of doors like this is worse than drinking unfiltered water."

Jeanne smiled down at him a little contemptuously.

"You are a child of the cities, Lord Ronald," she remarked. "Next year I am going to buy a yacht myself, but I shall not ask you to come with us."

Lord Ronald groaned.

"That is the worst of all heiresses," he said. "You have such queer tastes. I shall never summon up my courage to propose to you."

"There is always leap year," Jeanne reminded him.

"What a bewildering suggestion!" he murmured, looking uncomfortably over the side of the boat. "I say, Forrest, what do you think of this sort of thing?"

"Idyllic!" Forrest declared cynically. "To sit upon a hard plank and to have one's digestion unmercifully interfered with like this is unqualified rapture. If only there were cabins one might sleep."

"There will be cabins on my yacht," Jeanne declared laughing, "but I shall not ask either of you. You are both of you knights of the candle light. I shall get some great strong fisherman to be captain, and I shall go round the world and forget the days and the months."

Forrest shivered slightly.

"The country," he remarked to the Princess, "is having a terrible effect upon your stepdaughter."

The Princess nodded and thrust a bonbon into the languid jaws of the dog she was holding.

"It is my fault," she declared. "It is I who have set this fashion. It was a whim, and I am tired of it. Tell our host that we will go back."

They tacked a few minutes later, and swept shoreward. Jeanne, still standing in the bows, was gazing steadfastly upon the little island at the entrance of the estuary.

"I should like," she declared, pointing it out to Cecil, "to land there and have some tea."

Cecil looked at her doubtfully.

"We shall be home in a little more than an hour," he said, "and I don't suppose we could get any tea there, even if we were able to land."

"I have a conviction that we should," Jeanne declared. "Mother," she added, turning round to the older woman, "there is an island just ahead of us with a delightful looking cottage. I believe my preserver of this morning lives there. Wouldn't it be lovely to go and beg him to give us all tea?"

"Charming!" the Princess declared, sitting up amongst her cushions. "I should love to see him, and tea is the one thing in the world I want to make me happy."

Cecil de la Borne stood silent for a moment or two, looking steadfastly at the whitewashed cottage upon the island. It seemed impossible, after all, to escape from Andrew!

"The man lives there alone, I believe," he said. "I don't suppose there is any one to get us tea. He would only be embarrassed by our coming, and not know what to do."

Jeanne smiled reflectively.

"I do not think," she said, "that it would be easy to embarrass Mr. Andrew. However, if you like we will put it off to another afternoon, on one condition."

"Let me hear the condition at any rate," Cecil asked.

"That we go straight back, and that you show us that subterranean passage," Jeanne declared.

"Agreed!" Cecil answered. "I warn you that you will find it only damp and mouldy and depressing, but you shall certainly see it."

The girl moved toward the side of the boat, and stood leaning over, with her eyes fixed upon the island. Standing on the small grass plot in front of the cottage she could see the tall figure of a man with his face turned toward them. A faint smile parted her lips as she watched. She took out her handkerchief and waved it. The man for a moment stood motionless, and then raising his cap, held it for a moment above his head. The boat sped on, and very soon they were out of sight. She stood there, however, watching, until they had rounded the sandy spit and entered the creek which led into the harbour. There was something unusually piquant to her in the thought of that greeting with the man. whose response to it had been so unwilling, almost ungracious.

CHAPTER VIII

"Not another step!" the Princess declared. "I am going back at once."

"I too," Forrest declared. "Your smuggling ancestors, my dear De la Borne, must indeed have loved adventure, if they spent much of their time crawling about here like rats."

"As you will," Cecil answered. "The expedition is Miss Jeanne's, not mine."

"And I am going on," Jeanne declared. "I want to see where we come out on the beach."

"This way, then," Cecil said. "You need not be afraid to walk upright. The roof is six feet high all the way. You must tread carefully, though. There are plenty of holes and stones about."

The Princess and Forrest disappeared. Jeanne, with her skirts held high in one hand, and an electric torch in the other, followed Cecil slowly along the gloomy way. The walls were oozing with damp, glistening patches, like illuminated salt stains, and queer fungi started out from unexpected places. Sometimes their footsteps fell on the rock, awaking strange echoes down the gallery. Sometimes they sank deep into the sand. Cecil looked often behind, and once held out his hand to help his companion over a difficult place. At last he paused, and she heard him struggling to turn a key in a great worm-eaten door on their right.

"This is the room," he explained, "where they held their meetings, and where the stuff was hidden. It was used for more than twenty years, and the Customs' people never seemed to have had even an inkling of its existence."

He pushed the door open with difficulty. They found themselves in a gloomy chamber, with vaulted roof and stone floor. A faint streak of daylight from an opening somewhere in the roof, partially lit the place. Here, too, the walls were damp and the odour appalling. There were some fragments of broken barrels at one end, and an oak table in the middle of the floor. Jeanne looked round and shivered.

"Let us go on to the end," she said.

Cecil nodded, and they made their way on down the passage.

"The roof is getting lower now," he said. "You had better stoop a little."

She stopped short.

"What is that?" she asked fearfully.

A sound like rolling thunder, faint at first, but growing more distinct at every step, broke the chill silence of the place.

"The sea," Cecil answered. "We are getting near to the beach."

Jeanne nodded and crept on. Louder and louder the sound seemed to become, until at last she paused, half terrified.

"Where are we?" she gasped. "It sounds as though the sea were right over our heads."

Cecil shook his head.

"It is an illusion," he said. "The sound comes from the air-hole there. We are forty yards from the cliff still."

They crept on, until at last, after a turn in the gallery, they saw a faint glimmering of light. A few more yards and they came to a standstill.

"The entrance is boarded up, you see," Cecil said, "but you can see through the chinks. There is the sea just below, and the rope ladder used to hang from these staples."

She looked out. Sheer below was the sea, breaking upon the rocks and sending a torrent of spray into the air with every wave.

"We can't get out this way, then?" she asked.

He shook his head.

"No, we should want a rope ladder," he said, "and a boat. Have you seen enough?"

"More than enough," Jeanne answered. "Let us get back."

* * *

Jeanne sank into a garden seat a few minutes later with a little exclamation of relief.

"Never," she declared, "have I appreciated fresh air so much. I think, Mr. De la Borne, that smuggling, though it was a very romantic profession, must have had its unpleasant side."

Cecil nodded.

"There were more air-holes in those days," he said, "but our ancestors were a tougher race than we. Coarse brutes, most of them, I imagine," he added, lighting a cigarette. "Drank beer for breakfast, and smoked clay pipes before meals. Fancy if one had their constitutions and our tastes!"

"The two would scarcely go together," Jeanne remarked. "But after all I should think that absinthe and cigarettes are more destructive. I am dying for some tea. Let us go in and find the others."

Tea was set out in the hall, but only Engleton was there. Forrest and the Princess were walking slowly up and down the avenue.

"I imagine," the latter was saying drily, "that we are fairly free from eavesdroppers here. Now tell me what it is that you have to say, Nigel."

"I am bothered about Engleton," Forrest said. "I didn't like his insisting upon cutting last night. What do you think he meant by it?"

The Princess shrugged her shoulders.

"Nothing at all," she answered. "He may have thought that we were lucky together, and of course he knows that you are the best player. There is no reason why he should be willing to play with Cecil de la Borne, when by cutting with you he would be more likely to win."

"You think that that is all?" Forrest asked.

"I think so," the Princess answered. "What had you in your mind?"

"I wondered," Forrest said thoughtfully, "whether he had heard any of the gossip at the club."

The Princess frowned impatiently.

"For Heaven's sake, don't be imaginative, Nigel!" she declared. "If you give way like this you will lose your nerve in no time."

"Very well," Forrest said. "Let us take it for granted, then, that he did it only because he preferred to play with me to playing against me. What is to become of our little scheme if we cut as we did last night all the time?"

The Princess smiled.

"You ought to be able to manage that," she said carelessly. "You are so good at card tricks that you should be able to get an ace when you want it. I always cut third from the end, as you know."

"That's all very well," Forrest answered, "but we can't go on cutting two aces all the time. I ran it pretty fine last night, when for the second time I gave you a three or a four, and drew a two myself. But he seems to have the devil's own luck. They cut under us, as you know."

The Princess looked up toward the house. She had seen Jeanne and Cecil appear.

"Those people are back from their underground pilgrimage," she remarked. "Have you anything definite to suggest? If not, we had better go in."

"There is only one way, Ena," Forrest said, "in which we could improve matters."

"And what is that?" she asked quickly.

"Don't you think we could get our host in?"

The Princess was silent for several moments.

"It is a little dangerous, I am afraid," she said.

"I don't see why," Forrest answered. "If he were once in he'd have to hold his tongue, and you can do just what you like with him. He seems to me to be just one of those pulpy sort of persons whom you could persuade into a thing before he had had time to think about it."

"I will drop him a hint if you like," the Princess said thoughtfully, "and see how he takes it. Are you sure that the game is worth the candle?"

"Absolutely," Forrest answered eagerly. "I saw Engleton drop two thousand playing baccarat one night, and he never turned a hair. I wasn't playing, worse luck."

"If I can get Cecil alone before dinner," the Princess said, "I will sound him. I think we had better go back now. We are a little old for romantic wanderings, and the wind is beginning to disarrange my hair."

"See what you can do with him, then," Forrest said, as they retraced their steps. "I'll call in and hear if you've anything to tell me on my way down for dinner."

The Princess nodded. They entered the hall, and Cecil at once drew an easy-chair to the tea-table.

"My good people," the Princess declared, "I am famished. Your sea air, Cecil, is the most wonderful thing in the world. For years I have not known what it was like to be hungry. Hot cakes, please! And, Jeanne, please make my tea. Jeanne knows just how I like it. Tell us about the smuggler's cave, Jeanne. Was it really so wonderful?"

Jeanne laughed.

"It was very, very weird and very smelly," she said. "I think that you were wise to turn back."

CHAPTER IX

Andrew came face to face with his brother in the village street on the next morning. He looked at him for a moment in surprise.

"What have you been doing?" he asked, drily. "Sitting up all night?"

Cecil nodded dejectedly.

"Pretty well," he admitted. "We played bridge till nearly five o'clock."

"You lost, I suppose?" Andrew asked.

"Yes, I lost!" Cecil admitted.

"Your party," Andrew said, "does not seem to me to be an unqualified success."

"It is not," Cecil admitted. "Miss Le Mesurier has been quite unapproachable the last few days. She's just civil to me and no more. She isn't even half as decent as she was in town. I wish I hadn't asked them here. It's cost a lot more money than we can afford, and done no good that I can see."

Andrew looked away seaward for a moment. Was it his fancy, or was there indeed a slim white figure coming across the marshes from the Hall?

"Cecil," he said, "are you quite sure that your guests are worth the trouble you have taken to entertain them? I refer more particularly to the two men."

"They go everywhere," Cecil answered. "Lord Ronald is a bit of a wastrel, of course, and I am not very keen on Forrest, but we were all together when I gave the invitation, and I couldn't leave them out."

Andrew nodded.

"Well," he said, "I should be careful how I played cards with Forrest if I were you."

Cecil's face grew even a shade paler.

"You do not think," he muttered, "that he would do anything that wasn't straight?"

"On the contrary," Andrew answered, "I have reason to believe that he would. Isn't that one of your guests coming? You had better go and meet her."

Andrew passed on his way, and Cecil walked towards Jeanne. All the time, though, she was looking over his shoulder to where Andrew's tall figure was disappearing.

"What a nuisance!" she pouted. "I wanted to see Mr. Andrew, and directly I came in sight he hurried away."

"Can I give him any message?" Cecil asked with faint irony.

"He will no doubt be up with the fish later in the day."

She turned her back on him.

"I am going back to the house," she said. "I did not come out here to walk with you."

"Considering that I am your host," he began —

"You lose your claim to consideration on that score when you remind me of it," she answered. "Really the only man who has not bored me for weeks is Mr. Andrew. You others are all the same. You say the same things, and you are always paving the way toward the same end. I am tired of it. Stop!"

She turned suddenly round.

"I quite forgot," she said. "I must go into the village after all. I am going to send a telegram."

They retraced their steps in silence. As they entered the telegraph-office Andrew was just leaving, and the postmistress was wishing him a respectful farewell. He touched his hat as the two entered, and stepped on one side. Jeanne, however, held out her hand.

"Mr. Andrew," she said, "I am so glad to see you. I want to go out again in that great punt of yours. Please, when can you take me?"

"I am afraid," Andrew answered, "that I am rather busy just now. I — "

He stopped short, for something in her face perplexed him. It was impossible for her, of course, to feel disappointment to that extent, and yet she had all the appearance of a child about to cry. He felt suddenly awkward and ill at ease.

"Of course," he said, "if you really care about it, I should be very pleased to take you any morning toward the end of the week."

"Tomorrow morning, please," she begged.

He glanced towards his brother, who shrugged his shoulders.

"If Miss Le Mesurier is really inclined to go, Andrew," the latter said, "I am sure that you will take good care of her. Perhaps some of us will come, too."

She nodded her farewells to Andrew, and turned back with her host toward the Hall. Cecil looked at her a little curiously. It was certain that she seemed in better spirits than a short time ago. What a creature of caprices!

"Will you tell me, Mr. De la Borne," she asked, "why the postmistress called Mr. Andrew 'sir' if he is only a fisherman?"

"Habit, I suppose," Cecil answered carelessly. "They call every one sir and ma'am."

"I am not so sure that it was habit," she said thoughtfully. "I think that Mr. Andrew is not quite what he represents himself to be. No one who had not education and experience of nice people could behave quite as he does. Of course, he is rough and brusque at times, I know, but then many men are like that."

Cecil did not reply. A grey mist was sweeping in from the sea, and Jeanne shivered a little as they turned into the avenue.

"I wonder," she said pensively, "why we came here. My mother as a rule hates to go far from civilization, and I am sure Lord Ronald is miserable."

"I think one reason why your mother brought you here," Cecil said slowly, "is because she wanted to give me a chance."

She picked up her skirts and ran, ran so lightly and swiftly that Cecil, who was taken by surprise, had no chance of catching her. From the hall door she looked back at him, panting behind.

"Too many cigarettes," she laughed. "You are out of training. If you do not mind you will be like Lord Ronald, an old young man, and I would never let any one say the sort of things you were going to say who couldn't catch me when I ran away."

She went laughing up the stairs, and Cecil de la Borne turned into his study. The Princess was playing patience, and the two men were in easy-chairs.

"At last!" the Princess remarked, throwing down her cards. "My dear Cecil, do you realize that you have kept us waiting nearly an hour?"

"I thought, perhaps," he answered, "that you had had enough bridge."

"Absurd!" the Princess declared. "What else is there to do? Come and cut, and pray that you do not draw me for a partner. My luck is dead out — at patience, anyhow."

"Mine," Cecil remarked, with a hard little laugh, "seems to be out all round. Touch the bell, will you, Forrest. I must have a brandy and soda before I start this beastly game again."

The Princess raised her eyebrows.

"I trust," she said, "that my charming ward has not been unkind?"

"Your charming ward," Cecil answered, "has as many whims and fancies as an elf. She yawns when I talk to her, and looks longingly after one of my villagers. Hang the fellow!"

"A very superior villager," the Princess remarked, "if you mean Mr. Andrew."

Forrest looked up, and fixed his cold intent eyes upon his host.

"I suppose," he said, "you are sure that this man Andrew is

really what he professes to be, and not a masquerader?"

"I have known him," Cecil answered, "since I was old enough to remember anybody. He has lived here all his life, and only been away three or four times."

They played until the dressing-bell rang. Then Cecil de la Borne rose from his seat with a peevish exclamation.

"My luck seems dead out," he said.

The Princess raised her eyebrows.

"Possibly, my dear boy," she said, "but you must admit that you also played abominably. Your last declaration of hearts was indefensible, and why you led a diamond and discarded the spade in Lord Ronald's 'no trump' hand, Heaven only knows!"

"I still think that I was right," Cecil declared, a little sullenly.

The Princess said nothing, but turned toward the door.

"Any one dining tonight, Mr. Host?" she said.

"No one," he answered. "To tell you the truth there is no one to ask within a dozen miles, and you particularly asked not to be bothered with meeting yokels."

"Quite right," the Princess answered, "only I am getting a little bored, and if you had any yokels of the Mr. Andrew sort, with just a little more polish, they might be entertaining. You three men are getting deadly dull."

"Princess!" Lord Ronald declared reproachfully. "How can you say that? You never give any one a chance to see you until the afternoon, and then we generally start bridge. One cannot be brilliantly entertaining while one is playing cards."

The Princess yawned.

"I never argue," she said. "I only state facts. I am getting a little bored. Some one must be very amusing at dinner-time or I shall have a headache."

She swept up to her room.

"I suppose we'd better go and change," Cecil remarked, leading the way out into the hall.

Forrest, who was at the window, screwed his eyeglass in and leaned forward. A faint smile had parted the corner of his lips, and he beckoned to Cecil, who came over at once to his side. On the top of the sand-dyke two figures were walking slowly side by side. Jeanne, with the wind blowing her skirts about her small shapely figure, was looking up all the time at the man who walked by her side, and who, against the empty background of sea and sky, seemed of a stature almost gigantic.

"Quite an idyll!" Forrest remarked with a little sneer.

Cecil bit his lip, and turned away without a word.

CHAPTER X

"I don't think," Engleton said slowly, "that I care about playing any more — just now."

The Princess yawned as she leaned back in her chair. Both Forrest and De la Borne, who had left his place to turn up one of the lamps, glanced stealthily round at the speaker.

"I am not keen about it myself," Forrest said smoothly. "After all, though, it's only three o'clock."

Cecil's fingers shook, so that his tinkering with the lamp failed, and the room was left almost in darkness. Forrest, glad of an excuse to leave his place, went to the great north window and pulled up the blind. A faint stream of grey light stole into the room. The Princess shrieked, and covered her face with her hands.

"For Heaven's sake, Nigel," she cried, "pull that blind down! I do not care for these Rembrandtesque effects. Tobacco ash and cards and my complexion do not look at their best in such a crude light."

Forrest obeyed, and the room for a moment was in darkness. There was a somewhat curious silence. The Princess was breathing softly but quickly. When at last the lamp burned up again, every one glanced furtively toward the young man who was leaning back in his chair with his eyes fixed absently upon the table.

"Well, what is it to be?" Forrest asked, reseating himself. "One more rubber or bed?"

"I've lost a good deal more than I care to," Cecil remarked in a somewhat unnatural tone, "but I say another brandy and soda, and one more rubber. There are some sandwiches behind you, Engleton."

"Thank you," Engleton answered without looking up. "I am not hungry."

The Princess took up a fresh pack of cards, and let them fall idly through her fingers. Then she took a cigarette from the gold case which hung from her chatelaine, and lit it.

"One more rubber, then," she said. "After that we will go to bed."

The others came toward the table, and the Princess threw down the cards. They all three cut. Engleton, however, did not move.

"I think," he said, "that you did not quite understand me. I said that I did not care to play any more."

"Three against one," the Princess remarked lightly.

"Why not play cut-throat, then?" Engleton remarked. "It would be an excellent arrangement."

"Why so?" Forrest asked.

"Because you could rob one another," Engleton said. "It would be interesting to watch."

A few seconds intense silence followed Engleton's words. It was the Princess who spoke first. Her tone was composed but chilly. She looked toward Engleton with steady eyes.

"My dear Lord Ronald," she said, "is this a joke? I am afraid my sense of humour grows a little dull at this hour of the morning."

"It was not meant for a joke," Engleton said. "My words were spoken in earnest."

The Princess, without any absolute movement, seemed suddenly to become more erect. One forgot her rouge, her blackened eyebrows, her powdered cheeks. It was the great lady who looked at Engleton.

"Are we to take this, Lord Ronald," she asked, "as a serious accusation?"

"You can take it for what it is, madam," Engleton answered — "the truth."

Cecil de la Borne rose to his feet and leaned across the table. His cheeks were as pale as death. His voice was shaking.

"I am your host, Engleton," he said, "and I demand an explanation of what you have said. Your accusation is absurd. You must be drunk or out of your senses."

"I am neither drunk nor out of my senses," Engleton answered, "nor am I such an utter fool as to be so easily deceived. The fact that you, as my partner, played like an idiot, made rotten declarations, and revoked when one rubber was nearly won, I pass over. That may or may not have been your miserable idea of the game. Apart from that, however, I regret to have discovered that you, Forrest, and you, madam," he added, addressing the Princess, "have made use throughout the last seven rubbers of a code with your fingers, both for the declarations and for the leads. My suspicions were aroused, I must confess, by accident. It was remarkably easy, however, to verify them. Look here!"

Engleton touched his forehead.

"Hearts!" he said.

He touched his lip.

"Diamonds!" he added.

He passed his fingers across his eyebrows.

"Clubs!" he remarked.

He beat with his fourth finger softly upon the table.

"Spades!"

Major Forrest rose to his feet.

"Lord Ronald," he said, "I am exceedingly sorry that owing to my introduction you have become a guest in this house. As for your ridiculous accusation, I deny it."

"And I," the Princess murmured.

"Naturally," Engleton answered smoothly. "I really do not see what else you could do. I regret very much to have been the unfortunate means of breaking up such a pleasant little house-party. I am going to my room now to change my clothes, and I will trespass upon your hospitality, Mr. De la Borne, only so far as to beg you to let me have a cart, or something of the sort, to drive me into Wells, as soon as your people come on the scene."

Engleton rose to his feet, and with a stiff little bow, walked toward the door. He, too, seemed somehow during the last few minutes to have shown signs of a greater virility than was at any time manifest in his boyish, somewhat unintelligent, face. He carried himself with a new dignity, and he spoke with the decision of an older man. For a moment they watched him go. Then Forrest, obeying a lightning-like glance from the Princess, crossed the room swiftly and stood with his back to the door.

"Engleton," he said, "this is absurd. We can afford to ignore your mad behaviour and your discourtesy, but before you leave this room we must come to an understanding."

Lord Ronald stood with his hands behind his back.

"I had imagined," he said, "that an understanding was exactly what we had come to. My words were plain enough, were they not? I am leaving this house because I have found myself in the company of sharks and card-sharpers."

Forrest's eyes narrowed. A quick little breath passed between his teeth. He took a step forward toward the young man, as though about to strike him.

Engleton, however, remained unmoved.

"You are going to carry away a story like this?" he said hoarsely.

"I shall tell my friends," Engleton answered, "just as much or as little as I choose of my visit here. Since, however, you are curious, I may say that should I find you at any future time in any respectable house, it will be my duty to inform any one of my friends who are present of the character of their fellow-guest. Will you be so good as to stand away from that door?"

"No!" Forrest answered.

Engleton turned toward Cecil.

"Mr. De la Borne," he said, "may I appeal to you, as it is your house, to allow me egress from it?"

Cecil came hesitatingly up to the two. The Princess, with a sweep of her skirts, followed him.

"Major Forrest is right," she declared. "We cannot have this madman go back to London to spread about slanderous tales. Major Forrest will stand away from that door, Lord Ronald, as soon as you pass your word that what has happened tonight will remain a secret."

Engleton laughed contemptuously.

"Not I," he answered. "Exactly what I said to Major Forrest, I repeat, madam, to you, and to you, sir, my host. I shall give my friends the benefit of my experience whenever it seems to me advisable."

Forrest locked the door, and put the key into his pocket.

"We shall hope, Lord Ronald," he said quietly, "to induce you to change your mind."

CHAPTER XI

"Every one down for luncheon!" Jeanne declared. "What energy! Where is Lord Ronald, by the by?" she added, looking around the room. "He promised to take me out sailing this morning. I wonder if I missed him on the marshes."

The Princess yawned, and glanced at the clock.

"By this time," she remarked, "Lord Ronald is probably in London. He had a telegram or something in the middle of the night, and went away early this morning."

Jeanne looked at them in surprise.

"How queer!" she remarked. "I was down before nine o'clock. Had he left then?"

"Long before then, I believe," Forrest answered. "He is very likely coming back in a day or two."

Jeanne nodded indifferently. The intelligence, after all, was of little importance to her.

"Has the luncheon gong gone?" she asked. "I have been out since ten o'clock, and I am starving."

Cecil led the way across the hall into the dining-room.

"Come along," he said. "I wish we all had such healthy appetites."

She glanced at him, and then at the others.

"Well," she said, "you certainly look as though you had been up very late last night. What is the matter with you all?"

"We were very foolish," Major Forrest said softly. "We sat up a great deal too late, and I am afraid that we all smoked too many cigarettes. You see it was our last night, for without Engleton our bridge is over."

"We must try," Cecil said, "and find some other form of entertainment for you. Would you like to sail again this afternoon, Princess?"

"I believe," she answered, "that I should like it if I may have plenty of cushions and a soft place for my head, so that if I feel like it I can go to sleep. Really, these late nights are dreadful. I am almost glad that Lord Ronald has gone. At least there will be no excuse for us to sit up until daylight." "Tonight," Major Forrest remarked, "let us all be primitive. We will go to bed at eleven o'clock, and get up in the morning and walk with Miss Le Mesurier upon the marshes. What do you find upon the sands, I wonder," he added, turning a little suddenly toward the girl, "to bring such a colour to your cheeks, and to keep you away from us for so many hours?"

Jeanne looked at him for a moment without change of features.

"It would not be easy," she said, "for me to tell you, for I find things there which you could not appreciate or understand."

"You find them alone?" Major Forrest asked smiling.

She turned her left shoulder upon him and addressed her host.

"Major Forrest is very impertinent," she said. "I think that I will not talk with him any more. Tell me, Mr. De la Borne, do you really mean that we can go sailing this afternoon?"

"If you will," he answered. "I have sent down to the village to tell them to bring the boat up to our harbourage."

She nodded.

"I shall love it," she declared. "It will be such a good thing for you three, too, because it will make you all sleepy, and then you will be able to go to bed and not worry about your bridge. When is Lord Ronald coming back?"

"He was not quite sure," the Princess remarked. "It depends upon the urgency of his business which summoned him away."

"How odd," Jeanne remarked, "to think of Lord Ronald as having any business at all. I cannot understand even now why I did not hear the car go. My room is just over the entrance to the courtyard."

"It is a proof," Major Forrest remarked, "that you sleep as soundly as you deserve."

"I am not so sure about that," Jeanne said. "Last night, for instance, it seemed to me that I heard all manner of strange sounds."

Cecil de la Borne looked up quickly.

"Sounds?" he repeated. "Do you mean noises in the house?"

She nodded.

"Yes, and voices! Once I thought that you must be all quarrelling, and then I thought that I heard some one fall down. After that there was nothing but the opening and shutting of doors."

"And after that," the Princess remarked smiling, "you probably went to sleep."

"Exactly," Jeanne admitted. "I went to sleep listening for footsteps. I think it was very rude of Ronald to go away without saying good-bye to me."

"You would have thought it still ruder," Cecil remarked, "if he had had you roused at five o'clock or so to make his adieux."

The Princess and Jeanne left the table together a few minutes before the other two, and Jeanne asked her stepmother a question.

"How long are we going to stop here?" she inquired. "I thought that our visit was for two or three days only."

The Princess hesitated.

"Cecil is such a nice boy," she said, "and he is so anxious to have us stay a little longer. What do you say? You are not bored?"

"I am not bored," Jeanne answered, "so long as you can keep him from saying silly things to me. On the contrary, I like to be here. I like it better than London. I like it better than any place I have been in since I left school."

The Princess looked at her a little curiously.

"I wonder," she said, "whether I ought to be looking after you a little more closely, my child. What do you do on the marshes there all the time? Do you talk with this Mr. Andrew?"

"I went with him in his boat this morning," Jeanne answered composedly. "It was very pleasant. We had a delightful sail."

The Princess shrugged her shoulders.

"Well," she said, "one must amuse oneself, and I suppose it is only reasonable that we should all choose different ways. I think I need not tell even such a child as you that men are the same all the world over, and that even a fisherman, if he is encouraged, may be guilty sometimes of an impertinence."

Jeanne raised her eyebrows.

"I have not the slightest fear," she said, "that Mr. Andrew would ever be guilty of anything of the sort. I wish I could say the same of some of the people whom I have met in our own circle of society."

The Princess smiled tolerantly.

"Nowadays," she remarked, "it is perfectly true that men do take too great liberties. Well, amuse yourself with your fisherman, my dear child. It is your legitimate occupation in life to make fools of all manner of men, and there is no harm in your beginning as low down as you choose if it amuses you."

Jeanne walked deliberately away. The Princess laughed a little uneasily. As she watched Jeanne ascend the stairs, Forrest and Cecil came out into the hall. They all three moved together into the further corner, where coffee was set out upon a small table, and it was significant that they did not speak a word until they were there, and even then Major Forrest looked cautiously around before he opened his lips.

"Well?" he asked.

The Princess smiled scornfully at their white, anxious faces.

"What are you afraid of?" she asked contemptuously. "Jeanne suspects nothing, of course. There is nothing which she could suspect. She has not mentioned his name even."

Cecil drew a little breath of relief. His face seemed to have grown haggard during the last few hours.

"I wish to God," he muttered, "we were out of this!"

The Princess turned her head and looked at him coldly.

"My young friend," she said, "you men are all the same. You have no philosophy. The inevitable has happened, or rather the inevitable has been forced upon us. What we have done we did deliberately. We could not do otherwise, and we cannot undo it. Remember that. And if you have a grain of philosophy or courage in you, keep a stouter heart and wear a smile upon your face."

Cecil rose to his feet.

"You are right," he said. "Are you ready, Forrest? Will you come with me?"

Forrest rose slowly to his feet.

"Of course," he said. "By the by, a sail this afternoon was a good idea. We must develop an interest in country pursuits. It is possible even," he added, "that we may have to take to golf."

The Princess, too, rose.

"Come into my room, one of you," she said, "and see me for a moment, afterwards. I suppose we shall start for our sail about three?"

Cecil nodded.

"The boat will be here by then," he said.

"And I will come up and bring you the news, if there is any," Forrest added.

CHAPTER XII

The man who stood with a telescope glued to his eye watching the coming boat, shut it up at last with a little snap. He walked round to the other side of the cottage, where Andrew was sitting with a pipe in his mouth industriously mending a fishing net.

"Andrew," he said, "there are some people coming here, and I am almost sure that they mean to land."

Andrew rose to his feet and strolled round to the little stretch of beach in front of the cottage. When he saw who it was who approached, he stopped short and took his pipe from his mouth.

"By Jove, it's Cecil," he exclaimed, "and his friends!"

His companion nodded. He was a man still on the youthful side of middle age, with bronzed features, and short, closely-cut beard. He looked what he was, a traveller and a sportsman.

"So I imagined," he said, "but I don't see Ronald there."

Andrew shaded his eyes with his hand.

"No!" he said. "There is the Princess and Cecil, and Major Forrest and Miss Le Mesurier. No one else. They certainly do look as though they were going to land here."

"Why not?" the other man remarked. "Why shouldn't Cecil come to visit his hermit brother?"

Andrew frowned.

"Berners," he said, "I want you to remember this. If they land here and you see anything of them, will you have the goodness to understand that I am Mr. Andrew, fisherman, and that you are my lodger?"

Andrew's companion looked at him in surprise.

"What sort of a game is this, Andrew?" he asked.

Andrew de la Borne shrugged his shoulders and smiled good-naturedly.

"Never mind about that, Dick," he answered. "Call it a whim or anything else you like. The fact is that Cecil had some guests coming whom I did not particularly care to meet, and who certainly would not have been interested in me. I thought it would be best to clear out altogether, so I have left Cecil in possession of the Hall, and they don't even know that I exist."

The man named Berners looked up at his host with twinkling eyes.

"Right!" he said. "So far as I am concerned, you shall be Mr. Andrew, fisherman. Will you also kindly remember that if any curiosity is evinced as to my identity, I am Mr. Berners, and that I am here for a rest-cure. By the by, how are you going to explain that elderly domestic of yours?"

"He is your servant, of course," Andrew answered. "He understands the position. I have spoken to him already. Yes, they are coming here right enough! Suppose you help me to pull in the boat for them."

The two men sauntered down to the shelving beach. The boat was close to them now, and Cecil was standing up in the bows.

"We want to land for a few minutes," he called out.

"Throw a rope, then," Andrew answered briefly. "You had better come in this side of the landing-stage."

The rope was thrown, and the boat dragged high and dry upon the pebbly beach. The Princess, after a glance at him through her lorgnette, surrendered herself willingly to Andrew's outstretched hands.

"I am quite sure," she said, "that you will not let me fall. You must be the wonderful person whom my daughter has told me about. Is this queer little place really your home?"

"I live here," Andrew de la Borne said simply.

Jeanne leaned over towards him.

"Won't you please help me, Mr. Andrew?" she said, smiling down at him.

He held out his arms, and she sprang lightly to the ground.

"I hope you don't mind our coming," she said to him. "I was so anxious to see your cottage."

"There is little enough to see," Andrew answered, "but you are very welcome."

"We are sorry to trouble you," Cecil said, a little uneasily, "but would it be possible to give these ladies some tea?"

"Certainly," Andrew answered. "I will go and get it ready."

"Oh, what fun!" Jeanne declared. "I am coming to help. Please, Mr. Andrew, do let me help. I am sure I could make tea."

"It is not necessary, thank you," Andrew answered. "I have a lodger who has brought his own servant. As it happens he was just preparing some tea for us. If you will come round to the other side, where it is a little more sheltered, I will bring you some chairs."

They moved across the grass-grown little stretch of sand. The Princess peered curiously at Berners.

"Your face," she remarked, "seems quite familiar to me."

Berners did not for the moment answer her. He was looking towards Forrest, who was busy lighting a cigarette.

"I am afraid, madam," he said, after a slight pause, "that I cannot claim the honour of having met you."

The Princess was not altogether satisfied. Jeanne had gone on with Andrew, and she followed slowly walking with Berners.

"I have such a good memory for faces," she remarked, "and I am very seldom mistaken."

"I am afraid," Berners said, "that this must be one of those rare occasions. If you will allow me I will go and help Andrew bring out some seats."

He disappeared into the cottage, and came out again almost directly with a couple of chairs. This time he met Forrest's direct gaze, and the two men stood for a moment or two looking at one another. Forrest turned uneasily away.

"Who the devil is that chap?" he whispered to Cecil. "I'll swear I've seen him somewhere."

"Very likely," Cecil answered wearily, throwing himself down on the turf. "I've no memory for faces."

Jeanne had stepped into the cottage, and gave a little cry of delight as she found herself in a small sitting-room, the walls of which were lined with books and guns and fishing-tackle.

"What a delightful room, Mr. Andrew!" she exclaimed. "Why — "

She paused and looked up at him, a little mystified.

"Do the fishermen in Norfolk read Shakespeare and Keats?" she asked. "And French books, too, De Maupassant and De Musset?"

"They are my lodger's," Andrew answered. "This is his room. I sit in the kitchen when I am at home."

His dialect was more marked than ever, and his answer had been delivered without any hesitation. Nevertheless, Jeanne was still a little puzzled.

"May I come into the kitchen, please?" she asked.

"Certainly," he answered. "You will find Mr. Berners' servant there getting tea ready."

Jeanne peeped in, and looked back at Andrew, who was standing behind her.

"What a lovely stone floor!" she exclaimed. "And your copper kettle, too, is delightful! Do you mean that when you have not a lodger here, you cook and do everything for yourself?"

"There are times," he answered composedly, "when I have a little assistance. It depends upon whether the fishing season has been good."

Berners came in, and threw himself into an easychair in the sitting-room.

"Make what use you like of my man, Andrew," he said. "I will have a cup of tea in here afterwards."

"I'm very much obliged, sir," Andrew answered.

The Princess called out to him, and he stepped back once more to where they were all sitting.

"It is a shame," she said, "that we drive your lodger away from his seat. Will you not ask him to take tea with us?"

"I am afraid," Andrew answered, "that he is not a very sociable person. He has come down here because he wants a complete rest, and he does not speak to any one unless he is obliged. He has just asked me to have his tea sent into his room."

"Where does he come from, this strange man?" the Princess asked. "It is all the time in my mind that I have met him somewhere. I am sure that he is one of us."

"I believe that he lives in London," Andrew answered, "and his name is Berners, Mr. Richard Berners."

"I do not seem to remember the name," the Princess remarked, "but the man's face worries me. What a delightful looking tea-tray! Mr. Andrew, you must really sit down with us. We ought to apologize for taking you by storm like this, and I have not thanked you yet for being so kind to my daughter." Andrew stepped back toward the cottage with a firm refusal upon his lips, but Jeanne's hand suddenly rested upon the arm of his coarse blue jersey.

"If you please, Mr. Andrew," she begged, "I want you to sit by me and tell me how you came to live in so strange a place. Do you really not mind the solitude?"

Andrew looked down at her for a moment without answering. For the first time, perhaps, he realized the charm of her pale expressive face with its rapid changes, and the soft insistent fire of her beautiful eyes. He hesitated for a moment and then remained where he was, leaning against the flag-staff.

"It is very good of you, miss," he said. "As to why I came to live here, I do so simply because the house belongs to me. It was my father's and his father's. We folk who live in the country make few changes."

She looked at him curiously. The men whom she had known, even those of the class to whom he might be supposed to belong, were all in a way different. This man talked only when he was obliged. All the time she felt in him the attraction of the unknown. He answered her questions and remarks in words, the rest remained unspoken. She looked at him contemplatively as he stood by her side with a tea-cup in his hand, leaning still a little against the flag-staff. Notwithstanding his rough clothes and heavy fisherman's boots, there was nothing about his attitude or his speech, save in its dialect, to denote the fact that he was of a different order from that in which she had been brought up. She felt an immense curiosity concerning him, and she felt, too, that it would probably never be gratified. Most men were her slaves from the moment she smiled upon them. This one she fancied seemed a little bored by her presence. He did not even seem to be thinking about her. He was watching steadily and with somewhat bent eyebrows Cecil de la Borne and Forrest. Something struck her as she looked from one to the other.

"I read once," she remarked, "that people who live in a very small village for generation after generation grow to look like one another. In a certain way I cannot conceive two men more unlike, and yet at that moment there was something in your face which reminded me of Mr. De la Borne."

He looked down at her with a quick frown. Decidedly he was annoyed.

"You are certainly the first," he said drily, "who has ever discovered the likeness, if there is any."

"It does not amount to a likeness," she answered, "and you need not look so angry. Mr. De la Borne is considered very good-looking. Dear me, what a nuisance! Do you see? We are going!"

Andrew de la Borne took the cup from her hand and helped to prepare the boat. With a faint smile upon his lips he heard a little colloquy between Cecil and the Princess which amused him. The Princess, as he prepared to hand her into the boat, showed herself at any rate possessed of the instincts of her order. She held out her hand and smiled sweetly upon Andrew.

"We are so much obliged to you for your delightful tea, Mr. Andrew," she said. "I hope that next time my daughter goes wandering about in dangerous places you may be there to look after her."

Andrew looked swiftly away towards Jeanne. Somehow or other the Princess' words seemed to come to him at that moment charged with some secondary meaning. He felt instinctively that notwithstanding her thoroughly advanced airs, Jeanne was little more than a child as compared with these people. She met his eyes with one of her most delightful smiles.

"Some day, I hope," she said, "that you will take me out in the punt again. I can assure you that I quite enjoyed being rescued."

The little party sailed away, Cecil with an obvious air of relief. Andrew turned slowly round, and met his friend issuing from the door of the cottage.

"Andrew," he said, "no wonder you did not care about being

host to such a crowd!"

There was meaning in his tone, and Andrew looked at him thoughtfully.

"Do you know — anything definite?" he asked.

Berners nodded.

"About one of them," he said, "I certainly do. I wonder what on earth has become of Ronald. He was with them yesterday."

"Had enough, perhaps," Andrew suggested.

Berners shook his head.

"I am afraid not," he answered slowly. "I wish I could think that he had so much sense."

CHAPTER XIII

Cecil came into the room abruptly, and closed the door behind him. He was breathing quickly as though he had been running. His lips were a little parted, and in his eyes shone an unmistakable expression of fear. Forrest and the Princess both looked towards him apprehensively.

"What is it, Cecil?" the latter asked quickly. "You are a fool to go about the house looking like that."

Cecil came further into the room and threw himself into a chair.

"It is that fellow upon the island," he said. "You remember we all said that his face was familiar. I have seen him again, and I have remembered."

"Remembered what?" the Princess asked.

"Where it was that I saw him last," Cecil answered. "It was in Pall Mall, and he was walking with — with Engleton. It was before I knew him, but I knew who he was. He must be a friend of Engleton's. What do you suppose that he is doing here?"

Cecil was shaking like a leaf. The Princess looked towards him contemptuously.

"Come," she said, "there is no need for you to behave like a terrified child. Even if you have seen him once with Lord Ronald, what on earth is there in that to be terrified about? Lord Ronald had many friends and acquaintances everywhere. This one is surely harmless enough. He behaved quite naturally on the island, remember."

Cecil shook his head.

"I do not understand," he said. "I do not understand what he can be doing in this part of the world, unless he has some object. I saw him just now standing behind a tree at the entrance to the drive, watching me drive golf balls out on to the marsh. I am almost certain that he was about the place last night. I saw some one who looked very much like him pass along the cliffs just about dinner-time."

"You are frightened at shadows," the Princess declared contemptuously. "If he were one of Lord Ronald's friends, and he had come here to look for him, he wouldn't play about watching you from a distance. Besides, there has been no time yet. Lord Ronald only — left here yesterday morning."

"What is he doing, then, watching this house?" Cecil asked. "That is what I do not like."

The Princess raised her eyebrows contemptuously.

"My dear Cecil," she said, "it is just a coincidence, and not a very remarkable one at that. Lord Ronald had the name, you know, of having acquaintances in every quarter of the world."

Cecil drew a little breath.

"It may be all right," he said, "but I am not used to this sort of thing, and it gives me the creeps."

"Of course it is all right," the Princess said composedly. "One would think that we were a pack of children, to take any notice of such trifles. It is too early, my dear Cecil, by many a day, to look for trouble yet. Lord Ronald always wandered about pretty much as he chose. It will be months before — "

"Don't go on," Cecil interrupted. "I suppose I am a fool, but all the time I am fancying things."

Forrest moved away with a little laugh, and the Princess rose and thrust her arm through Cecil's.

"Silly boy!" she said. "You have nothing to be frightened about, I can assure you."

"I am not frightened," Cecil answered. "I don't think that I was ever a coward. All the same, there are some things about this fellow which I don't quite understand."

The Princess laughed as she swept from the room.

"Don't be foolish, Cecil," she said. "Remember that we are all here, and that nothing can go wrong unless we lose our nerve."

Forrest found the Princess alone a little later in the evening, waiting in the hall for the dinner-gong. He drew her into a corner, under pretext of showing her one of the old engravings, dark with age, which hung upon the wall.

"Ena," he said, "I suppose that you trust Cecil de la Borne? You haven't any fear about him, eh?"

The Princess shrugged her shoulders.

"No!" she answered. "He is a coward at heart, but he has enough vanity, I believe, to keep him from doing anything foolish. All the same, I think it is wiser not to leave him alone here."

"He would not stay," Forrest remarked. "He told me so only this morning."

"You suggested leaving?" the Princess asked.

Forrest nodded.

"I couldn't help it," he said, a little sullenly. "There is something about these great empty rooms, and the silence of the place, that's getting on my nerves. I start every time that great front-door bell clangs, or I hear an unfamiliar footstep in the hall. God! What fools we have been," he added, with a sudden bitter strength. "I couldn't have believed that I could ever have done anything so clumsy. Fancy giving ourselves away to a fool like Engleton, a self-opinionated young cub scarcely out of his cradle."

He felt his damp forehead. The Princess was watching him curiously.

"Don't be a fool, Nigel," she said. "We underrated Engleton, that was all. If ever a man looked an idiot, he did, and you must remember that we were in a corner. Yet," she added, leaning a little forward in her chair and gazing with hard, set face into the fire, "it was foolish of me. With Jeanne to play with, I ought to have had no such difficulties. I never counted upon the trades-people being so unreasonable. If they had let me finish the season it would have been all right."

Forrest walked restlessly across the room, and stood for a moment looking out of the window. Outside, the wind had suddenly changed. The sunshine had departed, and a grey fog was blowing in from the sea. He turned away with a shiver.

"What a cursed place this is!" he muttered. "I've half a mind even now to turn my back upon it and to run."

The Princess watched his pale face scornfully.

"I thought, Nigel," she said, "that you were a more reasonable person. Remember that if we show the white feather now, it is the end of everything — the Colonies, if you like, or a little cheap watering-place at the best. As for me, I might have a better chance of brazening it out, but remember that I could never afford to be seen in the company of a suspected person."

"It was the fear of losing you," he muttered, "which made me so rash."

The Princess laughed very softly.

"My dear friend," she said, "I do not believe you. I may seem to you sometimes very foolish, but at least I understand this. Life with you is self, self, self, and nothing more. You have scarcely a generous instinct, scarcely a spark of real affection left in you."

"And yet — " he began quietly.

"And yet," she whispered, repulsing him with a little gesture, but with a suddenly altered look in her face, "and yet we women are fools!"

She turned round to meet her host, who was crossing the hall, and almost simultaneously the dinner gong rang out. Their party was perhaps a little more cheerful than it had been on any of the last few evenings. Forrest drank more wine than usual, and exerted himself to entertain. Cecil followed his example, and the Princess, who sat by his side, looked often into his face, and whispered now and then in his ear. Jeanne was the only one who was a little distrait. She left the table early, as usual, and slipped out into the garden. The Princess, contrary to her custom, rose from the table and followed her. A sudden change of wind had blown the fog away, and the night was clear. The wind, however, had gathered force, and the Princess held down her elaborately coiffured hair and cried out in dismay.

"My dear Jeanne," she exclaimed, "but it is barbarous to wander about outside a night like this!"

Jeanne laughed. Her own more simply arranged hair was blown all over her face.

"I love it," she explained. "You don't want me indoors. I am going to walk down the grove and look at the sea."

"Come back into the hall one moment," the Princess said. "I want to speak to you."

Jeanne turned unwillingly round, and her step-mother drew her into the shelter of the open door.

"Jeanne," she said, "you seem to meet your friend the fisherman very often. If you should see anything of him tomorrow, I wish you would inquire particularly as to his lodger. You know whom I mean, the man who was on the island with him yesterday afternoon."

Jeanne looked at her stepmother curiously.

"What am I to ask about him?" she demanded.

"Where he comes from, and what he is doing here," the Princess said. "Find out if you can if Berners is really his name. I have a curious idea about him, and Cecil fancies that he has seen him before."

Jeanne looked for a minute interested.

"You are not usually so curious about people," she remarked.

The Princess lowered her voice a little.

"Jeanne," she said, "I will tell you something. Lord Ronald, when he left here, was very angry with us all. There was a quarrel, and he behaved very absurdly. Cecil fancies that this man Berners is a friend of Lord Ronald's. We want to know if it is so."

Jeanne raised her head and looked her stepmother steadily in the face.

"This is all very mysterious," she said. "I do not understand it at all. We seem to be almost in hiding here, seeing no one and going nowhere. And I notice that Major Forrest, whenever he walks even in the garden, is always looking around as though he were afraid of something. What did you quarrel with Lord Ronald about?"

"It is no concern of yours," the Princess answered, a little sharply. "Major Forrest has had a somewhat eventful career, and he has made enemies. It was chiefly his quarrel with Lord Ronald, and it was over a somewhat serious matter. He has an idea that this man Berners is connected with it in some way or other. Do find out if you can, there's a dear child."

"I do not suppose," Jeanne said, "that Mr. Andrew would know anything. However, when I see him I will ask him."

The Princess turned away from the open door, shivering.

"You are not really going out?" she said.

"Certainly I am," Jeanne answered. "I suppose you three will play cards, and it does not interest me to watch you. There is nothing which interests me here at all except the gardens and the sea. I am going down to the beach, and then I shall sit there behind the hollyhocks until it is bedtime."

The Princess looked at her curiously.

"You're a queer child," she said, turning away.

"It is not strange, that," Jeanne answered, with a little curl of the lips.

The Princess went back to the library. Coffee and liqueurs had already been served, and the card-table was set out, although none of the three had the slightest inclination to play. Jeanne walked along the beach and then came back to her favourite seat, sheltered by the little grove of stunted trees and the tall hollyhocks which bordered the garden. Her eyes were fixed upon the darkening sea, whitened here and there by the long straight line of breakers. The marshes on her right hand were hung with grey mists, floating about like weird phantoms, and here and there between them shone the distant lights of the village. She half closed her eyes. The soft falling of the waves upon the sand below, and the murmur of the wind through the bushes and scanty trees was like a lullaby. She sat there she scarcely knew how long. She woke up with a start, conscious that two men were standing talking together within a few yards of her in the rough lane that led down to the sea.

CHAPTER XIV

The Princess was attempting a new and very complicated form of patience. Forrest was watching her. Their host was making an attempt to read the newspaper.

"In five minutes," the Princess declared, "I shall have achieved the impossible. This time I am quite sure that I am going to do it."

A breathless silence followed her announcement. The Princess, looking up in surprise, found that the eyes of her two companions were fixed not upon her but upon the door. She laid down her cards and turned her head. It was Jeanne who stood there, her hair tossed and blown by the wind, her face ashen white.

"What is the matter, child?" the Princess demanded.

Jeanne came a little way into the room.

"There were two men," she faltered, "talking in the shrubbery close to where I was sitting behind the hollyhocks. I could not understand all that they said, but they are coming here. They were speaking of Lord Ronald."

"Go on," Forrest muttered, leaning forward with dilated eyes.

"They spoke as though something might have happened to him here," the girl whispered. "Oh! it is too horrible, this! What do you think that they meant?"

She looked at the three people who confronted her. There was nothing reassuring in the faces of the two men. The Princess leaned back in her chair and laughed.

"My dear child," she said, "you have been asleep and dreamed these foolish things; or if not, these yokels to whom you have been listening are mad. What harm do you suppose could come to Lord Ronald here?"

"I do not know," Jeanne said, speaking in a low tone, and with the fear still in her dark eyes.

"I told you," the Princess continued, "that there was some sort of a quarrel. What of it? Lord Ronald simply chose to go away. Do you suppose that there is any one here who would think of trying to hinder him? Look at us three and ask yourself if it is likely. Look at Major Forrest here, for instance, who never loses his temper, and whose whole life is a series of calculations. Or our host. Look at him," the Princess continued, with a little wave of her hand. "He may have secrets that we know nothing of, but if he is a desperate criminal, I must say that he has kept the knowledge very well to himself. As for me, you know very well that I quarrel with no one. Le jeu ne vaut pas la peine."

Jeanne drew a little breath. Her face was less tragic. There was a moment's silence. Then Cecil de la Borne moved toward the fireplace. He was pale, but his manner was more composed. The Princess' speech, drawn out, and very slowly spoken, of deliberate intent, had achieved its purpose. The first terror had passed away from all of them.

"I will ring the bell," Cecil said, "and find out who these trespassers are, wandering about my grounds at this hour of the night. Or shall we all go out and look for them ourselves?"

"As you will," Forrest answered. "Personally, I should think that Miss Jeanne has overheard some gossip amongst the servants, and misunderstood it. However, this sort of thing is just as well put a stop to."

A sudden peal rang through the house. The front-door bell, a huge unwieldy affair, seldom used, because, save in the depths of winter, the door stood open, suddenly sent a deep resonant summons echoing through the house. The bareness and height of the hall, and the fact that the room in which they were was quite close to the front door itself, perhaps accounted for the unusual volume of sound which seemed created by that one peal. It was more like an alarm bell, ringing out into the silent night, than any ordinary summons. Coming in the midst of those tense few seconds, it had an effect upon the people who heard it which was almost indescribable. Cecil de la Borne was pale with the nervousness of the coward, but Forrest's terror was a real and actual thing, stamped in his white face, gleaming in his sunken eyes, as he stood behind the card-table with his head a little thrust forward toward the door, as though listening for what might come next. The Princess, if she was in any way discomposed, did not show it. She sat erect in her chair, her head slightly thrown back, her eyebrows a little contracted. It was as though she were asking who had dared to break in so rudely upon her pastime. Jeanne had sunk back into the window, and was sitting there, her hands clasped together.

Cecil de la Borne glanced at the clock.

"It is nearly eleven o'clock," he said. "The servants will have gone to bed. I must go and see who that is."

No one attempted to stop him. They heard his footsteps go echoing down the silent hall. They heard the harsh clanking of the chain as he drew it back, and the opening of the heavy door. They all looked at one another in tense expectation. They heard Cecil's challenge, and they heard muffled voices outside. Then there came the closing of the door, and the sound of heavy footsteps in the hall. Forrest grasped the table with both hands, and his face was bloodless. The Princess leaned towards him.

"For God's sake, Nigel," she whispered in his ear, "pull yourself together! One look into your face is enough to give the whole show away. Even Jeanne there is watching you."

The man made an effort. Even as the footsteps drew near he dashed some brandy into a tumbler and drank it off. Cecil de la Borne entered, followed by the man who had been Andrew's guest and another, a small dark person with glasses, and a professional air. Cecil, who had been a little in front, turned round to usher them in.

"I cannot keep you out of my house, gentlemen, I suppose," he said, "although I consider that your intrusion at such an hour is entirely unwarrantable. I regret that I have no other room in which I can receive you. What you have to say to me, you can say here before my friends. If I remember rightly," he added, "your name is Berners, and you are lodging in this neighbourhood."

The man who had called himself Berners bowed to the Princess and Jeanne before replying. His manner was grave, but not in any way threatening. His companion stood behind him and remained silent.

"I have called myself Berners," he said, "because it is more convenient at times to do so. I am Richard Berners, Duke of Westerham. A recent guest of yours — Lord Ronald — is my younger brother."

The silence which reigned in the room might almost have been felt. The Duke, looking from one to the other, grew graver.

"I suppose," he continued, "I ought to apologize for coming here so late at night, but my solicitor has only just arrived from London, and reported to me the result of some inquiries he has been making. Ronald is my favourite brother, although I have not seen much of him lately. I trust, therefore," he continued, still speaking to Cecil de la Borne, "that you will pardon my intrusion when I explain that from the moment of quitting your house my brother seems to have completely disappeared. I have come to ask you if you can give me any information as to the circumstances of his leaving, and whether he told you his destination."

Cecil de la Borne was white to the lips, but he was on the point of answering when the Princess intervened. She leaned forward toward the newcomer, and her face expressed the most genuine concern.

"My dear Duke," she said, "this is very extraordinary news that you bring. Lord Ronald left here for London. Do you mean to say that he has never arrived there?"

The Duke turned towards his companion.

"My solicitor here, Mr. Hensellman," he said, "has made the most careful inquiries, and has even gone so far as to employ detectives. My brother has certainly not returned to London. We have also wired to every country house where a visit from him would have been a probability, without result. Under those circumstances, and others which I need not perhaps enlarge upon, I must confess to feeling some anxiety as to what has become of him."

"Naturally," the Princess answered at once. "And yet," she continued, "it is only a few days ago since he left here. Your brother, Duke, who seemed to me a most delightful young man, was also distinctly peculiar, and I do not think that the fact of your not being able to hear of him at his accustomed haunts for two or three days is in any way a matter which need cause you any anxiety."

The Duke bowed.

"Madam," he said, "I regret having to differ from you. I beg that you will not permit anything which I say to reflect upon yourself or upon Mr. De la Borne, whose honour, I am sure, is above question. But you have amongst you a person whom I am assured is a very bad companion indeed for boys of my brother's age. I refer to you, sir," he added, addressing Forrest.

Forrest bowed ironically.

"I am exceedingly obliged to you, sir," he said, "for your amiable opinion, although why you should go out of your way to volunteer it here, I cannot imagine."

"I do so, sir," the Duke answered, "because during the last two or three days cheques for a considerable amount have been honoured at my brother's bank, bearing your endorsement. I may add, sir, that I came down here to see my brother. I wished to explain to him that you were not a person with whom it was advisable for him to play cards."

Forrest took a quick step forward.

"Sir," he exclaimed, "you are a liar!"

The Duke bowed.

"I do not quote my own opinion," he said. "I speak from the result of the most careful investigations. Your reputation you cannot deny. Even at your own clubs men shrug their shoulders when your name is mentioned. I will give you the benefit of any doubt you wish. I will simply say that you are a person who is suspected in any assembly where gentlemen meet together, and that being so, as my brother has disappeared from this house after several nights spent in playing cards with you, I am here to learn from you, and from you, sir," he added, turning to Cecil de la Borne, "some further information as to the manner of my brother's departure, or to remain here until I have acquired that information for myself."

The Princess rose to her feet and laid her hand upon Forrest's shoulder. The veins were standing out upon his forehead, and his face was black with anger. He seemed to be in the act of springing upon the man who made these charges against him.

"Nigel," she said, "please let me talk to the Duke. Remember that, after all, from his own point of view, what he is saying is not so outrageous as it seems to us. Cecil, please don't interfere," she added turning towards him. "Duke," she continued, speaking firmly, and with much of the amiability gone from her tone, "you are playing the modern Don Quixote to an extent which is unpardonable, even taking into account your anxiety concerning your brother. Lord Ronald was a guest here of Mr. De la Borne's, and to the best of my knowledge he lost little more than he won all the time he was here. In any case, on Major Forrest's behalf, and as an old friend, I deny that there was any question whatever as to the fairness of any games that were played. Your brother received a telegram, and asked to be allowed the use of the car to take him to Lynn Station early on the following morning. He promised to return within a week."

"You have heard from him since he left?" the Duke asked quickly.

"We have not," the Princess answered. "Only yesterday morning I remarked that it was slightly discourteous. Your brother left here on excellent terms with us all. You can interview, if you will, any member of the household. You can make your inquiries at the station from which he departed. Your appearance here at such an untimely hour, and your barely veiled accusations, remind me of the fable of the bull in the china shop. If you think that we have locked your brother up here, pray search the house. If you think," she added, with curling lip, "that we have murdered him, pray bring down an army of detectives, invest the place, and pursue your investigations in whatever direction you like. But before you leave, I should advise you, if you wish to preserve your reputation as a person of breeding, to apologize to Mr. De la Borne for your extraordinary behaviour here tonight, and the extraordinary things at which you have hinted."

The Duke smiled pleasantly.

"Madam," he said, "I came here tonight not knowing that you were amongst the difficulties which I should have to deal with. I wish to speak to Mr. De la Borne. You will permit me?"

The Princess shrugged her shoulders and turned away.

"I have ventured to speak for both of them," she remarked, "for the sake of peace, because I am a woman and can keep my temper, and they are men who might have resented your impertinence."

The Duke remained as though he had not heard her speech. He laid his hand upon Cecil's shoulder.

"De la Borne," he said, "you and I are scarcely strangers, although we have never met. There have been friendships in our families for many years. Don't be afraid to speak out if anything has gone a little wrong here and you are ashamed of it. I want to be your friend, as you know very well. Tell me, now. Can't you help me to find Ronald. Haven't you any idea where he is?"

"None at all," Cecil answered.

"Tell me this, then," the Duke said, his clear brown eyes fixed steadily upon Cecil's miserable white face. "Were there any unusual circumstances at all connected with his leaving here?"

"None whatever," Cecil answered, with an uneasy little laugh, "except that I had to get up to see him off, and it was a beastly cold morning."

The lawyer, who had been standing silent all this time, drew the Duke for a moment on one side.

"I should recommend, sir," he whispered, "that we went away. If they know anything they do not mean to tell, and the less we let them know as to whether we are satisfied or not, the better."

The Duke nodded, and turned once more to Cecil.

"I am forced to accept your word, Mr. De la Borne," he said, "and when my brother confirms your story I shall make a special visit here to offer you my apologies. Madam," he added, bowing to the Princess, "I regret to have disturbed your interesting occupation."

Forrest he completely ignored, turning his back upon him almost immediately. Cecil went out with them into the hall. In a moment the great front door was opened and closed. Cecil came back into the room, and the perspiration stood out in great beads upon his forehead. Now that the Duke had departed, something seemed to have fallen from their faces. They looked at one another as the ghosts of their real selves might have looked. Forrest stumbled toward the sideboard. Cecil was already there.

"The brandy!" he muttered. "Quick!"

CHAPTER XV

Bareheaded, Jeanne walked upon the yellow sands close to the softly breaking waves. Inland stretched the marshes, with their patches of vivid green, their clouds of faintly blue wild lavender, their sinuous creeks stealing into the bosom of the land. She climbed on to a grassy knoll, warm with the sun's heat, and threw herself down upon the turf. She turned her back upon the Hall and looked steadily seawards, across the waste of sands and pasture-land to where sky and sea met. Here at least was peace. She drew a long breath of relief, cast aside the book which she had never dreamed of reading, and lay full length in the grass, with her eyes upturned to where a lark was singing his way down from the blue sky.

Andrew came before long, speeding his way out of the village harbour in his little catboat. She watched him cross the sandy bar of the inlet, and run his boat presently upon the beach below where she sat. Then she shook out her skirts and made room for him by her side.

"Really, Mr. Andrew," she said, resting her chin upon her hands, and looking up at him with her full dark eyes, "you are becoming almost gallant. Until now, when I have been weary, and have wished to talk to you, I have had almost to come and fetch you. Today it is you who come to me. That is a good sign."

"It is true," he admitted. "I have kept my telescope fixed upon the sands here for more than an hour. I wanted to see you."

"You have something to tell me about last night?" she asked gravely.

"No!" he answered, "I did not come here to talk about that."

"Did you know," she asked, "who your lodger really was?"

"Yes," he said, "I guessed! I will be frank with you, Miss Jeanne, if you will allow me. I do not like your stepmother and I do not like Major Forrest, but I think that the Duke is going altogether too far when he suspects them of having anything to do with the disappearance of his brother."

She drew a little sigh of relief.

"Oh! I am glad to hear you say that," she declared. "It is all so horrible. I could not sleep last night for thinking about it."

"Lord Ronald will probably turn up in a day or two," Andrew said gravely. "We will not talk any more about him."

She settled herself a little more comfortably, and smoothed out her skirts. Then she looked up at him with faintly parted lips.

"What shall we talk about, Mr. Andrew?" she said softly.

"About ourselves," he answered, "or rather about you. It seems to me that we both stand a little outside the game of life, as your friends up there understand it."

He waved his large brown hand in the direction of the Hall.

"You are a child, fresh from boarding-school, too young to understand, too young to know where to look for your friends, or discriminate against your enemies. I am a rough sort of fellow, also, outside their lives, from necessity, from every reason which the brain of man could evolve. Sometimes we outsiders see more than is intended. Is the Princess of Strurm really your stepmother?"

"Of course she is," Jeanne answered. "She was married to my father when I was quite a little girl, and she has visited me at the convent where I was at school, all my life, and when I left last year it was she who came for me. Why do you ask so strange a question?"

"Because," he said, "I should consider her about the worst possible guardian that a child like you could have. Tell me, what is it that goes on all day up at the Hall there — or rather what was it that did go on before Engleton went away? — eating and drinking, cards, and God knows what sort of foolishness! Nothing else, nothing worth doing, not a thing said worth listening to! It's a rotten life for a child like you. They tell me you're an heiress. Are you?"

She smoothed her crumpled skirts, and looked steadily at the tip of her brown shoe.

"One of the greatest in Europe," she answered. "No one knows how rich I am. You see all the money was left to me when I was six years old, and it is so strictly tied up that no one has had power to touch a single penny until I am of age. That is why it has gone on increasing and increasing."

"And when are you of age?" he asked.

"Next year," she answered.

"By that time, I imagine," Andrew continued, "your stepmother will have sold you to some broken-down hanger-on of hers. Haven't you any other relations, Miss Jeanne?"

She laughed softly.

"You are a ridiculous person," she said. "I am very fond of my stepmother. I think that she is a very clever woman."

"Bah!" he exclaimed in disgust. "A clever woman she may be, but a good woman, no! I am sure of that. You may judge a person by the company they keep. Neither she or this man Forrest are fit associates for a child of your age."

She laughed softly.

"They don't do me any harm," she said. "Mr. De la Borne and Lord Ronald have asked me to marry them, of course, but then every young man does that when he knows who I am. My step-mother has promised me at least that I shall not be bothered by any of them just yet. I am going to be presented next season, we are going to have a house in town, and I am going to choose a husband of my own."

It was Andrew now who looked long and steadily out sea-wards. She watched him covertly from under her heavily lidded eyes.

"Mr. Andrew," she said softly, "I wish very much — "

Then she stopped short, and he looked at her a little abruptly.

"What is it that you wish?" he asked.

"I wish that you did not wear such strange clothes and that you did not talk the dialect of these fishermen, and that you had more money. Then you too might come and see me, might you not, when we have that house in London?"

He laughed boisterously.

"I fancy I see myself in London, paying calls," he declared. "Give me my catboat and fishing line. I'd rather sail down the home creek, with a northeast gale in my teeth, than walk down Piccadilly in patent boots."

She sighed.

"I am afraid," she admitted, "that as a town acquaintance you are hopeless."

"I am afraid so," he answered, looking steadily seawards. "We country people have strong prejudices, you see. It seems to us that all the sin and all the unhappiness and all the decadence and all the things that mar the beauty of the world, come from the cities and from life in the cities. No wonder that we want to keep away. It isn't that we think ourselves better than the other folk. It is simply that we have realized pleasures greater than we could find in paved streets and under smoke-stained skies. We know what it is to smell the salt wind, to hear it whistling in the cords and the sails of our boats, to feel the warmth of the sun, to listen to the song of the birds, to watch the colouring of God's land here. I suppose we have the thing in our bloods; we can't leave it. We hear the call of the other things sometimes, but as soon as we obey we are restless and unhappy. It is only an affair of time, and generally a very short time. One cannot fight against nature."

"No!" she answered softly. "One cannot fight against nature. But there are children of the cities, children of the life artificial as well as children of nature. Look at me!"

He turned toward her quickly.

"Look at me!" she commanded, and he obeyed.

He saw her pale skin, which the touch of the sun seemed to have no power to burn or coarsen. The clear, wonderful eyes, the delicate eyebrows, the masses of dark hair, the scarlet lips. He saw her white throat swelling underneath her muslin blouse. The daintiness of her gown, airy and simple, yet fresh from a Paris workshop. The stockings and shoes, exquisite, but strangely out of place with their high heels buried in the sand.

"How do I know," she demanded, "that I am not one of the children of the cities, that I was not fashioned and made for the gas-lit life, to eat unreal food at unreal hours, and feed my brain upon the unreal epigrams of the men whom you would call decadents. Two days here, a week — very well. In a month I might be bored. Who shall guarantee me against it?"

"No one," he answered. "And yet there is something in your blood which calls for the truth, which hates the shams, which knows real beauty. Why don't you try and cultivate it? In your heart you know where the true things lie. Consider! Every one with great wealth can make or mar many lives. You enter the world almost as a divinity. Your wealth is reckoned as a quality. What you do will be right. What you condemn will be wrong. It is a very important thing for others as well as yourself, that you should see a clear way through life."

A moment's intense dejection seized upon her. The tears stood in her eyes as she looked away from him.

"Who is there to show it me?" she asked. "Who is there to help me find it?"

"Not those friends whom you have left to play bridge in a room with drawn curtains at this hour of the day," he answered. "Not your stepmother, or any of her sort. Try and realize this. Even the weakest of us is not dependent upon others for support. There is only one sure guide. Trust yourself. Be faithful to the best part of yourself. You know what is good and what is ugly. Don't be coerced, don't be led into the morass."

She looked at him and laughed gaily. Her mood had changed once more with chameleon-like swiftness.

"It is all very well for you," she declared. "You are six foot four, and you look as though you could hew your way through life with a cudgel. One could fancy you a Don Quixote amongst the shams, knocking them over like ninepins, and moving aside neither to the right nor to the left. But what is a poor weak girl to do? She wants some one, Mr. Andrew, to wield the cudgel for her."

It was several seconds before he turned his head. Then he found that, although her lips were laughing, her eyes were longing and serious. She sprang suddenly to her feet and leaned towards him.

"This is the most delightful nonsense," she whispered. "Please!"

She was in his arms for a moment, her lips had clung to his. Then she was away, flying along the sands at a pace which seemed to him miraculous, swinging her hat in her hands, and humming the maddening refrain of some French song, which it seemed to him was always upon her lips, and which had haunted him for days. He hesitated, uncertain whether to follow, ashamed of himself, ashamed of the passion which was burning in his blood. And while he hesitated she passed out of sight, turning only once to wave her hand as she crossed the line of grass-grown hillocks which shut him out from her view.

CHAPTER XVI

"Tomorrow," the Princess said softly, "we shall have been here a fortnight."

Cecil de la Borne came and sat by her side upon the sofa.

"I am afraid," he said, "that leaving out everything else, you have been terribly bored."

"I have been nothing of the sort," she answered. "Of course, the last week has been a strain, but we are not going to talk any more about that. You prepared us for semi-barbarism, and instead you have made perfect sybarites of us. I can assure you that though in one way to go will be a release, in another I shall be very sorry."

"And I," he said, in a low tone, "shall always be sorry."

He let his hand fall upon hers, and looked into her eyes. The Princess stifled a yawn. This country style of love-making was a thing which she had outgrown many years ago.

"You will find other distractions very soon," she said, "and besides, the world is a small place. We shall see something of you, I suppose, always. By the by, you have not been particularly attentive to my stepdaughter during the last few days, have you?"

"She gives me very little chance," he answered, in a slightly aggrieved tone.

"She is very young," the Princess said, "too young, I suppose, to take things seriously. I do not think that she will marry very early."

Cecil bent over his companion till his head almost touched hers.

"Dear lady," he said, "I am afraid that I am not very interested in your stepdaughter while you are here."

"Absurd!" she murmured. "I am nearly twice your age."

"If you were," he answered, "so much the better, but you are not. Do you know, I think that you have been rather unkind to me. I have scarcely seen you alone since you have been here."

She laughed softly, and took up her little dog into her arm as though to use him for a shield.

"My dear Cecil," she said earnestly, "please don't make love to me. I like you so much, and I should hate to feel that you were boring me. Every man with whom I am alone for ten minutes thinks it his duty to say foolish things to me, and I can assure you that I am past it all. A few years ago it was different. Today there are only three things in the world I care for — my little spaniel here, bridge, and money."

His face darkened a little.

"You did not talk like this in London," he reminded her.

"Perhaps not," she admitted. "Perhaps even now it is only a mood with me. I can only speak as I feel for the moment. There are times when I feel differently, but not now."

"Perhaps," he said jealously, "there are also other people with whom you feel differently."

"Perhaps," she admitted calmly.

"When I came into the room the other day," he said, "Forrest was holding your hand."

"Major Forrest," she said, "has been very much upset. He needed a little consolation. He has some other engagements, and he ought to have left before now, but, as you know, we are all prisoners. I wonder how long it will last."

"I cannot tell," Cecil answered gloomily. "Forrest knows more about it than I do. What does he say to you?"

"He thinks," the Princess said slowly, "that we may be able to leave in a few days now."

"Then while you do stay," Cecil begged, "be a little kinder to me."

She withdrew her hand from her dog and patted his for a moment.

"You foolish boy," she said. "Of course I will be a little kinder to you, if you like, but I warn you that I shall only be a disappointment. Boys of your age always expect so much, and I have so little to give."

"Why do you say that?" he asked.

She shrugged her shoulders.

"Because it is the truth," she answered. "You must not expect anything more from me than the husk of things. Believe me, I am not a poseuse. I really mean it."

"You may change your mind," he said.

"I may," she answered. "I have no convictions, and my enemies would add, no principles. If any one could make me feel the things which I have forgotten how to feel, I myself am perfectly willing! But don't hope too much from that. And do, there's a dear boy, go and stop my maid. I can see her on her way down the drive there. She has some telegrams I gave her, and I want to send another."

Cecil hurried out, and the Princess, moving to the window, beckoned to Forrest, who was lounging in a wicker chair with a cigarette in his mouth.

"Nigel," she said, "how much longer?"

Forrest looked despondently at his cigarette.

"I cannot tell," he answered. "Perhaps one day, perhaps a week, perhaps — "

"No!" the Princess interrupted, "I do not wish to hear that eventuality."

"You know that the Duke is still about?" Forrest said gloomily. "I saw him this morning. There has been a fellow, too — a detective, of course — enquiring about the car and who was able to drive it."

"But that," the Princess interrupted, "is all in our favour. You were seen to bring it back up the drive about ten o'clock in the morning."

Forrest nodded.

"Don't let's talk about it," he said. "Where is Jeanne? Do you know?"

The Princess pointed toward the lawn to where Cecil and Jeanne were just starting a game of croquet. Forrest watched them for a few minutes meditatively.

"Ena," he said, dropping his voice a little, "what are you going to do with that child? I have never quite understood your plans. You promised to talk to me about it while we were down here."

"I know," the Princess answered, "only this other affair has driven everything out of our minds. What I should like to do," she continued, "is to marry her before she comes of age, if I can find any one willing to pay the price."

"The price?" he repeated doubtfully.

The Princess nodded.

"Supposing," she continued, "that her fortune amounted to nearly four hundred thousand pounds, I think that twenty-five thousand pounds would be a very moderate sum for any one to pay for a wife with such a dowry."

"Have you any one in your mind?" he asked.

The Princess nodded.

"I have a friend in Paris who is making some cautious inquiries," she answered. "I am expecting to hear from her in the course of a few days."

"So far," he remarked, "you have made nothing out of your guardianship except a living allowance."

She nodded.

"And a ridiculously small one," she remarked. "All that I have had is two thousand a year. I need not tell you, my dear Nigel, that that does not go very far when it has to provide dresses and servants and a home for both of us. Jeanne is content, and never grumbles, or her lawyers might ask some very inconvenient questions."

"Supposing," he asked, "that she won't have anything to do with this man, when you have found one who is willing to pay?"

"Until she is of age," the Princess answered, "she is mine to do what I like with, body and soul. The French law is stricter than the English in this respect, you know. There may be a little trouble, of course, but I shall know how to manage her."

"She has likes and dislikes of her own," he remarked, "and fairly positive ones. I believe if she had her own way, she would spend all her time with this fisherman here."

The Princess smoothed the lace upon her gown, and gazed reflectively at the turquoises upon her white fingers.

"Jeanne's father," she remarked, "was bourgeois, and her mother had little family. Race tells, of course. I have never attempted to influence her. When there is a great struggle ahead, it is as well to let her have her own way in small things. Hush! She is coming. I suppose the croquet has been a failure."

Jeanne came across to them, swinging her mallet in her hand.

"Will some one," she begged, "take our too kind host away from me? He follows me everywhere, and I am bored. I have played croquet with him, but he is not satisfied. If I try to read, he comes and sits by my side and talks nonsense. If I say I am going for a walk, he wants to come with me. I am tired of it."

The Princess looked at her stepdaughter critically. Jeanne was dressed in white, with a great red rose stuck through her waistband. She was paler even than usual, her eyes were dark and luminous, and the curve of her scarlet lips suggested readily enough the weariness of which she spoke.

The Princess shrugged her shoulders and gathered up her skirts.

"Do what you like, my dear," she said. "I will tell Cecil to leave you alone. But remember that he is our host. You must really be civil to him."

She strolled across the lawn to where Cecil was still knocking the croquet balls about. Jeanne sank into her place, and Forrest looked at her for a few moments attentively.

"You are a strange child," he said at last.

She glanced towards him as though she found his speech an impertinence. Then she looked away across the old-fashioned, strangely arranged garden, with its irregular patches of many coloured flowers, its wind-swept shrubs, its flag-staff rising from the grassy knoll at the seaward extremity. She watched the seagulls, wheeling in from the sea, and followed the line of smoke of a distant steamer. She seemed to find all these things more interesting than conversation.

"You do not like me," he remarked quietly. "You have never liked me."

"I have liked very few of my stepmother's friends," she answered, "any more than I like the life which I have been compelled to lead since I left school."

"You would prefer to be back there, perhaps?" he remarked, a little sarcastically.

"I should," she answered. "It was prison of a sort, but one was at least free to choose one's friends."

"If," he suggested, "you could make up your mind that I was a person at any rate to be tolerated, I think that I could make things easier for you. Your stepmother is always inclined to follow my advice, and I could perhaps get her to take you to quieter places, where you could lead any sort of life you liked."

"Thank you," she answered. "Before very long I shall be my own mistress. Until then I must make the best of things. If you wish to do something for me you can answer a question."

"Ask it, then," he begged at once. "If I can, I shall be only too glad."

"You can tell me something which since the other night," she said, "has been worrying me a good deal. You can tell me who it was that drove Lord Ronald to the station the morning he went away. I thought that he sent his chauffeur away two days ago, and that there was no one here who could drive the car."

Forrest was momentarily taken aback. He answered, however, with scarcely any noticeable hesitation.

"I did," he answered. "I didn't make much of a job of it, and the car has been scarcely fit to use since, but I managed it somehow, or rather we did between us. He came and knocked me up about five o'clock, and begged me to come and try."

She looked at him with peculiar steadfastness. There was nothing in her eyes or her expression to suggest belief or disbelief in his words.

"But I have heard you say so often," she remarked, "that you knew absolutely nothing about the mechanism of a car, and that you would not drive one for anything in the world."

He nodded.

"I am not proud of my skill," he answered, "but I did try at Homburg once. There was nothing else to do, and I had some idea of buying a small car for touring in the Black Forest. If you doubt my words, you can ask any of the servants. They saw me bring the car up the avenue later in the morning."

"It was being dragged up," she reminded him. "The engine was not going."

He looked a little startled.

"It had only just gone wrong," he said. "I had brought it all the way from Lynn."

She rose to her feet.

"Thank you for answering my question," she said. "I am going for a walk now."

He leaned quite close to her.

"Alone?" he asked suggestively.

She swept away without even looking at him. He shrugged his shoulders as he resumed his seat.

"I am not sure," he said reflectively, as he lit a cigarette, "that Ena will find that young woman so easy to deal with as she imagines!"

CHAPTER XVII

Andrew looked up from his gardening, startled by the sudden peal of thunder. Absorbed in his task, he had not noticed the gathering storm. The sky was black with clouds, riven even while he looked with a vivid flash of forked lightning. The ground beneath his feet seemed almost to shake beneath that second peal of thunder. In the stillness that followed he heard the cry of a woman in distress. He threw down his spade and raced to the other side of the garden. About twenty yards from the shore, Jeanne, in a small boat, was rowing toward the island. She was pulling at the great oars with feeble strokes, and making no headway against the current which was sweeping down the tidal way. There was no time for hesitation. Andrew threw off his coat, and wading into the water, reached her just in time. He clambered into the boat and took the oars from her trembling fingers. He was not a moment too soon, for the long tidal waves were rushing in now before the storm. He bent to his task, and drove the boat safely on to the beach. Then he stood up, dripping, and handed her out.

"My dear young lady," he said, a little brusquely, and forgetting for the moment his Norfolk dialect, "what on earth are you about in that little boat all by yourself?"

She was still frightened, and she looked at him a little piteously.

"Please don't be angry with me," she said. "I wanted to come here and see you, to — to ask your advice. The boat was lying there, and it looked such a very short distance across, and directly I had started the big waves began to come in and I was frightened."

The storm broke upon them. Another peal of thunder was followed by a downpour of rain. He caught hold of her hand.

"Run as hard as you can," he said.

They reached the cottage, breathless. He ushered her into his little sitting-room.

"Has your friend gone?" she asked.

"Yes!" he answered. "He went last night."

"I am glad," she declared. "I wanted to see you alone. You said that he was lodging here, did you not?"

Andrew nodded.

"Yes," he said, "but he only stayed for a few days."

"You have an extra room here, then?" she asked.

"Certainly," he answered, wondering a little at the drift of her questions.

"Will you let it to me, please?" she asked. "I am looking for lodgings, and I should like to stay for a little time here."

He looked at her in amazement.

"My dear young lady!" he exclaimed. "You are joking!"

"I am perfectly serious," she answered. "I will tell you all about it if you like."

"But your stepmother!" he protested. "She would never come to such a place. Besides, you are Mr. De la Borne's guests."

"I do not wish to stay there any longer," she said. "I do not wish to stay with my stepmother any longer. Something has happened which I cannot altogether explain to you, but which makes me feel that I want to get away from them all. I have enough money, and I am sure I should not be much trouble. Please take me, Mr. Andrew."

He suddenly realized what a child she was. Her dark eyes were raised wistfully to his. Her oval face was a little flushed by her recent exertions. She wore a very short skirt, and her hair hung about her shoulders in a tangled mass. Her little foreign mannerisms, half inciting, half provocative, were forgotten. His heart was full of pity for her.

"My dear child," he said, "you are not serious. You cannot possibly be serious. Your stepmother is your guardian, and she certainly would not allow you to run away from her like this. Besides, I have not even a maid-servant. It would be absolutely impossible for you to stay here."

Her eyes filled with tears. She dropped her arms with a weary little gesture.

"But I should love it so much," she said. "Here I could rest, and forget all the things which worry me in this new life. Here I could watch the sea come in. I could sit down on the beach there and listen to the larks singing on the marshes. Oh! it would be such a rest — so peaceful! Mr. Andrew, is it quite impossible?"

He played his part well enough, laughing at her good-humouredly.

"It is more than impossible," he said. "If you stayed here for any time at all, your stepmother would come and fetch you back, and I should get into terrible disgrace. Mr. De la Borne would probably turn me out of my house," he added as an afterthought.

She sat down and looked out of the window in despair. The storm was still raging. The skies were black, and the window-pane streaming with rain-drops. She shivered a little.

"If I could help you in any other way," he continued, after a moment's pause, "I should be very glad to try."

She turned upon him quickly.

"How can you help me, or any one," she demanded, "unless you can take me away from these people? Listen! Until a few months ago I had scarcely seen my stepmother. She fetched me away from the convent, took me to Paris for some clothes, and since then I have done nothing but go to parties and houses where the people seem all to have fine names, but behave horribly. I know that I am rich. They told me that before I left the convent, so that I might be a little prepared, but is that any reason why every man, old and young, should say foolish things to me, and pretend that they have fallen in love, when I know all the time that it is my fortune they are thinking of. And my stepmother speaks of marrying me as though I were a piece of merchandise, to be disposed of to the highest bidder. I do not like her friends. I do not like the way they live. I have never liked Major Forrest. Last night your lodger and another man came to the Hall. They asked questions about Lord Ronald. They asked questions and they were told lies. I am sure of it. It got on my nerves. I thought I should shriek. Major Forrest said that it was he who drove Lord Ronald into Lynn, thirty-five miles away, at six o'clock in the morning. I am sure that he could not have driven the car a hundred yards."

"Good God!" Andrew muttered.

"I am sure of it," Jeanne continued. "Two days before Lord Ronald disappeared, he wanted the car to take us over to Sandringham, and he could not find the chauffeur. It seems that he was down at the public-house at the village, and he came back intoxicated. Lord Ronald was angry, and he sent the man away. The car was there in the coach-house, and there was no one who could drive it."

"But," Andrew protested, "Major Forrest was seen returning in the car."

"He was pulled up the avenue in it," Jeanne answered. "How he got the car there I don't know, but I do not believe that it had ever been any further."

"Why do you not believe that?" Andrew asked.

She leaned towards him.

"Because," she said, "I was up early. The car was there at eight o'clock, alone, just outside the gates. There were the marks where it had come down from the house, but there were no marks on the other side. I am sure that it had been no further. I felt the engine and it was cold. I do not believe that it had been started at all."

Andrew was looking very serious.

"Then," he said, "if Lord Ronald was not taken to Lynn that morning, what do you suppose has become of him?"

"I do not know," she cried. "I am afraid. I dare not stay there. They all look at one another and leave off talking when I come into the room unexpectedly. They all seem as though some trouble were hanging over them. I am afraid to be there, Mr. Andrew."

Andrew was very serious indeed now.

"I will go up to the Hall at once," he said, "and I will see Mr. De la Borne. I have some influence with him, and I will get to the bottom of the whole matter. I will take you back, and I will make inquiries at once."

She settled down in his easy chair. Her dark eyes were full of pleading.

"But, Mr. Andrew," she said, "I do not want to go back to the Hall. I am afraid of them all, and I am afraid of my stepmother more than any of them. Why may I not stay here? I will be very good, and I will give you no trouble at all."

"My child," he said firmly, "you are talking nonsense. I am only a village fisherman, but you could not possibly stay in my house here. I have not even a housekeeper."

"That," she declared calmly, "is an excellent reason why I should stop. I will be your housekeeper. Come and sit here by me and let us talk about it."

He walked instead to the window. He did not choose at that moment that she should see his face.

"You do not wish to have me!" she cried.

He turned round. She slid out of her chair and came over to his side.

"I can only tell you," he said gravely, "that it is impossible for you to stay here, and that I must take you home at once."

She took his arm and looked up into his face.

"At once, Mr. Andrew?" she asked timidly.

"As soon as the storm goes down," he answered, glancing uneasily towards the clock. "Listen, please, Miss — "

"Jeanne," she whispered.

"Miss Jeanne, then," he said. "There are some things which you do not yet understand very well, because you have been brought up differently to most English girls. I have some influence with Mr. De la Borne, and I shall do what I can for you up at the house. But it is very certain that you must not think of leaving your stepmother unless you have some other relative who is willing to take you. A child of your age cannot live alone. It is unheard of."

She sighed, and turned away.

"Very well, Mr. Andrew," she said. "If you do not wish to be troubled with me I will go back. I am ready when you are."

Andrew looked once more out of the window.

"We cannot cross just yet," he said. "The tide is coming in very fast, and even here there is a big sea."

"It is magnificent," she answered, stealing back to his side. "I only wish that we were outside."

"You could not stand up," he answered. "Listen!"

The thunder of the incoming waves seemed to fill the room. Even while they stood there a little shower of pebbles and spray were dashed against the windows. Andrew looked anxiously across the estuary and tapped the barometer by his side.

"I am afraid," he said, "that you are going to be late for dinner tonight. You are a bona fide prisoner here for an hour or more at least."

"I am so glad," she answered.

There was a knock at the door. A man entered with a tea-tray. He was in plain clothes and was obviously a servant. Jeanne looked at him in surprise.

"Has Mr. Berners left his servant here?" she asked.

"For a day or two," Andrew answered hastily. "He may come back, you see, and he went away in a great hurry. Martin, bring another teacup, and make the tea. please."

The man set down the tray and bowed.

"Very good, sir," he answered.

Jeannie watched him disappear, perplexed. Was it because he was so perfectly trained a servant that he addressed the man at her side with the same respect that he would have shown to his own master?

"I may stay for tea, may I?" she asked. "That is something, at any rate. I am going to look round at your things. You don't mind, do you?"

"Certainly not," he answered. "That big fish on the wall was caught within fifty yards of this island. Those sea-birds, too, were all shot from here."

"What strange little creatures!" she murmured. "You seem to find quite a lot of time to read and do other things beside fish, Mr. Andrew," she remarked, as she looked over his bookcases. "You puzzle me very much sometimes. I had no idea," she added, looking at him hesitatingly, "that people who have to work, as you have to, for a living, understood and read books like this."

"Ah, well," he answered, "I had perhaps a little more education than some of them."

The servant returned with some more things upon a tray. Jeanne sat down with a little laugh in front of the teapot. She was very much afraid of saying more than was polite, and she felt that she was amongst utterly strange surroundings. Yet it seemed to her a most extraordinary thing that a fisherman in a country village should possess a silver teapot and old Worcester china, and should be waited upon by a man servant even though he were the man servant of a lodger.

CHAPTER XVIII

The storm died away with the coming of evening, but a great sea still broke upon the island beach and floated up the estuary. Andrew stood outside his door and looked across toward the mainland with a perplexed frown. It was barely a hundred yards crossing, but it was certain that no boat could live for half the distance. Jeanne, who had recovered her spirits, stood by his side, and smiled as she saw the white crested waves come rolling up.

"It is beautiful, this," she declared. "Do you not love to feel the spray on your cheeks, Mr. Andrew? And how salt it smells, and fresh!"

"That is all very well," Andrew answered, "but I am wondering how we are going to get over to the other side there."

"I do not think," she answered, "that it will be possible for a long, long time. You will have to take me as a lodger whether you want to or not. I would not trust myself in a boat even with you, upon a sea like that."

"It will be high tide in half an hour," Andrew said, "and the sea will go down fast enough then."

"It may not," she answered hopefully. "I rather believe that there is another storm blowing up."

"There will be no dinner for you," he warned her.

"That I can endure cheerfully," she declared. "I am sick of dinners. I hate them. They come much too soon, and one has always the same things to eat. I am quite sure that I shall dine quite nicely with you, Mr. Andrew."

He glanced at his watch and looked out seaward. It was even as she had said. There were indications of another storm. Even while they stood there the large raindrops fell.

"We had better go in," Andrew said. "It is going to rain again."

She clapped her hands, and danced lightly back into the house. She subsided into his easy chair and clasped her hands over her head.

"Come and stand there on the hearthrug," she demanded, "and tell me stories — stories of fishing adventures and storms, and things that have happened to yourself. Never mind how ordinary they may seem. I want to hear them. Remember that everything is new to me. Everything is interesting." He accepted the inevitable at last, and they talked until the twilight filled the room. It was strange how much and yet how little she knew. The fascination of her worldly ignorance was a thing which grew continually upon him. Suddenly she burst into a little peal of laughter.

"I was wondering," she remarked, "whether they are waiting dinner for me. I can just imagine how frightened they all are."

"I had forgotten all about them," Andrew confessed. "Wait a moment."

He left the room and walked out on to the beach. The sea was still dashing its spray high over the roof of the little cottage. The stones outside were wet to within a few feet of his door. He looked across toward the mainland. Far away he fancied that he could see men carrying lanterns like will-o'-the-wisps, in that part of the marshes near the Hall. He retraced his steps to the sitting-room.

"I am afraid," he said, "that it will not be possible to take you back tonight. The sea is still too rough for my boat, and shows no sign of going down."

She clapped her hands.

"I am very glad," she declared frankly. "I would very much rather stay here than go back. Shall we go and see what there is for dinner? I can cook quite well. I learnt at the convent, but I have never had a chance to really try what I can do."

He smiled.

"Well," he said, "you can do exactly what you like with the contents of my larder, but so far as I am concerned, I must go."

"Go?" she repeated wonderingly. "If I cannot leave the island, surely you cannot!"

"Yes!" he answered. "There is another way. I am going to swim over to the mainland and let them know at the Hall where you are."

She was suddenly serious, serious as well as disappointed.

"You must not," she declared. "It is too dangerous. I will not have you try it. You must stay here with me. I am not used to being left alone. I should be very lonely indeed. You must please not think of going."

"Miss Jeanne," he said quietly, "there are many things which you do not know, and you must let me tell you this, that it is not possible for me to keep you here as my guest until tomorrow. You cannot leave the island, so I am going to. I can assure you that it is nothing whatever of a swim, and I shall get to the other side quite easily. Then I am going down to the village to get some dry clothes, and I shall go up to the Hall and talk to your stepmother."

"If you make me go back," she declared, "I shall run away the first time I have an opportunity, and if you will not have me, I dare say I can find some one else who has a room to let, who will."

"I am not your keeper," he answered, "but please don't do anything rash until I tell you what your stepmother says."

"It is you who are rash," she declared. "I do not think that I can let you go. I am afraid, and the water looks so cruel tonight."

He laughed as he stepped outside.

"I am going round to leave some orders with Mr. Berners' servant," he said, "and after that I am going. You must ring for anything you want, and the man will show you your room if you want to lie down. I dare say, though, that some one will come from the Hall presently. The sea will be calmer in a few hours' time."

She walked with him to the edge of the beach. When he drew off his coat and turned up his sleeves she trembled with anxiety.

"Oh, I am afraid," she muttered. "I don't like your going in. I don't like your doing this. I am sorry that I ever came."

He laughed a little scornfully, and plunged in. She watched his head appear and disappear, her heart beating fast all the time. Once she lost sight of it altogether and screamed. Almost immediately he came up to the surface again, and turning round waved his hand to her.

"I am all right," he sang out. "Going strong. It's quite easy."

A few minutes later she saw him wading, and directly afterwards he stood upon the sands opposite to her. He waved his hand. She put her fingers to her lips and threw him a kiss. He pretended not to notice, and started off toward the village, and her low laugh came floating to him in a momentary lull of the wind.

Half-way across the marshes he changed his course, clambered up a high bank on to the road, and turned toward the Hall. Barer than ever the great gaunt building seemed to stand out against the sky line, but from every window lights were flashing, and the windows of the dining-room seemed to reflect a perfect blaze of light. Andrew made his way to the back entrance, and entering unobserved, made his way up to his own room.

* * *

Dinner was over, and the little party of three were settling down to their coffee and cigarettes when the Princess' maid came down and whispered in her mistress' ear. The Princess turned to her host perplexed.

"Has any one seen anything of Jeanne?" she inquired. "Reynolds has just told me that she has not returned at all."

"I thought you said that she was lying down with a headache," Cecil interposed eagerly.

"I thought so myself," the Princess answered. "Early this afternoon she told me that she had no sleep last night, that she had a very bad headache, and that she was going to bed. As a matter of fact she went out almost at once, and has not returned." Cecil was already on his way to the door.

"We will send out into the village at once," he said, "and some one must go on the marshes. There are plenty of places there where it would have been absolutely unsafe for her in such a storm as we have had. Ring the bell, Forrest, will you?"

Andrew stepped in and closed the door behind him.

"It is not necessary," he said. "I can tell you all about Miss Le Mesurier."

CHAPTER XIX

There was a moment's breathless silence as Andrew stood there looking in upon the little group. Then he left his position at the door and came up to the table round which they were seated.

"Madam," he said to the Princess, "your daughter is safe. She came down to the island this afternoon, and was unable to return owing to the storm."

The Princess gave a little sigh of relief.

"Foolish child!" she said. "But where is she now, Mr. Andrew?"

"She is still at the island," Andrew answered. "It was impossible for her to leave, so I came here to tell you of her whereabouts."

"It was extremely thoughtful of you," the Princess said graciously.

"If Miss Le Mesurier was unable to leave the island, how was it that you came?" Major Forrest asked, looking at Andrew through his eyeglass as though he were some sort of natural curiosity.

"I swam over," Andrew answered. "It was a very short distance."

It was about this time that they all noticed the fact that Andrew was wearing clothes of an altogether different fashion to the fisherman's garb in which they had seen him previously. The Princess looked at him perplexed. Cecil felt instinctively that the event which he had most dreaded was about to happen.

"And you came up here purposely to relieve our minds, Mr. Andrew," the Princess said. "Really it is most kind of you. I wish that there were some way — "

She hesitated, a slight note of question in her tone, expressed also by her upraised eyebrows.

"I had a further reason for coming," Andrew said slowly. "I am very sorry indeed to seem inhospitable or discourteous, but there is a certain matter which must be cleared up, and at once. I refer to the disappearance of Lord Ronald."

There was an instant's dead silence. Then Forrest, with white face, leaned across the table.

"Who the devil are you?" he asked.

"I am Andrew de la Borne," Andrew answered, "the owner of these poor estates, which I am very well content to leave for the greater part of the time in my brother's care, only that he is young, and is liable to make mistakes. He has made one, sir, I fear, in offering you the hospitality of the Red Hall."

Forrest rose slowly to his feet. The Princess held out her hand as though to beg him not to speak. She turned towards Andrew.

"I do not understand, sir," she said, "why you have chosen to masquerade under another name, and why you come now to insult your brother's guests in such a manner. Is what he says true, Cecil?" she added, turning towards him. "Is this man your brother?"

"Yes!" Cecil answered sullenly. "He tells the truth. It is just like him to make such a thundering idiot of himself."

"I beg your pardon," Andrew answered. "It is not I, Cecil, who desire to come here and say these things to any guest of yours. It is you who are sheltering under this roof one man at least to whom you should never have offered your hospitality. The Duke of Westerham, who has been my guest for the last few days, told me all that one needs to know about you, sir, and your career."

Forrest asked no more questions. He turned to Cecil.

"Mr. De la Borne," he said, "I have understood that you were my host, and I appeal to you. Is this person indeed your elder brother?"

"Yes!" Cecil answered.

"You know what this means," Forrest continued, speaking to Cecil. "I cannot remain in this house any longer. I could only accept hospitality from those who have at least learned to comport themselves as gentlemen."

Andrew smiled.

"I will not grudge you, sir," he said, "any reasonable excuse for leaving this house as quickly as may be, but before you go, I insist upon knowing what has become of Lord Ronald."

Cecil turned towards his brother angrily.

"I am sick of hearing about Engleton!" he declared. "I tell you that he left here, Andrew, on Wednesday morning, and caught the 9-5 train to London, or at any rate to Peterboro'. Whether he went north, south, east, or west, is no concern of ours. We only know that he promised to come back and has not come."

"There is more to be learnt then," Andrew answered. "How did he get to Lynn Station that morning?"

"In the motor car," Cecil answered.

"Who drove it?" Andrew asked.

"Major Forrest," Cecil answered.

"It is a lie!" Andrew declared. "The car never went a hundred yards beyond the gates. I know that for a fact."

Again there was silence. The Princess intervened.

"Mr. Andrew," she began — "I beg your pardon, Mr. De la Borne — supposing Lord Ronald did wish to keep his departure and the manner of it a great secret, why should it trouble you? You don't suppose, I presume, that there has been a fight, or anything of that sort?"

"I only know," Andrew answered, "that the brother of one of my dearest friends has disappeared from this house, after spending several days in the company of a man of bad reputation. That is quite enough for me. I am determined to get to the bottom of the matter."

"It is a very little matter, after all," the Princess said calmly. "Perhaps — "

She hesitated, and looked at the two other men.

"Perhaps," she continued slowly, "it would be as well to tell you the truth."

"If you do not, madam," Andrew answered, "it is more than probable that I shall speedily elicit it."

Both Forrest and Cecil seemed stricken speechless, and before they could recover themselves the Princess had commenced her story, talking with easy and convincing fluency.

"Lord Ronald," she said, "did leave here at the time you and the Duke have been told, and Major Forrest did try to drive him in the motor to Lynn Station. When he found that that was impossible, that they could not get the engine to go, Lord Ronald left his luggage here and walked to Wells. That is the last we have heard of him. He asked that his luggage should be sent to his rooms in London, and we sent it off the next day. He left here on good terms with everybody, but he told us distinctly that the business on which he was summoned away was of a very unpleasant nature. I think that some one was trying to blackmail him. Now you can make what inquiries you like, but I am very certain of one thing, that anything you may discover is more likely to bring discredit upon Lord Ronald himself than anybody else."

"Madam," Andrew said, "your story, of course, I am bound to accept as the truth, but I must tell you frankly that I shall pass it on to the Duke, who will take up his inquiries from the point you name. If he finds that the facts do not correspond with what you have told me, I fear that the consequences will be disagreeable for all of you."

"Of what on earth do you suspect us?" Major Forrest asked sharply. "Do you think that we have made away with Engleton? Why should we? We may be the adventurers you delicately suggest, but at least we should have an object in our crimes. Engleton had not a ten-pound note of ready money with him. I know that for a fact, because I lent him some money to pay his chauffeur's wages when he sent him away."

"You are perhaps holding some of his IOU's?" Andrew asked.

"I certainly am," Forrest answered, "and the sooner I hear from him the better. If you are really the owner of this house, I shall leave tomorrow morning."

Andrew bowed coldly.

"That," he said, "would certainly seem to be your best course. On the contrary," he added, "I am not altogether sure that I am justified in letting you go."

The Princess frowned at him indignantly.

"You talk nonsense, my dear Mr. Andrew, or Mr. Andrew de la Borne," she said. "If you tried to retain Major Forrest on such a cock and bull pretext, you would be probably very soon sorry for it. Besides you have no power to do anything of the sort."

"Madam," Andrew answered, "I am a magistrate, and I could sign a warrant on the spot. I do not, however, feel justified in going to such lengths. I feel sure that if Major Forrest is wanted, we shall be able to find him."

"Of course you will," the Princess intervened calmly. "Men like Major Forrest do not run away just because some one chooses to make a ridiculous charge against them. If only I could get Jeanne, I would leave myself tonight."

"My dear Princess," Cecil said, "I hope that you do not mean it. My brother has said more than he means, I am sure."

"I have said less." Andrew replied. "I have the very best reasons for believing that Major Forrest has lied his way into whatever friendship he may have had with Lord Ronald and my brother."

Forrest moved toward the door.

"Mr. De la Borne," he said to Cecil, "you will forgive me if I decline to remain here to be insulted by your brother."

The Princess followed him from the room. Cecil and Andrew were alone.

"Damn you, Andrew!" the former said, turning upon him, whitefaced, and with a sort of petulant anger. "Why do you come here and spoil things like this?"

Andrew stood upon the hearthrug, and looked at his brother, black and forbidding.

"Cecil," he said, "my life has been spoilt by paying for your excesses. Ever since I came of age I have been hampered all the time by paying your debts and providing you with money. I even let you pose here as the master of the Red Hall because it pleased you. I have had enough of it. If you run up any more debts, you must pay them yourself. I am master here and I intend to remain so."

Cecil was suddenly pale.

"Do you mean," he asked, "that you intend to remain here now?"

Andrew hesitated.

"Your guests are leaving," he said. "Why not?"

"But they may not go until tomorrow or the next day," Cecil said. "I cannot turn them out."

Andrew stood for a moment looking thoughtfully at the door.

"They cannot stay more than a day," he said, "if Major Forrest is really their friend. In any case, I shall not return until they are gone."

Cecil's face cleared a little, but he was still perplexed.

"They had just promised," he said, "to stay another week."

"If you wish to entertain the Princess and Miss Le Mesurier," Andrew said, "and they are willing to stop after what has passed, I have nothing, of course, to say against it. But the man Forrest I will not have here. If ever cheat and coward were written in a man's face, your friend carries the marks in his."

"He has won nothing to speak of from me here," Cecil declared.

"You are probably too small game," Andrew answered. "How about Engleton? Did he lose?"

"I am not sure," Cecil answered. "Not very much, if anything."

The Princess came rustling back. She held her little spaniel up to her cheek, and she affected not to notice the somewhat strained attitude of the two men. She went at once to Andrew.

"Mr. De la Borne," she said, "I think that you have been very unjust and very rude to Major Forrest, who is an old friend of mine. I am sure that you have been misled, and I am sure that some day you will ask his pardon."

Andrew bowed slightly, and looked her straight in the face.

"Princess," he said, "may I ask how long you have known the gentleman who has just left us?"

"For a very great many years," she answered. "Why?"

"Are you sure of your own knowledge," Andrew asked, "that he is really a person of good repute and against whom there have been no scandalous reports?"

"I do not listen to gossip," the Princess answered. "Major Forrest goes everywhere in London, and I have seen nothing in his deportment at any time to induce me to withdraw my friendship."

"I fancy, then," Andrew said, "that some day you will find you have been a little deceived."

"What about Lord Ronald?" the Princess asked. "Perhaps, Mr. De la Borne, you think that we are all a little company of adventurers. This is such a likely spot for our operations, isn't it?"

"Lord Ronald," Andrew said, "is the brother of my old friend, and he is, of course, above suspicion, but Lord Ronald appears to have left you somewhat abruptly, I might almost say mysteriously."

"He was here for some time," the Princess said, "and he is coming back."

"In the meantime," Andrew continued, "he appears to have vanished from the face of the earth."

The Princess turned away carelessly.

"That," she said, "is scarcely our affair. I have not the slightest doubt but that he will turn up again."

"If it should turn out that I am mistaken," Andrew said stiffly, "I should be glad to ask your pardons, but from my present information I can only say I do not care to extend the hospitality of my house to Major Forrest, nor do I consider him a fit associate, madam, for you and your step-daughter."

"May I ask," the Princess inquired, "who Major Forrest's traducers have been?"

"My information," Andrew answered, "comes from the Duke of Westerham. I have every reason to believe that the case against him has been understated."

"The Duke," Cecil declared, "is a pig-headed old fool!"

Andrew shrugged his shoulders.

"I have always found him a man of remarkably keen judgment," he said.

"What are you going to do about Jeanne?" the Princess asked, changing the subject abruptly.

"I should suggest," Andrew answered, "that you have a maid pack a bag and prepare to go with me over to the island early in the morning. There is no chance to cross before then, as the tide would be high."

"But how nervous she will be there all alone!" the Princess exclaimed.

"My servant is there," Andrew answered, "and also an old woman who cooks for me. They will, I am sure, do everything they can to make her comfortable. I shall go myself and bring her back here as soon as it is daylight."

"We are giving you a great deal of trouble, I am afraid, Mr. De la Borne," the Princess said stiffly. "Tomorrow, as soon as my maid can pack, we will return to London."

Andrew bowed as he turned to leave the room.

"I trust," he said, "that you will not let my presence interfere with your plans. I shall remain on the island myself tomorrow, after I have brought your daughter back."

CHAPTER XX

Jeanne awoke the next morning to find herself between lavender scented sheets in a small iron bedstead, with a soft sea-wind blowing in through the half-open window. Her maid was ready to wait upon her, and her bath was of salt water fresh from the sea. She descended to find Andrew at work in the garden, the sun already high in the heavens, and the sea as blue and placid as though the storm of the night before were a thing long past and forgotten.

"I am never going away," she declared, as they sat at breakfast. "I take your rooms, Monsieur Andrew. I will import as many chaperons as you please, but I will not leave this island."

"I am afraid," he answered smiling, "that there are other people who would have something to say about that. Your stepmother is already anxious. I have promised that you shall be back at the Hall by ten o'clock."

The gaiety suddenly faded from her face. Her lips, which had been curved in laughter, quivered.

"You mean that?" she faltered.

"Most assuredly," he answered. "I have no place for lodgers here. As a matter of fact, if you knew the truth, you would admit that your staying here is quite impossible."

"Well," she said, "I should like to know the truth. Suppose you tell it me."

"I must confess, then," Andrew answered, "that I am somewhat of a fraud. Berners was my friend, not my lodger, and I am Andrew de la Borne, Cecil's elder brother."

She looked at him for several moments steadily.

"I think that you might have told me," was all she said.

He shrugged his shoulders.

"Why?" he asked, a little brusquely. "I am not of your world, or your stepmother's. When Cecil told me that he had invited some of his fashionable friends down here to stay, I begged him to leave me out of it. I chose to retire here, and I preferred not to see any of you. Mine are country ways, Miss Le Mesurier. I am at heart what I pretended to be, fisherman, countryman, yokel, call me what you will. The other side of life, Cecil's side, doesn't appeal to me a bit. I felt that it would be more comfortable for you people and for me, if I kept out of the way."

"You class me with them," she remarked quietly, "a little ruthlessly. I think you forget that as yet I have not chosen my way in life."

"That is true," he answered, "but how can you help but choose what every one of those who call themselves your friends regards as inevitable. You must dance in many ballrooms, and make your bow before the great ones of the earth. It is a part of the penalty that you must pay for your name and riches. All that I can wish you is that you lose as little of yourself as possible in the days that lie before you."

"I thank you," she answered quietly. "You will let me know when you are ready to take me back."

"Have I offended you?" he asked, as they rose from the table. "I am clumsy, I know, and the words do not come readily to my mouth. But after all, you must understand."

"Yes," she said sadly, "I do understand."

They went down to the beach and he helped her into the boat. Her maid sat by her side, and he rowed them across with a few powerful strokes.

"Storm and sunshine," he remarked, "follow one another here as swiftly as in any corner of the world. Yesterday we had wind and thunder and rain. Today, look! The sky is cloudless, the birds are singing everywhere upon the marshes, the waves can do no more than ripple in upon the sands. Will you walk across the marshes, Miss Jeanne, or will you come to the village and wait while I send for a carriage?"

"We will walk," she answered. "It may be for the last time."

The maid fell behind. Andrew and his companion, who seemed smaller and slimmer than ever by his side, started on their tortuous way, here and there turning to the right and to the left to follow the course of some tidal stream, or avoid the swampy places. The faint odour of wild lavender was mingled with the brackish scent of the sea. The ground was soft and spongy beneath their feet, and a breeze as soft as a caress blew in their faces. Up before them always, gaunt and bare, surrounded by its belts of weather-stricken trees, stood the Red Hall. Andrew looked toward it gloomily.

"Do you wonder," he asked, "that a man is sometimes depressed who is born the heir to a house like that, and to fortunes very similar?"

"Are you poor?" she asked him. "I thought perhaps you were, as your brother tried to make love to me."

He frowned impatiently at her words.

"For Heaven's sake, child," he said, "don't be so cynical! Don't fancy that every kind word that is spoken to you is spoken for your wealth. There are sycophants enough in the world,

Heaven knows, but there are men there as well. Give a few the credit of being honest. Try and remember that you are — "

He looked at her and away again toward the sea.

"That you are," he repeated, "young enough and attractive enough to win kind words for your own sake."

"Then," she whispered, leaning towards him, "I do not think that I am very fortunate."

"Why not?" he asked.

"Because," she answered, "one person who might say kind things to me, and whom my money would never influence a little bit in the world, does not say them."

"Are you sure," he asked, "that you believe that there is any one in the world who would be content to take you without a penny?"

She shook her head.

"Not that," she said sadly. "I am not what you call conceited enough for that, but I would like to believe that I might have a kind word or two on my own account."

She tried hard to see his face, but he kept it steadfastly turned away. She sighed. Only a few yards behind the maid was walking.

"Mr. Andrew," she said, "it was you whom I meant. Won't you say something nice to me for my own sake?"

They were nearing the Hall now, and it seemed natural enough that he should hold her hand for a minute in his.

"I will tell you," he said quietly, "that your coming has been a pleasure, and your going will be a pain, and I will tell you that you have left an empty place that no one else can fill. You have made what our people here call the witch music upon the marshes for me, so that I shall never walk here again as long as I live without hearing it and thinking of you."

"Is that all?" she whispered.

He pretended not to hear her.

"I am nearly double your age," he said, "and I have lived an idle, perhaps a worthless, life. I have done no harm. My talents, if I have any, have certainly been buried. If I had met you out in the world, your world, well, I might have taught myself to forget — "

He broke off abruptly in his sentence. Cecil stood before them, suddenly emerged from the hand-gate leading into the Hall gardens. "At last!" he exclaimed, taking Jeanne by the hands. "The Princess is distracted. We have all been distracted. How could you make us so unhappy?"

She drew her hands away coldly.

"I fancy that my stepmother," she said, "will have survived my absence. I was caught in a storm. I expect that your brother has already told you about it."

He looked from one to the other.

"So you have told her, Andrew," he said simply.

Andrew nodded. The three walked up toward the house in somewhat constrained silence. She was trying her hardest to make Andrew look at her, and he was trying his hardest to resist. The Princess came out to them. The morning was warm, and she was wearing a white wrapper. Her toilette was not wholly completed, but she was sufficiently picturesque.

"My dear Jeanne," she cried, "you have nearly sent us mad with anxiety. How could you wander off like that!"

Jeanne stood a little apart. She avoided the Princess' hands. She stood upon the soft turf with her hands clasped, her cheeks very pale, her eyes bright with some inward excitement.

"Do you wish me to answer that question?" she said.

The Princess stared.

"What do you mean, my child?" she exclaimed.

"You ask me," Jeanne said, "why I went wandering off into the marshes. I will tell you. It is because I am unhappy. It is because I do not like the life into which you have brought me, nor the people with whom we live. I do not like late hours, supper parties and dinner parties, dances where half the people are bourgeois, and where all the men make stupid love to me. I do not like the shops, the vulgar shop people, fashionable clothes, and fashionable promenading. I am tired of it already. If I am rich, why may I not buy the right to live as I choose?"

The Princess rarely allowed herself to show surprise. At this moment, however, she was completely overcome.

"What is it you want, then, child?" she demanded.

"I should like," Jeanne answered, "to buy Mr. De la Borne's house upon the island, and live there, with just a couple of maids, and my books. I should like some friends, of course, but I should like to find them for myself, amongst the country people, people whom I could trust and believe in, not people whose clothes and manners and speech are all hammered out into a type, and whose real self is so deeply buried that you cannot tell whether they are honest or rogues. That is what I should like, stepmother, and if you wish to earn my gratitude, that is how you will let me live."

The Princess stared at the child as though she were a lunatic.

"Jeanne," she exclaimed weakly, "what has become of you?"

"Nothing," Jeanne answered, "only you asked me a question, and I felt an irresistible desire to answer you truthfully. It would have come sooner or later."

Andrew turned slowly toward the girl, who stood looking at her stepmother with flushed cheeks and quivering lips.

"Miss Le Mesurier," he said, "on one condition I will sell you the island, but on only one."

"And that is?" she asked.

The Princess recovered herself just in time, and sailed in between them.

"Mr. De la Borne," she said, "my daughter is too young for such conversations. For two years she is under my complete guidance. She must obey me just as though she were ten years older and married, and I her husband. The law has given me absolute control over her. You understand that yourself, don't you, Jeanne?"

"Yes," Jeanne answered quietly, "I understand."

"Go indoors, please," the Princess said. "I have something to say to Mr. De la Borne."

"And I, too," Jeanne said. "Let me stay and say it. I will not be five minutes."

The Princess pointed toward the door.

"I will not have it," she said coldly. "Cecil, take my daughter indoors. I insist upon it."

She turned away unwillingly. The Princess took Andrew by the arm and led him to a more distant seat.

"Now, if you please, my dear Mr. Andrew," she said, "will you tell me what it is that you have done to my foolish little girl?"

CHAPTER XXI

The Princess arranged her skirts so that they drooped grace-fully, and turned upon her companion with one of those slow mysterious smiles, which many people described but none could imitate.

"Mr. De la Borne," she said, "I can talk to you as I could not talk to your brother, because you are an older and a wiser man. You may not have seen much of the world, but you are at any rate not a young idiot like Cecil. Will you listen to me, please?"

"It seems to me," Andrew answered drily, "that I am already doing so."

"I am not going to ask you," she continued, "whether you are in love with my little girl or not, because the whole thing is too ridiculous. I have no doubt that she has some sort of a fancy for you. It is evident that she has. I want you to remember that she is fresh from school, that as yet she has not entered life, and that a few months ago she did not know a man from a gate-post."

"An admirable simile," Andrew murmured.

"What I want you to understand is," the Princess continued, "that as yet she cannot possibly be in a position to make up her mind as to her future. She has seen nothing of the world, and what she has seen has been the least favourable side. She has a perfectly enormous fortune, so ridiculously tied up that although I am never out of debt and always borrowing money, I cannot touch a penny of it, not even with her help. Very soon she will be of age, and the amount of her fortune will be known. I can assure you that it will be a surprise to every one."

Andrew bowed his head indifferently.

"Very possibly," he answered, "and yet, madam, if your daughter has the wisdom to see that the matter of her wealth is after all but a trifle amongst the conditions which make for happi-ness, why should you deny her the benefits of that wisdom?"

"My dear friend," she continued earnestly, "for this reason — because Jeanne today is too young to choose for herself. She has not got over that sickly sentimental age, when a girl makes a hero of anything unusual in the shape of a man, and finds a sort of unwholesome satisfaction in making sacrifices for his sake. It may be that Jeanne may, after all, look to what you call the simple life for happiness. Well, if she does that after a year or so, well and good. But she shall not do so with my consent, without indeed my downright opposition, until she has had an opportunity of testing both sides, of weighing the matter thoroughly from every point of view. Do you not agree with me, Mr. De la Borne?"

"You speak reasonably, madam," he assented.

"Jeanne," she continued, "has perhaps charmed you a little. She is, after all, just now a child of nature. She is something of an artist, too. Beautiful places and sights and sounds appeal to her.

"She is ready, with her imperfect experience, to believe that there is nothing greater or better worth cultivating in life. But I want you to consider the effects of heredity. Jeanne comes from restless, brilliant people. Her mother was a leader of society, a pleasure-loving, clever, unscrupulous woman. Her father was a financier and a diplomat, many-sided, versatile, but with as complex a disposition as any man I ever met. Jeanne will ripen as the years go on; something of her mother, something of her father will appear. It is my place, knowing these things, to see that she does not make a fatal mistake. All that I say to you, Mr. De la Borne, is to let her go, to give her her chance, to let her see with both eyes before she does anything irremediable. I think that I may almost appeal to you, as a reasonable man and a gentleman, to help me in this."

Andrew de la Borne looked out through the wizened branches of his stunted trees, to the white-flecked sea rolling in below. The Princess was right. He knew that she was right. Those other thoughts were little short of madness. Jeanne was no coquette at heart, but she was a child. She had great responsibilities. She was turned into the world with a heavy burden upon her shoulders. It was not he or any man who could help her. She must fight her own battle, win or lose her own happiness. A few years' time might see her the wife of a great statesman or a great soldier, proud and happy to feel herself the means by which the man she loved might climb one step higher upon the great ladder of fame. How like a child's dream these few days upon the marshes, talking to one who was no more than a looker-on at the great things of life, must seem! He could imagine her thinking of them with a shiver as she remembered her escape. The Princess was right, she was very right indeed. He rose to his feet.

"Madam," he said, "I have not pretended to misunderstand you. I think that you have spoken wisely. Your stepdaughter must solve for herself the great riddle. It is not for any one of us to handicap her in her choice while she is yet a child."

"You are going, Mr. De la Borne?" she asked.

He pointed to a brown-sailed fishing-boat passing slowly down from the village toward the sea.

"That is one of my boats," he said. "I shall signal to her from the island to call for me. I need a change, and she is going out into the North Sea for five weeks' fishing."

The Princess held out her hand, and Andrew took it in his.

"You are a man," she said. "I wish there were more of your sort in the world where I live."

The Princess stood for a moment on the edge of the lawn, watching Andrew's tall figure as he strode across the marsh toward the village. Never once did he look back or hesitate on his swift, vigorous way. Then she sighed a little and turned away toward the house. After all, this was a man, although he was so far removed from the type she knew and understood.

Cecil was walking restlessly up and down the hall when she entered. He drew her eagerly into the library.

"Look here," he said, "Forrest declares that he is going. He is upstairs now packing his things."

"Your brother," the Princess answered, "scarcely left him much alternative."

"That's all very well," Cecil answered, "but if he goes I go. I am not going to be left here alone."

The Princess looked at him, and the colour came into his cheeks. It is never well for a man when he sees such a look upon a woman's face.

"It isn't that I'm afraid," Cecil declared. "I can stand any ordinary danger, but I am not going to be left shut up here alone, with the whole responsibility upon me. I couldn't do it. It wouldn't be fair to ask me."

"There is no fresh news, I suppose?" the Princess asked.

"None," Cecil answered gloomily. "If only we could see our way to the end of it, I shouldn't mind."

The Princess was thoughtful for a few moments.

"Well," she said, "I don't know, after all, if Forrest need go just yet. Your brother has made up his mind to go fishing for several weeks. I think that he is going to start today."

"Do you mean it?" Cecil exclaimed, incredulously.

The Princess nodded.

"He has been philandering with Jeanne," she said, "and his magnificent conscience is taking him out into the North Sea."

Cecil's features relaxed. After all, though he played at maturity, he was little more than a boy.

"Fancy old Andrew!" he exclaimed. "Gone on a child like Miss Jeanne, too! Well, anyhow, that makes it all right about Forrest staying, doesn't it?"

"He shall stop," the Princess answered slowly. "Jeanne and I will stay, too, until Monday. Perhaps by that time — "

"By that time," Cecil repeated, "something may have happened."

BOOK II

CHAPTER I

His Grace the Duke of Westerham stepped forward from the hearthrug, in the middle of which he had been standing, and held out both his hands. His lips were parted in a smile, and there was a twinkle in his eyes.

"My dear Andrew," he exclaimed, "it is delightful to see you. You seem to bring the salt of the North Sea into our frowsy city."

Andrew grasped his friend's hands.

"I have been fishing with some of my men for three weeks," he said, "off the Dogger Bank. The salt does cling to one, you know, and I suppose I am as black as a nigger."

The Duke sighed a little.

"My dear Andrew," he said, "you make one wonder whether it is worth while to count for anything at all in the world. You represent the triumph of physical fitness. You could break me, or a dozen like me, in your hands. You know what the faddists of the moment say? They declare that brains and genius have had their day — that the greatest man in the world nowadays is the strongest."

Andrew smiled as he settled down in the armchair which his friend had wheeled towards him.

"You do not believe in your own doctrines," he remarked. "You would not part with a tenth part of your brains for all my muscle."

The Duke paused to think.

"It is not only the muscle," he said. "It is this appearance of splendid physical perfection. You have but to show yourself in a London drawing-room, and you will establish a cult. Do you want to be worshipped, friend Andrew — to wear a laurel crown, and have beautiful ladies kneeling at your feet?"

"Chuck it!" Andrew remarked good humouredly. "I didn't come here to be chaffed. I came here on a serious mission."

The Duke nodded.

"It must indeed have been serious," he said, "for you to have had your hair cut and your beard trimmed, and to have attired yourself in the garments of civilization. You are the last man whom I should have expected to have seen in a coat which might have been cut by Poole, if it wasn't, and wearing patent boots."

"Jolly uncomfortable they are," Andrew remarked, looking at them. "However, I didn't want to be turned away from your doors, and I still have a few friends in town whom I daren't disgrace. Honestly, Berners, I came up to ask you something."

The Duke was sympathetic but silent.

"Well?" he remarked encouragingly.

"The fact is," Andrew continued, "I wonder whether you could help me to get something to do. We have decided to let the Red Hall, Cecil and I. The rents have gone down to nothing, and altogether things are pretty bad with us. I don't know that I'm good for anything. I don't see, to tell you the truth, exactly what place there is in the world that I could fill. Nevertheless, I want to do something. I love the villager's life, but after all there are other things to be considered. I don't want to become quite a clod."

The Duke produced a cigar box, passed it to Andrew, and deliberately lighted a cigar himself.

"Friend Andrew," he said, "you have set me a puzzle. You have set me a good many since I used to run errands for you at Eton, but I think that this is the toughest."

Andrew nodded.

"You'll think your way through it, if any one can," he remarked. "I don't expect anything, of course, that would enable me to afford cigars like this, but I'd be glad to find some work to do, and I'd be glad to be paid something for it."

The Duke was silent for a moment. He looked down at his cigar and then suddenly up again.

"Has that young idiot of a brother of yours been making a fool of himself?" he asked.

"Cecil is never altogether out of trouble," Andrew answered drily. "He seems to have taken bridge up with rather unfortunate results, and there were some other debts which had to be paid, but we needn't talk about those. The point is that we're jolly well hard up for a year or two. He's got to work, and so have I. If it wasn't for looking after him, I should go to Canada tomorrow."

"Damned young idiot!" the Duke muttered. "He's spent his own money and yours too, I suppose. Never mind, the money's gone."

"It isn't only the money," Andrew interrupted. "The fact is, I'm not altogether satisfied, as I told you before, with living just for sport. I'm not a prejudiced person. I know that there are greater things in the world, and I don't want to lose sight of them altogether. We De la Bornes have contributed poets and soldiers and sailors and statesmen to the history of our country, for many generations. I don't want to go down to posterity as altogether a drone. Of course, I'm too late for anything really worth doing. I know that just as well as you can tell me. At the same time I want to do something, and I would rather not go abroad, at any rate to stay. Can you suggest anything to me? I know it's jolly difficult, but you were always one of those sort of fellows who seem to see round the corner."

"Do you want a permanent job?" the Duke asked. "Or would a temporary one fit you up for a time?"

"A temporary one would be all right, if it was in my line," Andrew answered.

"We've got to send three delegates to a convention to be held at The Hague in a fortnight's time, for the revision of the International Fishing laws," the Duke remarked. "Could you take that on?"

"I should think so," Andrew answered. "I've been out with the men from our part of the world since I was a child, and I know pretty well all that there is to be known on our side about it. What is the convention about?"

"There are at least a dozen points to be considered," the Duke answered. "I'll send you the papers to any address you like, to-morrow. They're at my office now in Downing Street. Look 'em through, and see whether you think you could take it on. I have two men already appointed, but they are both lawyers, and I wanted some one who knew more about the practical side of it."

"I should think," Andrew remarked, "that this is my job down to the ground. What's the fee?"

"The fee's all right," the Duke answered. "You won't grumble about that, I promise you. You'll get a lump sum, and so much a day, but the whole thing, of course, will be over in a fortnight. What to do with you after that I can't for the moment think."

"We may hit upon something," Andrew said cheerfully. "What are you doing for lunch? Will you come round to the 'Travellers' with me? It's the only London club I've kept going, but I dare say we can get something fit to eat there."

"I'm jolly sure of it," the Duke answered, "but while you're in London you're going to do your lunching with me. We'll go to the Athenaeum and show these sickly-looking scholars and bishops what a man should look like. It's almost time for luncheon, isn't it?"

"Past," Andrew answered. "It was half-past twelve when I got here."

"Then we will leave at once," the Duke declared. "I have nothing to do this morning, fortunately. You don't care about driving, I know. We'll walk. It isn't half a mile."

They turned into the street together.

"By the by," the Duke asked, "what has become of your

brother's friends? I mean the little party that we broke into so unceremoniously."

"The Princess and Miss Le Mesurier are, I believe, in London," Andrew answered. "I was very surprised to hear this morning that Forrest was still down at the Red Hall with Cecil. By the by, Ronald has turned up again, of course?"

The Duke hesitated for so long that Andrew turned towards him, and noticed for the first time the anxious lines in his face.

"Since the day he left the Red Hall," the Duke said, "Ronald has neither been seen nor heard from. I forgot that you had been outside civilization for nearly a month. Although I have tried hard, I have not been able to keep the affair altogether out of the papers."

Andrew was thunderstruck.

"Good God!" he exclaimed. "Why, Berners, this is one of the strangest things I ever heard of. What are you doing about it?"

"I am employing detectives," the Duke answered. "I do not see what else I could do. They have been down to the Red Hall. In fact I believe one of them is still in the vicinity. Your brother's story as to his departure seems to be quite in order, although no one at the railway station is able to remember his travelling by that train. They seem to remember the car, however, which is practically the same thing, and several people saw Major Forrest bringing it back early in the morning."

"Did any one," Andrew asked slowly, "see Lord Ronald in the car on his way to the station?"

"Not a soul," the Duke answered.

Andrew was honestly perplexed. Jeanne's statement that she had seen Forrest leaving the Red Hall with the car empty except for himself, he had never regarded seriously. Even now he could only conclude that she had been mistaken.

"Have any large cheques been presented against your brother's account?" he asked.

The Duke shook his head.

"Not one," he answered.

"Have the detectives any clue at all?"

"Not the ghost of one," the Duke answered. "Ronald had a few harmless little entanglements, but absolutely nothing that could have proved of any anxiety to him. He had several engagements during the last ten days which I know that he meant to keep. Something must have happened to him, God knows when or where! But here we are at the club. Andrew, I see that you have no umbrella, so I need not repeat the old joke about the bishops."

"What a selfish fellow I am!" Andrew remarked, as they seated themselves at a small table in the luncheon room. "Here have I been bothering you about my affairs, and all the time you have had this thing on your mind. Berners, I want you to tell me something."

"Go ahead," the Duke answered.

"Have you any idea in your head that Ronald has come to any harm at the Red Hall?"

The Duke shook his head.

"No!" he answered decidedly. "Frankly, if he had been there with Forrest alone, that would have been my first idea, but with your brother there, and the Princess, it is impossible to suspect anything, even if one knew what to suspect. The only possible clue as to his disappearance which is connected in any way with the Red Hall is that I understand he was paying attentions to Miss Le Mesurier, which she was disinclined to accept."

Andrew nodded.

"I think," he said, "that is probable."

"On the other hand," the Duke continued, "Ronald isn't in the least the sort of man to make away with himself or hide, because a girl, whom he could not have known very well, refused to marry him."

"Have you seen anything of the Princess in town?" Andrew asked, a little irrelevantly.

"I met her with her stepdaughter at Hereford House last night," the Duke answered. "The Princess was looking as brilliant as ever, but the little girl was pale and bored. She had a dozen men around her, and not a smile for one of them. Dull little thing, I should think."

Andrew said nothing. He was looking out of the window upon Pall Mall, but his eyes saw a little sandy hillock with blades of sprouting grass. Behind, the lavender-streaked marsh; in front, the yellow sands and the rippling sea. The sun seemed to warm his cheeks, the salt wind blew in his face. Westerham wondered for a moment what his friend saw in the grey flagged street to bring that faint reminiscent smile to his lips.

A messenger from the hall outside came in, and respectfully addressed the Duke.

"Your Grace is wanted upon the telephone," he announced.

The Duke excused himself. He was absent only for a few minutes, and when he returned and took his place he leaned over towards Andrew.

"My message was from the detective," he said. "He wants to see me. In fact, he is coming round here directly."

CHAPTER II

Cecil came face to face with his brother in the room where refreshments were being dispensed by solemn-looking footmen and trim parlour-maids. He stared at him for a moment in surprise.

"What on earth are you doing here, Andrew?" he asked.

"Exactly what I was wondering myself," Andrew answered, setting down his empty glass. "I met Bellamy Smith this afternoon in Bond Street, and he asked me to dine, without saying anything about this sort of show afterwards. By the by, Cecil," he added, "what are you doing in town? I thought you said that you were not coming up until the late autumn."

"No more I am, for any length of time," Cecil answered. "I am up for the day, back tomorrow. There were one or two things I wanted, and it was easier to come up and see about them than to write."

"Is Forrest still with you?" Andrew asked.

Cecil hesitated, and his brother had an unpleasant conviction that for a moment he was uncertain whether to tell the truth or no.

"Yes!" Cecil answered, "he is still there. I know you don't like him, Andrew, but he really isn't a bad sort, and he's quite a sportsman."

"Does he play cards with you?" Andrew asked.

"Never even suggested it," Cecil declared eagerly. "Fact is, we're out shooting all day, duck shooting, or fishing, or motoring, and we go to bed soon after dinner."

"You can't come to much harm at that," Andrew admitted. "By the by, do you know that Engleton has never turned up?"

"I have heard so," Cecil admitted. "I am not so surprised."

"Why not?" Andrew asked.

Cecil raised his eyebrows in a superior manner.

"Well," he said, "I know he was very sick about his brother looking too closely into his concerns. He has a little affair on just now that he wants to keep to himself, and I think that that is the reason he went off so quietly."

"His brother is very upset about it," Andrew remarked.

"Oh! the Duke was always a heavy old stick," Cecil answered. "I see you've been doing your duty tonight," he added, making a determined effort to change the conversation.

Andrew nodded.

"Do I look so hot?" he asked. "I am not used to these close rooms, or dancing either. Unfortunately they seem short of men, and Mrs. Bellamy Smith had me set."

Cecil grinned.

"That's the worst of dining before a dance," he remarked. "You're pretty well cornered before the crowd comes. Upon my word, old chap," he added, looking his brother up and down with an air of kindly patronage, "you don't turn out half badly. Country tailor still, eh?"

"Mind your own business, you young jackanapes," Andrew answered. "Do you think that no one can wear town clothes except yourself?"

Cecil laughed. After all, considering everything, Andrew was a good-natured fellow.

"By the by," he said, "do you know who is here this evening?"

Andrew demolished another sandwich.

"Every one, I should think," he answered. "I never saw such a crowd in my life."

"The Princess and Jeanne are here," Cecil said. "I don't suppose we shall either of us get near them. People are getting to know about Jeanne's little dot, and they are fairly mobbed everywhere."

Andrew stood for a moment quite still. His first emotion was one of dismay, and Cecil, noticing it, laughed at him.

"You can go ahead with your little flirtation," he remarked. "I had quite forgotten that. You needn't consider me. I haven't a chance with Miss Jeanne. She's too cranky a young person for me. I like something with a little more go in it."

Cecil drifted away, and Andrew glanced at his card. There were two dances for which he was still engaged, and he made his way slowly back to the ballroom. There was a slight block at the entrance, and he had to stand aside to let several couples pass out. One of the last of these was Jeanne, on the arm of young Bellamy Smith. Andrew stood quite still looking at her. He saw her start for a moment as she recognized him, and her eyes swept him over with a half incredulous, half startled expression. She drew a little breath. And then Andrew saw her suddenly and instinctively stiffen. She looked him in the face and bowed very slightly, without the vestige of a smile.

"How do you do, Mr. De la Borne?" she said as she passed on, without taking the slightest notice of the hand, which, forgetting where he was, he had half extended towards her.

Andrew went on into the ballroom, found his partner, and danced with her. As soon as he could he made his adieux and hurried off to the cloakroom. His coat was already upon his arm when Cecil discovered him.

"What are you bolting off for, old man?" he asked.

"I've had enough," Andrew answered. "I can't stand the atmosphere, and I hate dancing, as you know. See you tomorrow, Cecil. I want to have a talk with you. I am going away for a few weeks."

"Right oh!" Cecil answered. "But you can't go just yet. Mademoiselle Le Mesurier sent me for you. She wants to speak to you at once."

Andrew hesitated.

"Do you mean this, Cecil?" he asked.

"Of course I do," Cecil answered. "I haven't been rushing about looking into every corner of the place for nothing. Come along. I'll take you to where she is."

Andrew handed back his coat and hat to the attendant, and followed Cecil into the ballroom. In a passage leading to the billiard-room, where several chairs had been arranged for sitting out, Jeanne was ensconced, with two men leaning over her. She waved them away when she saw who it was coming. Without a smile, or the vestige of one, she motioned to Andrew to take the vacant seat by her side.

"I have executed your commission, Miss Le Mesurier," Cecil said, bowing before her. "I will claim my reward when we meet again."

He sauntered away, leaving them alone. Jeanne turned at once towards her companion.

"I am sorry," she said, "if my sending for you was in any way an annoyance. I understand, of course, you have made it quite clear to me, that our little friendship, or whatever you may choose to call it, is at an end. But I do insist upon knowing what it was that you and my stepmother were discussing for nearly half an hour in the gardens of the Red Hall. The truth, mind. You and I should owe one another that."

"We talked of you," he answered. "What other subject can you possibly imagine your stepmother and I could have in common?"

"That is a good start," she answered. "Now tell me the rest."

"I am not sure," he answered, "that I feel inclined to do that."

She leaned forward and looked at him. Unwillingly he turned his head to meet her gaze.

"You must tell me, please," she said. "I insist upon knowing."

"Your stepmother," he said, "was perfectly reasonable and very candid. She reminded me that you were a great heiress, and that as yet you had seen nothing of the world. I do not know why she thought it necessary to point this out to me, except that perhaps she thought that in some mad moment I might have conceived the idea that you — "

"That I?" she repeated softly, as he hesitated.

He set his teeth hard and frowned.

"You know what I mean," he said coldly. "Your stepmother is a clever woman, and a woman of the world. She takes into account all contingencies, never mind how improbable they might be. She was afraid that I might think things were possible between us which after all must always remain outside serious consideration. She wanted to warn me. That was all. It was kindness, but I am sure that it was unnecessary."

"You are not very lucid," she murmured. "It is because I am a great heiress, then, that you go off fishing for three weeks without saying good-bye; that you leave our next meeting to happen by chance in the last place I should have expected to see you? What do you think of me, Mr. Andrew? Do you imagine that I am of my stepmother's world, or ever could be? Have the hours we have spent together taught you nothing different?"

"You are a child," he answered evasively. "You do not know as yet to what world you will belong. It is as your stepmother said to me. With your fortune you may marry into one of the great families of Europe. You might almost take a part in the world's history. It is not for such as myself to dream of interfering with a destiny such as yours may be."

"For that reason," she remarked, leaning a little towards him, "you went fishing in a dirty little boat with those common sailors for three weeks. For that reason you bow to me when you meet me as though I were an acquaintance whom you barely remembered. For that reason, I suppose, you were hurrying away when your brother found you."

"It was the inevitable thing to do," he answered. "You may think today one thing, but it is for others who are older and wiser than you to remember that you are only a child, and that you have not realized yet the place you fill in the world. If it pleases you to know it, let me tell you that I am very glad indeed that you came to Salthouse. You have made me think more seriously. You have made me understand that after all the passing life is short, that idle days and physical pleasures do not make up the life which is worthiest. I am going to try other things. For the inspiration which bids me seek them, I have to thank you."

She touched his great brown hand with the delicate tips of her fingers.

"Dear Mr. Andrew," she said, "you are very big and strong and obstinate. You will have your own way however I may plead. Go, then, and strike your great blows upon the anvil of life. You say that I am passing the threshold, that as yet I am ignorant. Very well, I will make my way in with the throng. I will look about me, and see what this thing, life, is, and how much more it may mean to me because I chance to be the possessor of many ill-earned millions. Before very long we will meet again and compare notes, only I warn you, Mr. Andrew, that if any change comes, it comes to you. I am one of the outsiders who has looked into life, and who knows very well what is there even from across the borders."

He rose at once. To stay there was worse torture than to go.

"So it shall be," he said. "We will each take our draught of experience, and we will meet again and speak of the flavour of it. Only remember that whatever may be your lot, hold fast to those simple things which we have spoken of together, and the darkest days of all can never come."

She gave him her hand, and flashed a look at him which he was not likely to forget.

"So!" she said simply. "I shall remember."

CHAPTER III

The Princess was enjoying a few minutes of well-earned repose. She had lunched with Jeanne at Ranelagh, where they had been the guests of a lady who certainly had the right to call herself one of the leaders of Society. The newspapers and the Princess' confidences to a few of her friends had done all that was really necessary. Jeanne was accepted, and the Princess passed in her wake through those innermost portals which at one time had come perilously near being closed upon her. She was lying on a sofa in a white negligee gown. Jeanne had just brought in a pile of letters, mostly invitations. The Princess glanced them through, and smiled as she tossed them on one side.

"How these people amuse one!" she exclaimed. "Eighteen months ago I was in London alone, and not a soul came near me. Today, because I am the guardian of a young lady whom the world believes to be a great heiress, people tumble over one another with their invitations and their courtesies."

Jeanne looked up.

"Why do you say 'believes to be?'" she asked quickly. "I am a great heiress, am I not?"

The Princess smiled, a slow, enigmatic smile, which might have meant anything, but which to Jeanne meant nothing at all.

"My dear child," she said, "of course you are. The papers have said so, Society has believed them. If I were to go out and declare right and left that you had nothing but a beggarly twenty thousand pounds or so, I should not find a soul to believe me. Every one would believe that I was trying to scare them off, to keep you for myself, or some one of my own choice. Really it is a very odd world!"

Jeanne was looking a little pensive. Her stepmother sometimes completely puzzled her.

"Who are the trustees of my money?" she asked, a little abruptly.

The Princess raised her eyebrows.

"Bless the child!" she exclaimed. "What do you know about trustees?"

"When I am of age," Jeanne said calmly, "which will happen sometime or other, I suppose, it will interest me to know exactly how much money I have and how it is invested."

The Princess looked a little startled.

"My dear Jeanne," she exclaimed, "pray don't talk like that until after you are married. Your money is being very well looked after. What I should like you to understand is this. You are going to meet tonight at dinner the man whom I intend you to marry."

Jeanne raised her eyebrows.

"I had some idea," she murmured, "of choosing a husband for myself."

"Impossible!" the Princess declared. "You have had no experience, and you are far too important a person to be allowed to think of such a thing. Tonight at dinner you will meet the Count de Brensault. He is a Belgian of excellent family, quite rich, and very much attracted by you. I consider him entirely suitable, and I have advised him to speak to you seriously."

"Thank you," Jeanne said, "but I don't like Belgians, and I do not mean to marry one."

The Princess laughed, a little unpleasantly.

"My dear child," she said, "you may make a fuss about it, but eventually you will have to marry whom I say. You must remember that you are French, not English, and that I am your guardian. If you want to choose for yourself, you will have to wait three or four years before the law allows you to do so."

"Then I will wait three or four years," Jeanne answered quietly. "I have no idea of marrying the Count de Brensault."

The Princess raised herself a little on her couch.

"Child," she said, "you would try any one's patience. Only a month or so ago you told me that you were quite indifferent as to whom you might marry. You were content to allow me to select some one suitable." "A few months," Jeanne answered, "are sometimes a very long time. My views have changed since then."

"You mean," the Princess said, "that you have met some one whom you wish to marry?"

"Perhaps so," Jeanne answered. "At any rate I will not marry the Count de Brensault."

The Princess' face had darkened.

"I do not wish to quarrel with you, Jeanne," she said, "but I think that you will. Whom else is it that you are thinking of? Is it our island fisherman who has taken your fancy?"

"Does that matter?" Jeanne answered calmly. "Is it not sufficient if I say that I will not marry the Count de Brensault."

"No, it is not quite sufficient," the Princess remarked coldly. "You will either marry the man whom I have chosen, or give me some definite and clear reason for your refusal."

"One very definite and clear reason," Jeanne remarked, "is that I do not like the Count de Brensault. I think that he is a noisy, forward, and offensive young man."

"His income is nearly fifty thousand a year," the Princess remarked, "so he must be forgiven a few eccentricities of manner."

"His income," Jeanne said, "scarcely matters, does it? If my money is ever to do anything for me, it should at least enable me to choose a husband for myself."

"That's where you girls always make such absurd mistakes," the Princess remarked. "You get an idea or a liking into your mind, and you hold on to it like wax. You forget that the times may change, new people may come, the old order of things may pass altogether away. Suppose, for instance, you were to lose your money?"

"I should not be sorry," Jeanne answered calmly. "I should at least be sure that I was not any longer an article of merchandise. I could lead my own life, and marry whom I pleased."

The Princess laughed scornfully.

"Men do not take to themselves penniless brides nowadays," she remarked.

"Some men — " Jeanne began.

The Princess interrupted her.

"Bah!" she said. "You are thinking of your island fisherman again. I see by the papers that he has gone away. He is very wise. He may be a very excellent person, but the whole world could not hold a less suitable husband for you."

Jeanne smiled.

"Well," she said, "we shall see. I certainly do not think that he will ever ask me to marry him. He is one of those whom my gold does not seem to attract."

"He is clumsy," the Princess remarked. "A word of encouragement would have brought him to your feet."

"If I had thought so," Jeanne remarked, "I would have spoken it."

The Princess looked across at her stepdaughter searchingly.

"Tell me the truth, Jeanne," she said. "Have you been idiot enough to really care for this man?"

"That," Jeanne answered, "is a subject which I cannot discuss with any one, not even you."

"It is all very well," the Princess answered, "but whatever happens, I must see that you do not make an idiot of yourself. It is very important indeed, for more reasons than you know of."

Jeanne looked up.

"Such as — ?" she asked.

The Princess hesitated. There were two evils before her. It was not possible to escape from both. She found herself weighing the chances of each of them, their nearness to disaster.

"Well," she said, "great fortunes even like yours are not above the chances of the money-markets. Your fortune, or a great part of it, might go. What would happen to you then? You would be a pauper."

Jeanne smiled.

"I can see nothing terrifying in that," she answered, "but at the same time I do not think that a fortune such as mine is a very fluctuating affair."

"You are right, of course," the Princess said. "You will be one of the richest young women in the country. There is nothing to prevent it. It is a good thing that you have me to look after you."

Jeanne leaned a little forward in her chair, and looked steadfastly at her stepmother.

"I suppose," she said, "that you are right. You know the world, at any rate, and you are clever. But often you puzzle me. Why at first did you want me to marry Major Forrest?"

The Princess' face seemed suddenly to harden.

"I never wished you to," she said coldly. "However, we will not talk about that. For certain reasons I think that it would be well for you to be married before you actually come of age. That is why I have invited the Count de Brensault here tonight."

Jeanne's dark eyes were fixed curiously upon the Princess.

"Sometimes," she said, "I do not altogether understand you. Why should there be all this nervous haste about my marriage? Do you know that it would trouble me a great deal more, only that I have absolutely made up my mind that nothing will induce me to marry any one whom I do not really care for."

The Princess raised her head, and for a moment the woman and the girl looked at one another. It was almost a duel — the Princess' intense, almost threatening regard, and Jeanne's set face and steadfast eyes.

"My father left me all this money," Jeanne said, "that I might be happy, not miserable. I am quite determined that I will not ruin my life before it has commenced. I do not wish to marry at all for several years. I think that you have brought me into what you call Society a good deal too soon. I would rather study for a little time, and try and learn what the best things are that one may get out of life. I am afraid, from your point of view, that I am going to be a failure. I do not care particularly about dances, or the people we have met at them. I think that in another few weeks I shall be as bored as the most fashionable person in London."

A servant knocked at the door announcing Major Forrest. Jeanne rose to her feet and passed out by another door. The Princess made no attempt to stop her.

CHAPTER IV

The Princess looked up with ill-concealed eagerness as Forrest entered.

"Well," she asked, "have you any news?"

Forrest shook his head.

"None," he answered. "I am up for the day only. Cecil will not let me stay any longer. He was here himself the day before yesterday. We take it by turns to come away."

"And there is nothing to tell me?" the Princess asked. "No change of any sort?"

"None," Forrest answered. "It is no good attempting to persuade ourselves that there is any."

"What are you up for, then?" she asked.

He laughed hardly.

"I am like a diver," he answered, "who has to come to the surface every now and then for fresh air. Life down at Salthouse is very nearly the acme of stagnation. Our only excitement day by day is the danger — and the hope."

"Is Cecil getting braver?" the Princess asked.

"I think that he is, a little," Forrest answered.

The Princess nodded.

"We met him at the Bellamy Smiths'," she said. "It was quite a reunion. Andrew was there, and the Duke."

Forrest's face darkened.

"Meddling fool," he muttered. "Do you know that there are two detectives now in Salthouse? They come and go and ask all manner of questions. One of them pretends that he believes Engleton was drowned, and walks always on the beach and hires boatmen to explore the creeks. The other sits in the inn and bribes the servants with drinks to talk. But don't let's talk about this any longer. How is Jeanne?"

"We are going," the Princess said quietly, "to have trouble with that child."

"Why?" Forrest asked.

"She is developing a conscience," the Princess remarked. "Where she got it from, Heaven knows. It wasn't from her father. I can answer for that."

"Anything else?" Forrest asked.

"It is a curious thing," the Princess replied, "but ever since those few days down at that tumbledown old place of Cecil de la Borne's, she seems to have developed in a remarkable manner. I don't know how much nonsense she talked with that fisherman of hers, but some of it, at any rate, seems to have stuck. I am sure," she added, with a little sigh, "that we are going to have trouble."

Forrest smiled grimly.

"So far as I'm concerned," he remarked, "the trouble has arrived. I've a good mind to chuck it altogether."

The Princess looked up. Worn though her face was, she possessed one feature, her eyes, which still entitled her to be called a beautiful woman. She looked at Forrest steadily, and he felt himself growing uncomfortable before the contempt of her steady regard.

"I wonder how it is," she said pensively, "that all men are more or less cowards. You shield yourselves by speaking of an attack of nerves. It is nothing more nor less than cowardice."

"I believe you are right," Forrest assented. "I'm not the man I was."

"You are not," the Princess agreed. "It is well for you that you have had me to look after you, or you would have gone to pieces altogether. You talk of giving up cards and retiring to the Continent. My dear man, what do you propose to live on?"

He did not answer. He had bullied this woman for a good many years. Now he felt that the tables were being turned upon him.

"What has become of the De la Borne money?" she asked. "I never thought that you would get it, but he paid up every cent, didn't he?"

Forrest nodded.

"He did," he admitted, "or rather his brother did for him. I lost four hundred at Goodwood, and there were some of my creditors I simply had to give a little to, or they would have pulled me up altogether. You talk about nerves, Ena, but, hang it all, it's enough to give anyone the hum to lead the sort of life I've had to lead for the last few years. I'm nothing more nor less than a common adventurer."

"Whatever you are," the Princess answered steadily, "you are too old to change your life or the manner of it. One can start again afresh on the other side of forty, but at fifty the thing is hopeless. Fortunately you have me."

"You!" he repeated bitterly. "You mean that I can dip into your purse for pocket-money when you happen to have any. I have done too much of it. You forget that there is one way into a new world, at any rate."

The Princess smiled.

"My dear Nigel," she said, "it is a way which you will never take. Don't think I mean to be unkind when I say that you have not the courage. However, we will not talk about that. I sent for you to tell you that De Brensault is really in earnest about Jeanne. He is dining here tonight. I will get some other people and we will have bridge. De Brensault is conceited, and a bad player, and what is most important of all, he can afford to lose."

Forrest began to look a little less gloomy.

"You were fortunate," he remarked, "to get hold of De Brensault. There are not many of his sort about. I am afraid, though, that he will not make much of an impression upon Jeanne."

The Princess' face hardened.

"If Jeanne is going to be obstinate," she said, "she must suffer for it. De Brensault is just the man I have been looking for. He wants a young wife, and although he is rich, he is greedy. He is the sort of person I can talk to. In fact I have already given him a hint."

Forrest nodded understandingly.

"But, Ena," he said, "if he really does shell out, won't you be sailing rather close to the wind?"

She shrugged her shoulders.

"I am not afraid," she said. "I know De Brensault and his sort. If he feels that he has been duped, he will keep it to himself. He is too vain a man to allow the world to know it. Poor Jeanne! I am afraid, I am very much afraid that he will take it out of her."

"I do not quite see," Forrest said reflectively, "how you are going to make Jeanne marry any one, especially in this country."

"Jeanne is French, not English," the Princess remarked, "and she is not of age. A mother has considerable authority legally, as I dare say you are aware. We may not be able to manage it in England, but I think I can guarantee that if De Brensault doesn't disappoint us, the wedding will take place."

Forrest helped himself to a cigarette from an open box by his side.

"I think," he said, "that if it comes off we ought to go to the States for a year or so. They don't know us so well there, and those people are the easiest duped of any in the world."

The Princess nodded.

"I have thought of that," she remarked. "There are only one or two little things against it. However, we will see. You had better go now. I have some callers coming and must make myself respectable."

She gave him her hands and he raised them to his lips. Her eyes followed him as he turned away and left the room. For a few moments she was thoughtful. Then she shrugged her shoulders.

"Well," she said, "all things must come to an end, I suppose."

She rang the bell and sent for Jeanne. It was ten minutes, however, before she appeared.

"What have you been doing?" the Princess asked with a frown.

"Finishing some letters," Jeanne answered calmly. "Did you want me particularly?"

"To whom were you writing?" the Princess demanded.

"To Monsieur Laplanche for one person," Jeanne answered calmly.

The Princess raised her eyebrows.

"And what had you," she asked, "to say to Monsieur Laplanche?"

"I have written to ask him a few particulars concerning my fortune," Jeanne answered.

"Such as?" the Princess inquired steadily.

"I want to know," Jeanne said, "at what age it becomes my own, and how much it amounts to. It seems to me that I have a right to know these things, and as you will not tell me, I have written to Monsieur Laplanche."

The Princess held out her hand.

"Give me the letter," she said.

Jeanne made no motion to obey.

"Do you object to my writing?" she asked.

"I object," the Princess said, "to your writing anybody on any subject without my permission, and so far as regards the information you have asked for from Monsieur Laplanche, I will tell you all that you want to know."

"I prefer," Jeanne said steadily, "to hear it from Monsieur Laplanche himself. There are times when you say things which I do not understand. I have quite made up my mind that I will have things made plain to me by my trustee."

The Princess was outwardly calm, but her eyes were like steel.

"You are a foolish child," she said. "I am your guardian. You have nothing whatever to do with your trustees. They exist to help me, not you. Everything that you wish to know you must learn from me. It is not until you are of age that any measure of control passes from me. Give me that letter."

Jeanne hesitated for a moment. Then she turned toward the door.

"No!" she said. "I am going to post it."

The Princess rose from her chair, and crossing the room locked the door.

"Jeanne," she said, "come here."

The girl hesitated. In the end she obeyed. The Princess reached out her hand and struck her on the cheek.

"Give me that letter," she commanded.

Jeanne shrank back. The suddenness of the blow, its indignity, and these new relations which it seemed designed to indicate, bewildered her. She stood passive while the Princess took the letter from her fingers and tore it into pieces. Then she unlocked the door.

"Go to your room, Jeanne," she ordered.

Jeanne heard the sound of people ascending the stairs, and this time she did not hesitate. The Princess drew a little breath and looked at the fragments of the letter in the grate. It was victory of a sort, but she realized very well that the ultimate issue was more doubtful than ever. In her room Jeanne would have time for reflection. If she chose she might easily decide upon the one step which would be irretrievable.

CHAPTER V

The Count de Brensault was a small man, with a large pale face. There were puffy little bags under his eyes, from which the colour had departed. His hair, though skilfully arranged, was very thin at the top, and his figure had the lumpiness of the man who has never known any sort of athletic training. He looked a dozen years older than his age, which was in reality thirty-five, and for the last ten years he had been a constant though cautious devotee of every form of dissipation. Jeanne, who sat by his side at dinnertime, found herself looking at him more than once in a sort of fascinated wonder. Was it really possible that any one could believe her capable of marrying such a creature! There were eight people at dinner, in none of whom she was in the least interested. The Count de Brensault talked a good deal, and very loudly. He spoke of his horses and his dogs and his motor cars, but he omitted to say that he had ceased to ride his horses, and that he never drove his motor car. Jeanne listened to him in quiet contempt, and the Princess fidgetted in her chair. The man ought to know that this was not the way to impress a child fresh from boarding-school!

"You seem," Jeanne remarked, after listening to him almost in silence for a long time, "to give most of your time to sports. Do you play polo?"

He shook his head.

"I am too heavy," he said, "and the game, it is a little dangerous."

"Do you hunt?" she asked.

"No!" he admitted. "In Belgium we do not hunt."

"Do you race with your motor cars?"

"I entered one," he answered, "for the Prix des Ardennes. It was the third. My driver, he was not very clever."

"You did not drive it yourself, then?" she asked.

He laughed in a superior manner.

"I do not wish," he said, "to have a broken neck. There are so many things in life which I still find very pleasant."

He smiled at her in a knowing manner, and Jeanne looked away to hide her disgust.

"Your interest in sport," she remarked, "seems to be a sort of second-hand one, does it not?"

"I do not know that," he answered. "I do not know quite what you mean. At Ostend last year I won the great sweepstakes."

"For shooting pigeons?" she asked.

"So!" he admitted, with content.

She smiled.

"I see that I must beg your pardon," she said. "Have you ever done any big game shooting?"

He shook his head.

"I do not like to travel very much," he answered. "I do not like the cooking, and I think that my tastes are what you would call very civilized."

The Princess intervened. She felt that it was necessary at any cost to do so.

"The Count," she told Jeanne, "has just been elected a member of the Four-in-Hand Club here. If we are very nice to him he will take us out in his coach."

"As soon," De Brensault interposed hastily, "as I have found another team not quite so what you call spirited. My black horses are very beautiful, but I do not like to drive them. They pull very hard, and they always try to run away."

The Princess sighed. The man, after all, was really a little hopeless. She saw clearly that it was useless to try and impress Jeanne. The affair must take its course. Afterwards in the drawing-room the Count came and sat by Jeanne's side.

"Always," he declared, "in England it is bridge. One dines with one's friends, and one would like to talk for a little time, and it is bridge. It must be very dull for you little girls who are not old enough to play. There is no one left to talk to you."

Jeanne smiled.

"Perhaps," she said, "I am an exception. There are very few people whom I care to have talk to me."

She looked him in the eyes, but he was unfortunately a very spoilt young man, and he only stroked the waxed tip of a scanty moustache.

"I am very glad to hear you say so, mademoiselle," he said. "That makes it the more pleasant that your excellent mother gives me one quarter of an hour's respite from bridge that we may have a little conversation. Have you ever been in my country, Miss Le Mesurier?"

"I have only travelled through it," Jeanne answered; "but I am afraid that you did not understand what I meant just now. I said that there were very few people with whom I cared to talk. You are not one of those few, Monsieur le Comte."

He looked at her with a half-open mouth. His eyes were suddenly like beads.

"I do not understand," he said.

"I am afraid," Jeanne answered, with a sigh, "that you are very unintelligent. What I meant to say was that I do not like to sit here and talk with you. It wearies me, because you do not say anything that interests me, and I should very much rather read my book."

The Count de Brensault was nonplussed. He looked at Jeanne, and he looked vaguely across the room at the Princess, as though wondering whether he ought to appeal to her.

"Have I offended you?" he asked. "Perhaps I have said something that you do not like. I am sorry."

"No, it is not that at all," Jeanne answered sweetly. "It is simply that I do not like you. You must not mind if I tell you the truth. You see I have only just come from boarding-school, and there we were always taught to be quite truthful."

De Brensault stared at her again. This was the most extraordinary young woman whom he had ever met in his life. Had not the Princess only an hour ago told him that although he might find her a little difficult at first, she was nevertheless prepared to receive his advances. He had imagined himself dazzling her a little with his title and possessions, gracefully throwing the handkerchief at her feet, and giving her that slight share in his life and affection which his somewhat continental ideas of domesticity suggested. Had she really meant to be rude to him, or was she nervous? He looked at her once more, still with that unintelligent stare. Jeanne was perfectly composed, with her pale cheeks and large serious eyes. She was obviously speaking the truth. Then as he looked the expression in his eyes changed. She was gradually becoming desirable, not only on account of her youth and dowry — there were other things. He felt a sudden desire to kiss those very shapely, somewhat full lips, which had just told him so calmly that their owner disliked him. Already he was telling himself in his mind that some day, when she was his altogether, for a plaything or what he chose to make of her, he would remind her of this evening.

"I am sorry," he said, "that you do not like me, but that is because you are not used to men. Presently you will know me better, and then I am sure it will be different. As for you," he continued, looking at her in a manner which he felt should certainly awaken some different feeling in her inexperienced heart, "I admire you very much indeed. I have seen you only once or twice, but I have thought of you much. Some day I hope that we shall be very much better friends."

He leaned a little toward her, and Jeanne calmly removed herself a little further away. She turned her head now to look at him, as she sat upright upon the sofa, very slim and graceful in her white gown.

"I do not think so," she said. "I do not care about being friendly with people whom I dislike, and I am beginning to dislike you very much indeed because you will not go away when I ask you."

He rose to his feet a little offended.

"Very well," he said, "I will go and talk to your stepmother, who wants me to play bridge, but very soon I shall come back, and before long I think that I am going to make you like me very much."

He crossed the room, and Jeanne's eyes followed his awkward gait with a sudden flash of quiet amusement. She watched him talk to her stepmother, and she saw the Princess' face darken. As a matter of fact De Brensault felt that he had some just cause for complaint.

"Dear Princess," he said, "you did not tell me that she was so very farouche, so very shy indeed. I speak to her quite kindly, and she tells me that she does not like me, and that she wished me to go away."

The Princess looked across the room towards Jeanne, who was calmly reading, and apparently oblivious of everything that was passing.

"My dear Count," she said, tapping his hand with her fan, "she is very, very serious. She would like to have been a nun, but of course we would not hear of it. I think that she was a little afraid of you. You looked at her very boldly, you know, and she is not used to the glances of men. At her age, perhaps — you understand?"

The Count was not quite sure that he did understand. He had a most unpleasant recollection of the firmness and decision with which Jeanne had announced her views with regard to him, but he looked towards her again and the look was fatal. Jeanne was certainly a most desirable young person, quite apart from her dowry.

"It may be as you say, Princess," he said. "I must leave her to you for a little time. You must talk to her. She is quite pretty," he added with an involuntary note of condescension in his tone. "I am very pleased with her. In fact I am quite attracted."

"You will remember," the Princess said, dropping her voice a little, "that before anything definite is said, you and I must have a little conversation."

De Brensault twirled his moustache. He looked up at the Princess as though trying to fathom the meaning of her words.

"Certainly," he answered slowly. "I have not forgotten what you said. Of course, her dot is very large, is it not?"

"It is very large indeed," the Princess answered, "and there are a great many young men who would be very grateful to me indeed if I were willing even to listen to them."

De Brensault nodded.

"Very well," he said. "We will have that little talk whenever you like."

The Princess nodded.

"I suppose," she said, "we must play bridge now. They are waiting for us."

De Brensault looked behind to where Jeanne was still sitting reading. Her head was resting upon a sofa pillow, deep orange coloured, against which the purity of her complexion, the delicate lines of her eyebrows, the shapeliness of her exquisite mouth, were all more than ever manifest. She read with interest, and without turning her head away from the pages of the book which she held in long, slender fingers. De Brensault sighed as he turned away.

"Certainly," he said. "We will go and play bridge. But I will tell you what it is, my dear Princess. I think I am very near falling in love with your little stepdaughter."

CHAPTER VI

Forrest crossed the room and waited his opportunity until the Princess was alone.

"Let me take you somewhere," he said. "I want to talk to you."

She laid her fingers upon his arm, and they walked slowly away from the crowded part of the ballroom.

"So you are up again," she remarked looking at him curiously. "Does that mean — ?"

"It means nothing, worse luck," he answered, "except that I have twenty-four hours' leave. I am off back again at eight o'clock tomorrow morning. Tell me about this De Brensault affair. How is it going on?"

"Well enough on his side," she answered. "The amusing part of it is that the more Jeanne snubs him, the keener he gets. He sends roses and chocolates every day, and positively haunts the house. I never was so tired of any one."

"Make him your son-in-law quickly," he said grimly. "You'll see little enough of him then."

"I'm not sure," the Princess said reflectively, "whether it is quite wise to hurry Jeanne so much."

"Wise or not," Forrest said, "it must be done. Even supposing the other affair comes out all right, London is getting impossible for me. I don't know who's at the bottom of it, but people have stopped sending me invitations, and even at my pothouse of a club the men seem to have as little to say to me as possible. Some one's at work spreading reports of some sort or another. I am not over sensitive, but the thing's becoming an impossibility."

"Do you suppose," she asked quietly, "that it is the Engleton affair?"

He nodded.

"People are saying all sorts of things," he answered. "I'd go abroad tomorrow and leave De la Borne to look out for himself, but I haven't even the money to pay my railway fare."

The Princess shrugged her shoulders expressively.

"Oh, I'm not begging!" he continued. "I know you're pretty well in the same box."

"That," the Princess remarked, "scarcely expresses it. I am a great deal worse off than you, because I have a houseful of unpaid servants, and a mob of tradespeople, who are just beginning to clamour. I see that you are looking at my necklace," she continued. "I can assure you that I have not a single real stone left. Everything I possess that isn't in pawn is of paste."

"Then don't you see, Ena," he said, "that this thing really must be hurried forward? De Brensault is ready enough, isn't he?"

"Quite," she answered.

"And he understands the position?"

"I think so," the Princess answered. "I have given him to understand it pretty clearly."

"Then have a clear business talk with him," Forrest said, "and then have it out with Jeanne. You could all go abroad together, and they could be married at the Embassy, say at Paris."

"Jeanne is the only difficulty," the Princess said. "It would suit me better, for upon my word I don't know where I could get credit for her trousseau."

"It isn't any use waiting," Forrest said. "I have watched them together, and I am sure of it. De Brensault isn't one of those fellows who improve upon acquaintance. Look, there they are. Nothing very lover-like about that, is there?"

De Brensault and Jeanne were crossing the room together. Only the very tips of her fingers rested upon his coat-sleeve, and there was a marked aloofness about her walk and the carriage of her head. He was saying something to her to which she seemed to be paying the scantiest of attention. Her head was thrown back, and in her eyes was a great weariness. Suddenly, just as they reached the entrance, they saw her whole expression change. A wave of colour flooded her cheeks. Her eyes were suddenly filled with life. They saw her lips part. Her hands were outstretched to greet the man who, crossing the room, had stopped at her summons. Both the Princess and Forrest frowned when they saw who it was. It was Andrew de la Borne.

"That infernal fisherman!" Forrest muttered. "I saw in the paper that he had returned this afternoon from The Hague."

The Princess made an involuntary movement forward, but Forrest checked her.

"You can do no good," he said. "Wait and see what happens."

What did happen was very simple, and for the Count de Brensault a little humiliating. Jeanne passed her arm through the newcomer's and with the curtest of nods to her late companion, disappeared through an open doorway. The Belgian stood looking after them, twirling his moustache with shaking fingers. His face was paler even than usual, and he was shaking with anger.

"Leave him alone for a few minutes," Forrest said to the Princess. "You will do no good at all by speaking to him just now. Ena, it is absolutely necessary that you make Jeanne understand the state of affairs."

"I think," the Princess said thoughtfully, "that it will be best to take her away from London. Lately I have noticed a development in Jeanne which I do not altogether understand. She has begun to think for herself most unpleasantly. She plays at being a child with De Brensault, but that is simply because it is the easiest way to repulse him."

Meanwhile Jeanne, whose face was transfigured, and whose whole manner was changed, was sitting with her companion in the quietest corner they could find.

"It is delightful to see you again," she said frankly. "I do not think that any one ever felt so lonely as I do."

He smiled.

"I can assure you that I find it delightful to be back again," he said, "although I have enjoyed my work very much. By the by, who introduced you to the man whom you were with when I found you?"

"My stepmother," she answered. "He is the man, by the by, whom I am told I am to marry."

Andrew looked as he felt for a moment, shocked.

"I am sorry to hear that," he said quietly.

"You need not be afraid," she answered. "I am not of age, and I was brought up in a country where one's guardians have a good deal of authority, but nothing in the world would ever induce me to marry a creature like that."

His face cleared somewhat.

"I am very surprised," he said, "that your stepmother should have thought of it. He is an unfit companion for any self-respecting woman."

"I do not understand," Jeanne said quietly, "why they are so anxious that I should marry quickly, but I know that my step-mother thinks of nothing else in connection with me. Look! They are coming through the conservatories. Let us go out by the other door."

They came face to face with a tall, grave-looking man, who wore an order around his neck. Andrew stopped suddenly.

"I should like," he said to Jeanne, "to introduce you to my friend. You have met him before down at the Red Hall, and on the island, but that scarcely counts. Westerham, this is Miss Le Mesurier. You remember that you saw her at Salthouse."

The Duke shook hands with the girl, looking at her attentively. His manner was kind, but his eyes seemed to be questioning her all the time.

"I am very glad to know you, Miss Le Mesurier," he said. "My friend Andrew here has spoken of you to me."

They remained talking together for some minutes, until, in fact, Forrest and the Princess, who were in pursuit of them, appeared. The Princess looked curiously at the Duke, and Forrest frowned heavily when he recognized him. There was a moment's almost embarrassed silence. Then Andrew did what seemed to him to be the reasonable thing.

"Princess," he said, "will you allow me to present my friend the Duke of Westerham. The Duke was staying with me a few weeks ago, as you know, and at that time he had a particular reason for not wishing his whereabouts to be known."

The Duke bowed over the Princess' hand, which was offered him at once, and without hesitation, but his greeting to Forrest was markedly cold. Forrest had evidently lost his nerve. He seemed tongue-tied, and he was very pale. It was the Princess alone who saved the situation from becoming an exceedingly embarrassing one.

"I have heard of you very often, Duke," she said. "Your brother, Lord Ronald, took us down to Norfolk, you know. By the by, have you heard from him yet?"

"Not yet, madam," the Duke said, "but I can assure you that it is only a matter of time before I shall discover his whereabouts. I wonder whether your ward will do me the honour of giving me this dance?" he added, turning to her. "I am afraid I am not a very skilful performer, but perhaps she will have a little consideration for one who is willing to do his best."

He led Jeanne away from them, and Andrew, after a moment's stereotyped conversation, also departed. The Princess and Forrest were alone.

"This is getting worse and worse," Forrest muttered. "He is suspicious. I am sure that he is. They say that young Engleton was his favourite brother, and that he is determined — "

"Hush!" the Princess said. "There are too many people about to talk of these things. I wonder why the Duke took Jeanne off."

"An excuse for getting away from us," Forrest said. "Did you see the way he looked at me? Ena, I cannot hang on like this any longer. I must have a few thousand pounds and get away."

The Princess nodded.

"We will go and talk to De Brensault," she said. "I should think he would be just in the frame of mind to consent to anything."

The Duke, who was well acquainted with the house in which they were, led Jeanne into a small retiring room and found her an easy chair.

"My dear young lady," he said, "I hope you will not be disappointed, but I have not danced for ten years. I brought you here because I wanted to say something to you."

Jeanne looked up at him a little surprised.

"Something to me?" she repeated.

He bowed.

"Andrew de la Borne is one of my oldest and best friends," he said, "and what I am going to say to you is a little for his sake, although I am sure that if I knew you better I should say it also for your own. You must not be annoyed or offended, because I am old enough to be your father, and what I say I say altogether for your own good. They tell me that you are a young lady with a great fortune, and you know that nowadays half the evil that is done in the world is done for the sake of money. Frankly, without wishing to say a word against your stepmother, I consider that for a young girl you are placed in a very difficult and dangerous position. The man Forrest — mind you must not be offended if he should be a friend of yours — but I am bound to tell you that I believe him to be an unscrupulous adventurer, and I am afraid that your stepmother is very much under his influence. You have no other relatives or friends in this country, and I hear that a man named De Brensault is a suitor for your hand."

"I shall never marry him," Jeanne said firmly. "I think that he is detestable."

"I am glad to hear you say so," the Duke continued, "because he is not a man whom I would allow any young lady for whom I had any shade of respect or affection, to become acquainted with. Now the fact that your stepmother deliberately encourages him makes me fear that you may find yourself at any moment in a very difficult position. I do not wish to say anything against your friends or your stepmother. I hope you will believe that. But nowadays people who are poor themselves, but who know the value and the use of money, are tempted to do things for the sake of it which are utterly unworthy and wrong. I want you to understand that if any time you should need a friend it will give me very great happiness indeed to be of any service to you I can. I am a bachelor, it is true, but I am old enough to be your father, and I can bring you into touch at once with friends more suitable for you and your station. Will you come to me, or send for me, if you find yourself in any sort of trouble?"

She said very little, but she looked at him for a moment with her wonderful eyes, very soft with unshed tears.

"You are very, very kind," she said. "I have been very unhappy, and I have felt very lonely. It will make everything seem quite different to know there is some one to whom I may come for advice if — if — "

"I know, dear," the Duke interrupted, rising and holding out his arm. "I know quite well what you mean. All I can say is, don't be afraid to come or to send, and don't let any one bully you into throwing away your life upon a scoundrel like De Brensault. I am going to give you back to Andrew now. He is a good fellow — one of the best. I only wish — "

The Duke broke off short. After all, he remembered, he had no right to complete his sentence. Andrew, he felt, was no more of a marrying man than he himself, and he was the last person in the world to ever think of marrying a great heiress. They found him waiting about outside.

"I must relinquish my charge," the Duke said smiling. "You will not forget, Miss Le Mesurier?"

"I am never likely to," she answered gratefully.

CHAPTER VII

The Count de Brensault had seldom been in a worse temper. That Jeanne should have flouted him was not in itself so terrible, because he had quite made up his mind that sooner or later he would take a coward's revenge for the slights he had been made to endure at her hands. But that he should have been flouted in the presence of a whole roomful of people, that he should have been deliberately left for another man, was a different matter altogether. His first impulse when Jeanne left him, was to walk out of the house and have nothing more to say to the Princess or Jeanne herself. The world was full of girls perfectly willing to tumble into his arms, and mothers only too anxious to push them there. Why should he put himself in this position for Jeanne, great heiress though she might be? But somehow or other, after he had tossed off two glasses of champagne at the buffet, he realized that his fancy for her was a real thing, and one from which he could not so readily escape. If she had wished to deliberately attract him, she could scarcely have chosen means more calculated to attain that end than by this avowed indifference, even dislike. He sat by himself in a small smoking-room and thought of her — her slim girlish perfection of figure and bearing, her perfect complexion, her beautiful eyes, her scarlet lips. All these things came into his mind as he sat there, until he felt his cheeks flush with the desire to succeed, and his eyes grow bright at the thought of the time when he should hold her in his arms and take what revenge he chose for these slights. No! he would not let her go, he determined. Dignified or undignified, he would pursue her to the end, only he must have an understanding with the Princess, something definite must be done. He would not run the risk again of being made a laughing-stock before all his friends. Forrest found him in exactly the mood most suitable for his purpose.

"Come and talk to the Princess," he said. "She has something to say to you."

De Brensault rose somewhat heavily to his feet.

"And I," he said, "I, too, have something to say to her. We will take a glass of champagne together, my friend Forrest, and then we will seek the Princess."

Forrest nodded.

"By all means," he said. "To tell you the truth I need it."

De Brensault looked at him curiously.

"You are very pale, my friend," he said. "You look as though things were not going too well with you."

"I have been annoyed," Forrest answered. "There is a man here whom I dislike, and it made me angry to see him with Miss Jeanne. I think myself that the time has come when something definite must be done as regards that child. She is too young to be allowed to run loose like this, and a great deal too inexperienced."

"I agree with you," De Brensault said solemnly. "We will drink that glass of wine together, and we will go and talk to the Princess."

They found the Princess where Forrest had left her. She motioned to De Brensault to sit by her side, and Forrest left them.

"My dear Count," the Princess said, "tonight has proved to me that it is quite time Jeanne had some one to look after her. Let me ask you. Are you perfectly serious in your suit?"

"Absolutely!" De Brensault answered eagerly. "I myself would like the matter settled. I propose to you for her hand."

The Princess bowed her head thoughtfully.

"Now, my dear Count," she said, "I am going to talk to you as a woman of the world. You know that my husband, in leaving his fortune entirely to Jeanne, treated me very badly. You may know this, or you may not know it, but the fact remains that I am a very poor woman."

De Brensault nodded sympathetically. He guessed pretty well what was coming.

"If I," the Princess continued, "assist you to gain my step-daughter Jeanne for your wife, and the control of all her fortune, it is only fair," she continued, "that I should be recompensed in some way for the allowance which I have been receiving as her guardian, and which will then come to an end. I do not ask for anything impossible or unreasonable. I want you to give me twenty thousand pounds the day that you marry Jeanne. It is about one year's income for her rentes, a mere trifle to you, of course."

"Twenty thousand pounds," De Brensault repeated reflectively.

The Princess nodded. She was sorry that she had not asked thirty thousand.

"I am not a mercenary woman," she said. "If I were not almost a pauper I would accept nothing. As it is, I think you will call my proposal a very fair one."

"The exact amount of Mademoiselle Jeanne's dot," he remarked, "has never been discussed between us."

"The figures are altogether beyond me," the Princess said. "To tell you the truth I have never had the heart to go into them. I have always thought it terribly unfair that my husband should have left me nothing but an annuity, and this great fortune to the child. However, as you are both rich, it seems to me that settlements will not be necessary. On your honeymoon you can go and see her trustees in Paris, and you yourself will, of course, then take over the management of her fortune."

De Brensault looked thoughtful for a moment or two.

"Perhaps," he said, "it would be better if I had a business interview with her trustees before the ceremony."

"Just as you like," the Princess answered carelessly. "Monsieur Laplanche is in Cairo just now, but he will be back in Paris in a few weeks' time. Perhaps you would rather delay everything until then?"

"No!" De Brensault said, after a moment's hesitation. "I would like to delay nothing. I would like to marry Mademoiselle Jeanne at once, if it can be arranged."

"To tell you the truth," the Princess said, "I think it would be much the best way out of a very difficult situation. I am finding Jeanne very difficult to manage, and I am quite sure that she will be happier and better off married. I am proposing, if you are willing, to exercise my authority absolutely. If she shows the slightest reluctance to accept you, I propose that we all go over to Paris. I shall know how to arrange things there."

De Brensault smiled. The prospect of winning Jeanne at any cost became more and more attractive to him. The Princess, who was looking at him through half closed eyes, saw that he was perfectly safe.

"And now, my dear Count," she said, "I am going to ask you a favour. I am doing for you something for which you ought to be grateful to me all your life. For a mere trifle which will not recompense me in the least for what I am giving up, I am finding you one of the most desirable brides in Europe. I want you to help me a little."

"What is it that I can do?" he asked.

"Let me have five thousand pounds on account of what you are going to give me, tomorrow morning," she said coolly.

De Brensault hesitated. He was prepared to pay for what he wanted, but five thousand pounds was nevertheless a great deal of money.

"I would not ask you," the Princess continued, "if I were not really hard up. I have been gambling, a foolish thing to do, and I do not want to sell my securities, because I know that very soon they will pay me over and over again. Will you do this for me? Remember, I am giving you my word that Jeanne is to be yours."

"Make it three thousand," De Brensault said slowly. "Three thousand pounds I will send you a cheque for, tomorrow morning."

The Princess nodded.

"As you will," she said. "I think if I were you, though, I should make it five. However, I shall leave it for you to do what you can. Now will you take me out into the ballroom. I am going to look for Jeanne."

They found her at supper with the Duke and Andrew and a very great lady, a connection of the Duke's, who was one of those few who had refused to accept the Princess. The Princess swept up to the little party and laid her hand upon Jeanne's shoulder.

"I do not want to hurry you, dear," she said, "but when you have finished supper I should be glad to go. We have to go on to Dorchester House, you know."

Jeanne sighed. She had been enjoying herself very much indeed.

"I am ready now," she said, standing up, "but must we go to Dorchester House? I would so much rather go straight home. I have not had such a good time since I have been in London."

The Duke offered her his arm, ignoring altogether Count De Brensault, who was standing by.

"At least," he said, "you will permit me to see you to your carriage."

The Princess smiled graciously. It was bad enough to be ignored, as she certainly was to some extent, but on the other hand it was good for De Brensault to see Jeanne held in such esteem. She took his arm and they followed down the room. The Duke was bending down and talking earnestly to Jeanne; this surprised the Princess.

"I wonder," she remarked, more to herself than to her companion, "what he is saying."

De Brensault shrugged his shoulders.

"I do not care," he said. "We will keep to our bargain, you and I. In a few days it will be my arm that she shall take, and nobody else's. Perhaps I shall be a little jealous. Who can say? In a little time she will not mind."

"Remember," the Duke was saying, as he drew Jeanne's hand through his arm, "that I was very much in earnest in what I said to you just now. I have seen a good deal of the world, and you nothing at all, and I cannot help believing that the time when you may need some one's help is a good deal nearer than you yourself imagine."

"I wonder," she asked, a little timidly, "why you are so kind to me?"

"I accept you upon trust," the Duke said, "for the sake of my friend Andrew. I know that he lives out of the world, and has not much experience in judging others, but I do believe that when he has made up his mind about anybody, he is generally right. Frankly, from what I have heard, and a little that I know, I am afraid that I should have been suspicious about even a child like you, because of your associates. But because I believe in you, I am all the more sure that very soon you are going to find yourself in trouble. It is agreed, remember, that when that time comes you will remember that I am your friend."

"I will remember," she murmured. "I am not likely to forget. Except for you and Mr. De la Borne, no one has been really kind to me since I left school. They all say foolish things, and try to make me like them, because I am a great heiress, but one understands how much that is worth."

The Duke looked at her, and seemed half inclined to say something. Whatever it may have been, however, he thought better of it. He contented himself with taking her hand in his and shaking it warmly.

"Good night," he said, "little Miss Jeanne, and remember, No. 51, Grosvenor Square. If I am not there, I have a very nice old housekeeper who will look after you until I turn up."

"No. 51," she repeated softly. "No, I shall not forget!"

CHAPTER VIII

The Princess and Jeanne drove homewards in a silence which remained unbroken until the last few minutes. The events of the evening had been somewhat perplexing to the former. She scarcely understood even now why a great personage like the Duke of Westerham had shown such interest in her charge.

"Tell me, Jeanne," she asked at last, "why is the Duke of Westerham so friendly with your fisherman?"

Jeanne raised her eyebrows slightly.

"'My fisherman,' as you call him," she answered, "is, after all, Andrew de la Borne! They were at school together."

"That is all very well," the Princess answered, "but I cannot see what possible sympathy there can be between them now. Their stations in life are altogether different. You talked with the Duke for some time, Jeanne?"

"He was very kind to me," Jeanne answered.

"Did he give you any idea," the Princess asked, "as to why he was staying down at Salthouse with Mr. Andrew?"

"None at all," Jeanne answered.

"You know very well," the Princess continued, "of what I am thinking. Did he speak to you at all of Major Forrest?"

"Not a word," Jeanne answered.

"Of his brother, then?"

"He did not mention his name," Jeanne declared.

"He asked you no questions at all about anything which may have happened at the Red Hall?"

Jeanne shook her head.

"Certainly not!"

"You do not think, then," the Princess persisted, "that it was for the sake of gaining information about his brother that he talked with you so much?"

"Why should I think so?" Jeanne asked. "He scarcely mentioned any of your names even. He talked to me simply out of kindness, and I think because he knew that Mr. Andrew and I were friends."

The Princess smiled.

"You seem," she remarked, "to have made quite a conquest. I congratulate you. The Duke has not the reputation of being an easy man to get on with."

The carriage pulled up before their house in Berkeley Square, and the Princess did not pursue the subject, but as Jeanne left her for the night, her stepmother called her back.

"Tomorrow morning," she said, "I should be glad if you would come to my room at twelve o'clock, I have something to say to you."

Jeanne slept well that night. For the first time she felt that she had lost the feeling of friendlessness which for the last few weeks had constantly oppressed her. Andrew de la Borne was back in London, and the Duke, who seemed to have some sort of understanding as to the troubles which were likely to beset her, had gone out of his way to offer her his help. She felt now that she would not have to fight her stepmother's influence unaided. Yet when she sought her room at twelve o'clock the next morning she had very little idea of the sort of fight which she might indeed have to make.

The Princess had already spent an hour at her toilette. Her hair was carefully arranged and her face massaged. She received her stepdaughter with some show of affection, and bade her sit close to her.

"Jeanne," she said, "you are now nearly twenty years old. For many reasons I wish to see you married. The Count de Brensault formally proposed for you last night. He is coming at three o'clock this afternoon for his answer."

Jeanne sat upright in her chair. Her stepmother noticed a new air of determination in the poise of her head, and the firm lines of her mouth.

"The Count might have spared himself the trouble," she said. "He knows very well what my answer will be. I think that you know, too. It is no, most emphatically and decidedly! I will not marry the Count de Brensault."

"Before you express yourself so irrevocably," the Princess said calmly, "I should like you to understand that it is my wish that you accept his offer."

"In all ordinary matters," Jeanne answered, "I am prepared to obey you. In this, no! I think that I have the right to choose my husband for myself, or at any rate to approve of whomever you may select. I do not approve of the Count de Brensault. I do not care for him, and I never could care for him, and I will not marry him!"

The Princess said nothing for several moments. Then she moved toward the door which led into her sleeping chamber, where her maid was still busy, and turned the key in the lock.

"Jeanne," she said when she returned, "I think it is time that you were told something which I am afraid will be a shock to you. This great fortune of yours, of which you have heard so much, and which has been so much talked about, is a myth."

"What do you mean?" Jeanne asked, looking at her step-mother with startled eyes.

"Exactly what I say," the Princess continued. "Your father made huge gifts to his relatives during the last few years of his life, and he left enormous sums in charity. To you he left the remainder of his estate, which all the world believed to amount to at least a million pounds. But when things came to be realized, all his securities seemed to have depreciated. The legacies were paid in cash. The depreciation of his fortune all fell upon you. When everything had been paid, there was something like twenty-five thousand pounds left. More than half of that has gone in your education, and in an allowance to myself since I have had the charge of you. There is a little left in the hands of Monsieur Laplanche, but very little indeed. What there is we owe for your dresses, the rent of this house, and other things."

"You mean," Jeanne interrupted bewildered, "that I have no money at all?"

"Practically none," the Princess answered. "Now you can see why it is so important that you should marry a rich man."

Jeanne was bewildered. It was hard to grasp these things which her stepmother was telling her.

"If this be true," she said, "how is it that every one speaks of me as being a great heiress?"

The Princess glanced at her with a contemptuous smile.

"You do not suppose," she said, "that I have found it necessary to take the whole world into my confidence."

"You mean," Jeanne said, "that people don't know that I am not a great heiress?"

"Certainly not," the Princess replied, "or we should scarcely be here."

"The Count de Brensault?" Jeanne asked.

"He does not know, of course," the Princess answered. "He is a rich man. He can afford quite well to marry a girl without a DOT."

Jeanne's head fell slowly between her hands. The suddenness of this blow had staggered her. It was not the loss of her fortune so much which affected her as the other contingencies with which she was surrounded. She tried to think, and the more she thought the more involved it all seemed. She looked up at last.

"If my fortune is really gone," she said, "why do you let people talk about it, and write about me in the papers as though I were still so rich?"

The Princess shrugged her shoulders.

"For your own sake," she answered. "It is necessary to find you a husband, is it not, and nowadays one does not find them easily when there is no DOT."

Jeanne felt her cheeks burning.

"I am to be married, then," she said slowly, "by some one who thinks I have a great deal of money, and who afterwards will be able to turn round and reproach me for having deceived him."

The Princess laughed.

"Afterwards," she said, "the man will not be too anxious to let the world know that he has been made a fool of. If you play your cards properly, the afterwards will come out all right."

Jeanne rose slowly to her feet.

"I do not think," she said, "that you have quite understood me. I should like you to know that nothing would ever induce me to marry any one unless they knew the truth. I will not go on accepting invitations and visiting people's houses, many of whom have only asked me because they think that I am very rich. Every one must know the truth at once."

"And how, may I ask, do you propose to live?" the Princess asked quietly.

"If there is nothing left at all of my money," Jeanne said, "I will work. If it is the worst which comes, I will go back to the convent and teach the children."

The Princess laughed softly.

"Jeanne," she said, "you are talking like a positive idiot. It is because you have had no time to think this thing out. Remember that after all you are not sailing under any false colours. You are your father's daughter, and you are also his heiress. If the newspapers and gossip have exaggerated the amount of his fortune, that is not your affair. Be reasonable, little girl," she added, letting her hand fall upon Jeanne's. "Don't give us all away like this. Remember that I have made sacrifices for your sake. I owe more money than I can pay for your dresses, for the carriage, for the house here. Nothing but your marriage will put us straight again. You must make up your mind to this. The Count de Brensault is so much in love with you that he will ask no questions. You must marry him."

Jeanne drew herself away from her stepmother's touch.

"Nothing," she said, "would induce me to marry the Count de Brensault, not even if he knew that I am penniless. If we cannot afford to live in this house, or to keep carriages, let us go away at once and take rooms somewhere. I do not wish to live under false pretences."

The Princess was very pale, but her eyes were hard and steely.

"Child," she said, "don't be a fool. Don't make me angry, or I may say and do things for which I should be sorry. It is no fault of mine that you are not a great heiress. I have done the next best thing for you. I have made people believe that you are. Be reasonable, and all will be well yet. If you are going to play the Quixote, it will be ruin for all of us. I cannot think how a child like you got such ideas. Remember that I am many years older and wiser than you. You should leave it to me to do what is best."

Jeanne shook her head.

"I cannot," she said simply. "I am sorry to disappoint you, but I shall tell every one I meet that I have no money, and I will not marry the Count de Brensault."

The Princess grasped her by the wrist.

"You will not obey me, child?" she said.

"I will obey you in everything reasonable," Jeanne said.

"Very well, then," the Princess answered, "go to your room at once."

Jeanne turned and walked toward the door. On the threshold, however, she paused. There were many times, she remembered, when her stepmother had been kind to her. She looked around at the Princess, sitting with her head resting upon her clasped hands.

"I am very sorry," Jeanne said timidly, "that I cannot do what you wish. It is not honest. Cannot you see that it is not honest?"

The Princess turned slowly round.

"Honest!" she repeated scornfully. "Who is there in our world who can afford to be honest? You are behaving like a baby, Jeanne. I only hope that before long you may come to your senses. Will you obey me if I tell you not to leave your room until I send for you?"

Jeanne hesitated.

"Yes!" she said. "I will obey you in that."

"Then go there and wait," the Princess said. "I must think what to do."

CHAPTER IX

The Count de Brensault called in Berkeley Square at three o'clock precisely that afternoon, but it was the Princess who received him, and the Princess was alone.

"Well?" he asked, a little eagerly. "Mademoiselle Jeanne is more reasonable, eh? You have good news?"

The Princess motioned him to a seat.

"I think," she said, "we had forgotten how young Jeanne really is. The idea of getting married to any one seems to terrify her. After all, why should we wonder at it? The school where she was brought up was a very, very strict one, and this plunge into life has been a little sudden."

"You think, then," De Brensault asked eagerly, "that it is not I personally whom she objects to so much?"

"Certainly not," the Princess answered. "It is simply you as the man whom it is proposed that she should marry that she dislikes. I have been talking to her for a long time this afternoon. Frankly, I do not know which would be best — to give up the idea of anything of the sort for some time, or to — to — "

"To what?" De Brensault demanded, as the Princess hesitated.

"To take extreme measures," the Princess answered slowly. "Mind, I would not consider such a thing for a moment, if I were not fully convinced that Jeanne, when she is a little older, would be perfectly satisfied with what we have done. On the other hand, one hesitates naturally to worry the child."

"She will not see me?" De Brensault asked. "It is possible that I might be able to persuade her."

"You would do more harm than good," the Princess answered decidedly. "She is terrified just now at the idea. She is in her room shaking like a schoolgirl who is going to be punished. Really, I don't know why I should have been plagued with such a charge. There are so many things I want to do, and I have to stay here to look after Jeanne, because she is too foolish to be trusted with any one else. I want to go to America, and a very dear friend of mine has invited me to go with her and some delightful people on a yachting cruise around the world."

"Then why not use those measures you spoke of?" De Brensault said eagerly. "I shall make Jeanne a very good husband, I assure you. I shall promise you that in a fortnight's time she will be only too delighted with her lot."

The Princess looked at him thoughtfully.

"I wonder," she said, "whether I could trust you."

"Trust me, of course you could, dear Princess!" De Brensault exclaimed eagerly. "I will be kind to her, I promise you. Be sensible. She would feel this way with any one. You yourself have said so. There can be no more suitable marriage for her than with me. Let us call it arranged. Tell me what it is that you propose. Perhaps I may be able to help."

"Jeanne is, of course, not of age," the Princess said thoughtfully, "and she is entirely under my control. In England people are rather foolish about these things, but abroad they understand the situation better."

"Why not in Belgium?" De Brensault exclaimed. "We might go to a little town I know of very near to my estates. Everything could be arranged there very easily. I am quite well-known, and no questions would be asked."

The Princess nodded thoughtfully.

"That might do," she admitted.

"Why not start at once?" De Brensault suggested. "There is nothing to be gained by waiting. We might even leave tomorrow."

The Princess shook her head.

"You are too impetuous, my dear Count," she said.

"But what is there to wait for?" he demanded.

"I must see my lawyers first," she answered slowly, "and before I leave London I must pay some bills."

The Count drew a cheque book from his pocket.

"I will keep my word," he said. "I will pay you on account the amount we spoke of."

The Princess opened her escritoire briskly.

"There is a pen and ink there," she said, "and blotting paper. Really your cheque will be a god-send to me. I seem to have had nothing but expenses lately, and Jeanne's guardians are as mean as they can be. They grumble even at allowing me five thousand a year."

De Brensault twirled his moustache as he seated himself at the table.

"Five thousand a year," he muttered. "It is not a bad allowance for a young girl who is not yet of age."

The Princess shrugged her shoulders.

"My dear Count," she said, "you do not know what our expenses are. Jeanne is extravagant, so am I extravagant. It is all very well for her, but for me it is another matter. I shall be a poor woman when I have resigned my charge."

De Brensault handed the cheque across.

"You will not find me," he said, "ungrateful. And now, my

dear lady, let us talk about Jeanne. Do you think that you could persuade her to leave London so suddenly?"

"I am going upstairs now," the Princess said, "to have a little talk with her. Dine with me here tonight quite quietly, and I will tell you what fortune I have had."

De Brensault went away, on the whole fairly content with his visit. The Princess endorsed his cheque, and with a sigh of relief enclosed it in an envelope, rang for a maid and ordered her carriage. Then she went upstairs to Jeanne, whom she found busy writing at her desk. She hesitated for a moment, and then went and stood with her hand resting upon the girl's shoulder.

"Jeanne," she said, "I think that we have both been a little hasty."

Jeanne looked up in surprise. Her stepmother's tone was altered. It was no longer cold and dictatorial. There was in it even a note of appeal. Jeanne wondered to find herself so unmoved.

"I am sorry," she said, "if I have said anything unbecoming. You see," she continued, after a moment's pause, "the subject which we were talking about did not seem to me to leave much room for discussion."

"There is no harm in discussing anything," the Princess said, throwing herself into a wicker chair by the side of Jeanne's table. "I am afraid that all that I said must have sounded very cruel and abrupt. You see I have had this thing on my mind for so long. It has been a trouble to me, Jeanne."

Jeanne raised her large eyes and looked steadily at her stepmother. She felt almost ashamed of her coldness and lack of sympathy. The Princess was certainly looking worn and worried.

"I am sorry," Jeanne said stiffly. "I cannot imagine how you could have supported life for a day under such conditions."

Her stepmother sighed.

"That," she said, "is because you have had so little experience of life, and you do not understand its practical necessities. Children like you seem to think that the commonplace necessaries of life drop into our laps as a matter of course, or that they are a sort of gift from Heaven to the deserving. As a matter of fact," the Princess continued, "nothing of the sort happens. Life is often a very cruel and a very difficult thing. We are given tastes, and no means to gratify them. How could I, for instance, face life as a lodging-house keeper, or at best as a sort of companion to some ill-tempered old harridan, who would probably only employ me to have some one to bully? You yourself, Jeanne, are fond of luxuries."

It was a new reflection to Jeanne. She became suddenly

thoughtful.

"I have noticed your tastes," the Princess continued. "You would be miserable in anything but silk stockings, wouldn't you? And your ideas of lingerie are quite in accord with the ideas of the modern young woman of wealth. You fill your rooms with flowers. You buy expensive books," she added, taking up for a moment a volume of De Ronsard, bound in green vellum, with uncut edges. "Your tastes in eating and drinking, too," she continued, "are a little on the sybaritic side. Have you realized what it will mean to give all these things up — to wear coarse clothes, to eat coarse food, to get your books from a cheap library, and look at other people's flowers?"

Jeanne frowned. The idea was certainly not pleasing.

"It will be bad for you," the Princess continued, "and it will be very much worse for me, because I have been used to these things all my life. You may think me very brutal at having tried to help you toward the only means of escape for either of us, but I think, dear, you scarcely realize the alternative. It is not only what you condemn yourself to. Remember that you inflict the same punishment on me."

"It is not I who do anything," Jeanne said. "It is you who have brought this upon both of us. All this money that has been spent upon luxuries, it was absurd. If I was not rich I did not need them. I think that it was more than absurd. It was cruel."

The Princess produced a few inches of lace-bordered cambric. A glance at Jeanne's face showed her that the child had developed a new side to her character. There was something pitiless about the straightened mouth, and the cold questioning eyes.

"Jeanne," the Princess said, "you are a fool. Some day you will understand how great a one. I only trust that it may not be too late. The Count de Brensault may not be everything that is to be desired in a husband, but the world is full of more attractive people who would be glad to become your slaves. You will live mostly abroad, and let me assure you that marriage there is the road to liberty. You have it in your power to save yourself and me from poverty. Make a little sacrifice, Jeanne, if indeed it is a sacrifice. Later on you will be glad of it. If you persist in this unreasonable attitude, I really do not know what will become of us."

Jeanne turned her head, but she did not respond in the least to the Princess' softened tone. There was a note of finality about her words, too. She spoke as one who had weighed this matter and made up her mind.

"If there was no other man in the world," she said, "or no

other way of avoiding starvation, I would not marry the Count de Brensault."

The Princess rose slowly to her feet.

"Very well," she said, "that ends the matter, of course. I hope you will always remember that it is you who are responsible for anything that may happen now. You had better," she continued, "leave off writing letters which will certainly never be posted, and get your clothes together. We shall go abroad at the latest tomorrow afternoon."

"Abroad?" Jeanne repeated.

"Yes!" the Princess answered. "I suppose you have sense enough to see that we cannot stay on here for you to make your interesting confessions. I should probably have some of these tradespeople trying to put me in prison."

"I will tell Saunders at once," Jeanne said. "I am quite ready to do anything you think best."

The Princess laughed hardly.

"You will have to manage without Saunders," she answered. "Paupers like us can't afford maids. I am going to discharge every one this afternoon. Have your boxes packed, please, tonight. Your dinner will be sent up to you."

The Princess left the room, and Jeanne heard the key turn in the lock.

CHAPTER X

Jeanne's packing was after all a very small matter. She ignored the cupboards full of gowns, nor did she open one of the drawers of her wardrobe. She simply filled her dressing-case with a few necessaries and hid it under the table. At eight o'clock one of the servants brought her dinner on a tray. Jeanne saw with relief that it was one of the younger parlour maids, and not the Princess' own maid.

"Mary," Jeanne said, taking a gold bracelet from her wrist and holding it out to her, "I am going to give you this bracelet if you will do just a very simple thing for me."

The girl looked at Jeanne and looked at the bracelet. She was too amazed for speech.

"I want you," Jeanne said, "when you go out to leave the door unlocked. That is all. It will not make any difference to you so far as your position here is concerned, because your mistress is sending you all away in a few days."

The girl looked at the bracelet and did not hesitate for a moment.

"I would do it for you without anything, Miss Jeanne," she said. "The bracelet is too good for me."

Jeanne laughed, and pushed it across the table to her.

"Run along," she said. "If you want to do something else, open the back door for me. I am coming downstairs."

The girl looked a little perplexed. The bracelet which she was holding still engrossed most of her thoughts.

"You are not doing anything rash, Miss Jeanne, I hope?" she asked timidly.

Jeanne shook her head.

"What I am doing is not rash at all," she said softly. "It is necessary."

Five minutes later Jeanne walked unnoticed down the back stairs of the house, and out into the street. She turned into Piccadilly and entered a bus.

"Where to, miss?" the man asked, as he came for his fare.

"I do not know," Jeanne said. "I will tell you presently."

The man stared at her and passed on. Jeanne had spoken the truth. She had no idea where she was going. Her one idea was to get away from every one whom she knew, or who had known her, as the Princess' ward and a great heiress. She sat in a corner of the bus, and she watched the stream of people pass by. Even there she shrank from any face or figure which seemed to her familiar. She almost forgot that she, too, had been a victim of her stepmother's deception. She remembered only that she had been the principal figure in it, and that to the whole world she must seem an object for derision and contempt. It was not her fault that she had played a false part in life. But nevertheless she had played it, and it was not likely that many would believe her innocent. The thought of appealing to the Duke, or to Andrew de la Borne, for help, made her cheeks burn with shame. In any ordinary trouble she would have gone to them. This, however, was something too humiliating, too impossible. She felt that it was a blow which she could ask no one to share.

The omnibus rolled on eastwards and reached Liverpool Street. A sudden overwhelming impulse decided Jeanne as to her destination. She remembered that peculiar sense of freedom, that first escape from her cramped surroundings, which had come to her walking upon the marshes of Salthouse. She would go there again, if it was only for a day or two; find rooms somewhere in the village, and write to Monsieur Laplanche from there. Visitors she knew were not uncommon in the little seaside village, and she would easily be able to keep out of the way of Cecil, if he were still there. The idea seemed to her like an inspiration. She went up to the ticket-office and asked for a ticket for Salthouse. The man stared at her.

"Never heard of the place, miss," he said. "It's not on our line."

"It is near Wells on the east coast," she said. "Now I think of it, I remember one has to drive from Wells. Can I have a ticket to there?"

He glanced at the clock.

"The train goes in ten minutes, miss," he said.

Jeanne travelled first, because she had never thought of travelling any other way. She sat in the corner of an empty carriage, looking steadily out of the window, and seeing nothing but the fragments of her little life. Now that she was detached from it, she seemed to realize how little real pleasure she had found in the life which the Princess had insisted upon dragging her into. She remembered how every man whom she had met addressed her with the same EMPRESSEMENT, how their eyes seemed to have followed her about almost covetously, how the girls had openly envied her, how the court of the men had been so monotonous and so unreal. She drew a little breath, almost of relief. When she was used to the idea she might even be glad that this great fortune had taken to itself wings and flitted away. She was no longer the heiress of untold wealth. She was simply a girl, standing on the threshold of life, and looking forward to the happiness which at that age seems almost a natural heritage.

The sense of freedom grew on her next morning, as she walked once more upon the marshes, listened to the larks, now in full song, and felt the touch of the salt wind upon her cheeks. She had found rooms very easily, and no one had seemed to treat her coming as anything but a matter of course. One old fisherman of whom she asked questions, told her many queer stories about the Red Hall and its occupants.

"As restless young men as them two as is there now," he admitted, "Mr. Cecil and his friend, I never did see. Fust one of them one day goes to London, back he comes on the next day, and away goes the other. Why they don't go both together the Lord only knows, but that is so for a fact, miss, and you can take it from me. Every week of God's year, one of them goes to London, and directly he comes back the other goes."

"And Mr. Andrew de la Borne?" she asked. "Has he gone back there yet?"

"He have not," the man answered, "but I doubt he'll be back again one day 'fore long. Sure he need be. They're beginning to talk about the shuttered windows at the Red Hall."

The girl turned and looked toward the house, bleak and desolate-looking enough now that the few encircling trees were shorn of their leaves.

"I shouldn't care to live there all the year round," she remarked.

"I've heerd others say the same thing," he answered, "and yet in Salthouse village we're moderate well satisfied with life. It's them as have too much," he continued, "who rush about trying to make more. A simple life and a simple lot is what's best in this world."

"Things were livelier up there," Jeanne remarked, seating herself on the edge of his boat, "when the smugglers used to bring in their goods."

The old man smiled.

"Why that's so, lady," he admitted. "Lord! When I was a boy I mind some great doings. One night there was a great fight. I mind it now. Fifteen of the King's men were lying hidden close to the cove there, and it looked for all the world as though the boats which were being rowed ashore must fall right into their hands. They were watching from the Hall, though, and the Squire's new alarm was set going. It were a cry like a siren, rising and falling like. The boats heerd it and turned back, but three of the Squire's men were set on, and a rare fight there was that night. There was broken heads to be mended, and no mistake. Mat Knowles here, the father of him who keeps the public now, he right forgot to shut his inn, and there it was open two hours past the lawful time, and all were drinking as though it were a great day of rejoicing, instead of being one of sorrow for the De la Bornes. I mind you were here a few weeks ago, miss. You know the two Mr. De la Bornes?"

"Yes!" Jeanne admitted. "I know them slightly."

"Mr. Andrew, he be one of the best," the man declared, "but Mr. Cecil we none of us can understand, him nor his friends. What he is doing up there now with this man what's staying with him, there's none can tell. Maybe they gamble at cards, maybe they just sit and look at one another, but 'tis a strange sort of life anyhow."

"I think it is a very interesting place to live in," Jeanne said. "What became of the siren which warned the smugglers?"

"There's no one here as can tell that, miss," the man answered, "There are them as have fancied on windy nights as they've heerd it, but fancy it have been, in my opinion. Five and twenty years have gone since I've heerd it mysen, and there's few 'as better ears.'"

"Mr. Andrew de la Borne is not here now, is he?" she asked.

The fisherman shook his head.

"Mr. Andrew," he said, "is mortal afraid of strangers and such like, and there's photographers and newspaper men round in these parts just now, by reason of the disappearance of this young lord that you heerd tell on. Some say he was drowned, and I have heerd folk whisper about a duel with the gentleman as is with Mr. Cecil now. Anyway, it was here that he disappeared from, and though I've not seen it in print, I've heerd as his brother is offering a reward of a thousand pounds to any as might find him. It's a power of money that, miss."

"It is a great deal of money," Jeanne admitted. "I wonder if Lord Ronald was worth it."

CHAPTER XI

The two men sat opposite to one another separated only by the small round table upon which the dessert which had followed their dinner was still standing. Even Forrest's imperturbable face showed signs of the anxiety through which he had passed. The change in Cecil, however, was far more noticeable. There were lines under his eyes and a flush upon his cheeks, as though he had been drinking heavily. The details of his toilette, usually so immaculate, were uncared for. He was carelessly dressed, and his hair no longer shone with frequent brushings. He looked like a person passing through the rapid stages of deterioration.

"Forrest," he said, "I cannot stand it any longer. This place is sending me mad. I think that the best thing we can do is to chuck it."

"Do you?" Forrest answered drily. "That may be all very well for you, a countryman, with enough to live on, and the whole world before you. As for me, I couldn't face it. I have passed middle age, and my life runs in certain grooves. It must run in them now until the end. I cannot break away. I would not if I could. Existence would simply be intolerable for me if that young fool were ever allowed to tell his story."

"We cannot keep him for ever," Cecil answered gloomily. "We cannot play the jailer here all our lives. Besides, there is always the danger of being found out. There are two detectives in the place already, and I am fairly certain that if they have been in the house while we have been out — "

"There is nothing for them to discover here," Forrest answered. "I should keep the doors open. Let them search if they want to."

"That is all very well," Cecil answered, "but if these fellows hang about the place, sooner or later they will hear some of the stories these villagers are only too anxious to tell."

Forrest nodded.

"There," he said, "I am not disinclined to agree with you. Hasn't it ever struck you, De la Borne," he continued, after a moment's slight hesitation, "that there is only one logical way out of this?"

"No!" Cecil answered eagerly. "What way? What do you mean?"

Forrest filled his glass to the brim with wine before he answered. Then he passed the decanter back to Cecil.

"We are not children, you and I," he said. "Why should we let a boy like Engleton play with us? Why do we not let him have the issue before him in black and white? We say to him now — 'Sign this paper, pledge your word of honour, and you may go.' He declines. He declines because the alternative of staying where he is is endurable. I propose that we substitute another alternative. Drink your wine, De la Borne. This is a chill house of yours, and one loses courage here. Drink your wine, and think of what I have said."

Cecil set down his glass empty.

"Well," he said, "what other alternative do you propose?"

"Can't you see?" Forrest answered. "We cannot keep Engleton shut up for ever. I grant you that that is impossible. But if he declines to behave like a reasonable person, we can threaten him with an alternative which I do not think he would have the courage to face."

"You mean?" Cecil gasped.

"I mean," Forrest answered, "what your grandfather would have told him, or your great grandfather, in half a dozen words weeks ago. At full tide there is sea enough to drown a dozen such as he within a few yards of where he lies. Why should we keep him carefully and safe, knowing that the moment he steps back into life you and I are doomed men?"

Cecil drew a little breath and lifted his hand to his forehead. He was surprised to find it wet. All the time he was gazing at Forrest with fascinated eyes.

"Look here," he said, in a hoarse whisper, "we mustn't talk like this. Engleton will turn round in a day or two. People would think, if they heard us, that we were planning a murder."

"In a woman's decalogue," Forrest said, "there is no sin save the sin of being found out. Why not in ours? No one ever had such a chance of getting rid of a dangerous enemy. The whole thing is in our hands. We could never be found out, never even questioned. If, by one chance in a thousand, his body is ever recovered, what more natural? Men have been drowned before on the marshes here many a time."

"Go on!" Cecil said. "You have thought this out. Tell me exactly what you propose."

"I propose," Forrest answered, "that we narrow the issues, and that we put them before him in plain English, now — tonight — while the courage is still with us. It must be silence or death. I tell you frankly how it is with me. I would as soon press a pistol to my forehead and pull the trigger as have this boy go back into the world and tell his story. For you, too, it would be ruin."

Cecil sank back into his chair, and looked with wide-open but unseeing eyes across the table, through the wall beyond. He saw his future damned by that one unpardonable accusation. He saw himself sent out into the world penniless, an outcast from all the things in life which made existence tolerable. He knew very well that Andrew would never forgive. There was no mercy to be hoped for from him. There was nothing to be looked for anywhere save disaster, absolute and entire. He looked across at Forrest, and something in his companion's face sent a cold shiver through his veins.

"We might go and see what he says," he faltered. "I haven't been there since the morning, have you?"

"No!" Forrest answered. "Solitude is good for him. Let us go now, together."

Without another word they rose from the table. Cecil led the way into the library, where he rang for a servant.

"Set out the card-table here," he ordered, "and bring in the whisky and soda. After that we do not wish to be disturbed. You understand?"

"Certainly, sir," the man answered.

They waited until the things were brought. Afterwards they locked the door. Cecil went to a drawer and took out a couple of electric torches, one of which he handed to Forrest. Then he went to the wall, and after a few minutes' groping, found the spring. The door swung open, and a rush of unwholesome air streamed into the room. They made their way silently along the passage until at last they reached the sunken chamber. Cecil took a key from his pocket and opened the door.

* * *

Engleton was in evil straits, but there was no sign of yielding in his face as he looked up. He was seated before a small table upon which a common lamp was burning. His clothes hung about him loosely. His face was haggard. A short, unbecoming beard disfigured his face. He wore no collar or necktie, and his general appearance was altogether dishevelled. Forrest looked at him critically.

"My dear Engleton!" he began.

"What the devil do you want with me at this time of night?" Engleton interrupted. "Have you come down to see how I amuse myself during the long evenings? Perhaps you would like to come and play cut-throat. I'll play you for what stakes you like, and thank you for coming, if you'll leave the door open and let me breathe a little better air."

"It is your own fault that you are here," Cecil de la Borne declared. "It is all your cursed obstinacy. Listen! I tell you once more that what you saw, or fancied you saw, was a mistake. Forget it. Give your word of honour to forget it, never to allude to it at any time in your life, and you can walk out of here a free man."

Engleton nodded.

"I have no doubt of it," he answered. "The worst of it is that nothing in the world would induce me to forego the pleasure I promise myself, before very long, too, of giving to the whole world the story of your infamy. I am not tractable tonight. You had better go away, both of you. I am more likely to fight."

Forrest sat down on the edge of a chest.

"Engleton," he said, "don't be a fool. It can do you no particular good to ruin Cecil here and myself, just because you happen to be suspicious. Let that drop. Tell us that you have decided to let it drop, and the world can take you into its arms again."

"I refuse," Engleton answered. "I refuse once and for always. I tell you that I have made up my mind to see you punished for this. How I get out I don't care, but I shall get out, and when I do, you two will be laid by the heels."

"We came here tonight," Forrest said slowly, "prepared to compromise with you."

"There is no compromise," Engleton answered fiercely. "There is nothing which you could offer which could repay me for the horror of the nights you have left me to shiver here in this damned vault. Don't flatter yourself that I shall ever forget it. I stay on because I cannot escape, but I would sooner stay here for ever than beg for mercy from either of you."

"Upon my word," Forrest declared, "our friend is quite a hero."

"I am hero enough, at any rate," Engleton answered, "to refuse to bargain with you. Get out, both of you, before I lose my temper."

Forrest came a little further into the room. The thunder of the sea seemed almost above their heads. The little lamp on the table by Engleton's side gave little more than a weird, unnatural light around the circle in which he sat.

"That isn't quite all that we came to say," Forrest remarked coldly. "To tell you the truth we have had enough of playing jailer."

"I can assure you," Engleton answered, "that I have had equally enough of being your prisoner."

"We are agreed, then," Forrest continued smoothly. "You will probably be relieved when I tell you that we have decided to end it."

Engleton rose to his feet.

"So much the better," he said. "You might keep me here till doomsday, and the end would be the same."

"We do not propose," Forrest continued, "to keep you here till doomsday, or anything like it. What we have come to say to you is this — that if you still refuse to give your promise — I need not say more than that — we are going to set you free."

"Do you mean that literally?" Engleton asked.

"Perhaps not altogether as you would wish to understand it," Forrest admitted. "We shall give you a chance at high tide to swim for your life."

Engleton shrunk a little back. After all, his nerves were a little shattered.

"Out there?" he asked, pointing to the seaward end of the passage.

Forrest nodded.

"It will be a chance for you," he said.

Engleton looked at them for a moment, dumbfounded.

"It will be murder," he said slowly.

Forrest shrugged his shoulders.

"You may call it so if you like," he answered. "Personally, I should not be inclined to agree with you. You will be alive when you go into the sea. If you cannot swim, the fault is not ours."

"And when, may I ask," Engleton continued, "do you propose to put into operation your amiable plan?"

"Just whensoever we please, you damned obstinate young puppy!" Forrest cried, suddenly losing his nerve. "Curse your silent tongue and your venomous face! You think you can get the better of us, do you? Well, you are mistaken. You'll tell no stories from amongst the seaweed."

Engleton nodded.

"I shall take particular good care," he said, "to avoid the seaweed."

"Enough," Forrest declared. "Listen! Here is the issue. We are tired of negative things. Tonight you sign the paper and give us your word of honour to keep silent, or before morning, when the tide is full, you go into the sea!"

"I warn you," Engleton said, "that I can swim."

"I will guarantee," Forrest answered suavely, "that by the time you reach the water you will have forgotten how."

CHAPTER XII

The days that followed were strange ones for Jeanne. Every morning at sunrise, or before, she would steal out of the little cottage where she was staying, and make her way along the top of one of the high dyke banks to the sea. Often she saw the sun rise from some lonely spot amongst the sandbanks or the marshes, heard the awakening of the birds, and saw the first glimpses of morning life steal into evidence upon the grey chill wilderness. At such times she saw few people. The house where she was staying was apart from the village, and near the head of one of the creeks, and there were times when she would leave it and return without having seen a single human being. She knew, from cautious inquiries made from her landlady's daughter, that Cecil and Major Forrest were still at the Red Hall, and for that reason during the daytime she seldom left the cottage, sitting out in the old-fashioned garden, or walking a little way in the fields at the back. For the future she made no plans. She was quite content to feel that for the present she had escaped from an intolerable situation.

The woman from whom Jeanne had taken the rooms, a Mrs. Caynsard, she had seen only once or twice. She was waited upon most of the time by an exceedingly diminutive maid servant, very shy at first, but very talkative afterwards, in broad Norfolk dialect, when she had grown a little accustomed to this very unusual lodger. Now and then Kate Caynsard, the only daughter of the house, appeared, but for the most time she was away, sailing a fishing boat or looking after the little farm. To Jeanne she represented a type wholly strange, but altogether interesting. She was little over twenty years of age, but she was strong and finely built. She had the black hair and dark brown eyes, which here and there amongst the villagers of the east coast remind one of the immigration of worsted spinners and silk weavers from Flanders and the North of France, many centuries ago. She was very handsome but exceedingly shy. When Jeanne, as she had done more than once, tried to talk to her, her abrupt replies gave little opening for conversation. One morning, however, when Jeanne, having returned from a long tramp across the sand dunes, was sitting in the little orchard at the back of the house, she saw her landlady's daughter come slowly out to her from the house. Jeanne put down her book.

"Good morning, Miss Caynsard!" she said.

"Good morning, miss!" the girl answered awkwardly. "You have had a long walk!"

Jeanne nodded.

"I went so far," she said, "that I had to race the tide home, or I should have had to wade through the home creek."

Kate nodded.

"The tide do come sometimes," she said, "at a most awful pace. I have been out after whelks myself, and had to walk home with the sea all round me, and nothing but a ribbon of dry land. One needs to know the ways about on this wilderness."

"One learns them by watching," Jeanne remarked. "I suppose you have lived here all your life."

"All my life," the girl answered, "and my father and grandfather before me. 'Tis a queer country, but them as is born and bred here seldom leaves it. Sometimes they try. They go to the next village inland, or to some town, or to foreign parts, but sooner or later if they live they come back."

Jeanne nodded sympathetically.

"It is a wonderful country," she said. "When I saw it first it seemed to me that it was depressing. Now I love it!"

"And I," the girl remarked, with a sudden passion in her tone, "I hate it!"

Jeanne looked at her, surprised.

"It sounds so strange to hear you say that," she remarked. "I should have thought that any one who had lived here always would have loved it. Every day I am here I seem to discover new beauties, a new effect of colouring, a new undertone of the sea, or to hear the cry of some new bird."

"It is beautiful sometimes," the girl answered. "I love it when the creeks are full, and the April sun is shining, and the spring seems to draw all manner of living things and colours from the marsh and the pasturage lands. I love it when the sea changes its colour as the clouds pass over the sun, and the wind blows from the west. The place is well enough then. But there are times when it is nothing but a great wilderness of mud, and the grey mists come blowing in, and one is cold here, cold to the bone. Then I hate the place worse than ever."

"Have you ever tried to go away for a time?" Jeanne asked.

"I went once to London," the girl said, turning her head a little away. "I should have stayed there, I think, if things had turned out as I had expected, but they didn't, and my father died suddenly, so I came home to take care of the farm."

Jeanne nodded sympathetically. She was beginning to wonder why this girl had come out from the house with the obvious intention of speaking to her. She stood by her side, not exactly awkward, but still not wholly at her ease, her hands clasped behind her straight back, her black eyebrows drawn together in a little uneasy frown. Her coarse brown skirt was not long enough to conceal her wonderfully shaped ankles. Sun and wind had done little more than slightly tan her clear complexion. She had somehow the appearance of a girl of some other nation. There was something stronger, more forceful, more brilliant about her, than her position seemed to warrant.

"There is a question, miss," she said at last, abruptly, "I should like to ask you. I should have asked you when you first came, if I had been in when you came to look at the rooms."

"What is it?" Jeanne asked quietly.

"I've a good eye for faces," Kate said, "and I seldom forget one. Weren't you the young lady who was staying up at the Red Hall a few weeks ago?"

Jeanne nodded.

"Yes," she said, "I was staying there. It was because I liked the place so much, and because I was so much happier here than in London, that I came back."

There was a moment's silence. Jeanne looked up and found Kate's magnificent eyes fixed steadfastly upon her face.

"Is it for no other reason, miss," she asked, "that you have come back?"

"For none other in the world," Jeanne answered. "I was unhappy in London, and I wanted to get somewhere where I should be quite unknown. That is why I came here."

"You didn't come back," Kate asked, "to see more of Mr. De la Borne, then?"

The simple directness of the question seemed to rob it of its impertinence. Jeanne laughed goodhumouredly.

"I can assure you that I did not," she answered. "To tell you the truth, and I hope that you will be kind and remember that I do not wish any one to know this, the reason why I only go out so early in the morning or late at night is because I do not wish to see any one from the Red Hall. I do not wish them to know that I am here."

"They do gossip in a small place like this most amazing," the girl said slowly. "When you and the other lady came down from London to stay up yonder, they did say that you were a great heiress, and that Mr. De la Borne was counting on marrying you, and buying back all the lands that have slipped away from the De la Bornes back to Burnham Market and Wells township."

Jeanne shrugged her shoulders.

"I cannot help," she said, "what people say. Every one has spoken of me always as being very rich, and a good many men have wanted to marry me to spend my money. That is why I came down here, if you want to know, Miss Caynsard. I came to escape from a man whom my stepmother was determined that I should marry, and whom I hated."

The girl looked at her wonderingly.

"It is a strange manner of living," she said, "when a girl is not to choose her own man."

"In any case," Jeanne said smiling, "if I had but one or two to choose from in the world, I should never choose Mr. De la Borne."

The girl was gloomily silent. She was looking up towards the Red Hall, her lips a little parted, her face dark, her brows lowering.

"'Tis a family," she said slowly, "that have come down well-nigh to their last acre. They hold on to the Hall, but little else. Folk say that for four hundred years or more the De la Bornes have heard the sea thunder from within them walls. 'Tis, perhaps, as some writer has said in a book I've found lately, that the old families of the country, when once their menkind cease to be soldiers or fighters in the world, do decay and become rotten. It is so with the De la Bornes, or rather with one of them."

"Mr. Andrew," Jeanne remarked timidly.

"Mr. Andrew," the girl interrupted, "is a great gentleman, but he is never one of those who would stop the rot in a decaying race. He is a great strong man is Mr. Andrew, and deceit and littleness are things he knows nothing of. I wish he were here today."

The girl's face wore a troubled expression. Jeanne began to suspect that she had not as yet come to the real object of this interview.

"Why do you wish that Mr. Andrew were here?" Jeanne asked. "What could he do for you that Mr. Cecil could not?"

A strange look filled the girl's eyes.

"I think," she said, "that I would not go to Mr. Cecil whatever might betide, but there is a matter — "

She hesitated again. Jeanne looked at her thoughtfully.

"You have something on your mind, I think, Miss Caynsard," she said. "Can I help you? Do you wish to tell me about it?"

The girl seemed to have made up her mind. She was standing quite close to Jeanne now, and she spoke without hesitation.

"You remember the young lord," she said, "of whom there has been so much in the papers lately? He was staying at the Red Hall when you were, and is supposed to have left for London early one morning and disappeared."

"Lord Ronald Engleton," Jeanne said. "Yes, I know all about that, of course."

"Sometimes," Kate said slowly, "I have had strange thoughts about him. Mr. Cecil and the other man, Major Forrest they call him, are still at the Hall, and the servants say that they do little but drink and swear at one another. I wonder sometimes why they are there, and why Mr. Andrew stays away."

Jeanne leaned a little forward in her chair. Something in the other's words had interested her.

"There is something," she said, "behind in your thoughts. What is it?"

The girl was silent for a moment.

"Tonight," she said, "if you have the courage to come with me, I will show you what I mean."

CHAPTER XIII

"I am afraid," Jeanne declared, "that I cannot go on. I have not the eyes of a cat. I cannot see one step before me."

Her companion laughed softly as she turned round.

"I forgot," she said. "You are town bred. To us the darkness is nothing. Do not be afraid. I know the way, every inch of it. Give me your hand."

"But I cannot see at all," Jeanne declared. "How far is this place?"

"Less than a mile," Kate answered. "Trust to me. I will see that nothing happens to you. Hold my hand tightly, like that. Now come."

Jeanne reluctantly trusted herself to her companion's guidance. They made their way down the rough road which led from the home of the Caynsards, half cottage, half farmhouse, to the lane at the bottom. There was no moon, and though the wind was blowing hard, the sky seemed everywhere covered with black clouds. When Kate opened the wooden gate which led on to the marshes, Jeanne stopped short.

"I am not going any farther," she declared. "Even you, I am sure, could not find your way on the marshes tonight. Didn't you hear what the fisherman said, too, that it was a flood tide? Many of the paths are under water. I will not go any farther, Kate. If there is anything you have to tell me, say it now."

She felt a hand suddenly tighten upon her arm, a hand which was like a vice.

"You must come with me," Kate said. "As to the other things, do not be foolish. On these marshes I am like a cat in a dark room. I could feel my way across every inch of them on the blackest night that ever was. I know how high the tide is. I measured it but half an hour since by Treadwell's pole. You come with me, miss. You'll not miss your way by a foot. I promise you that."

Even then Jeanne was reluctant. They were on the top of the grass-grown dyke now, and below she could dimly see the dark, swelling water lapping against the gravel bottom.

"But you do not understand," she declared. "I do not even know where to put my feet. I can see nothing, and the wind is enough to blow us over the sides. Listen! Listen how it comes booming across the sand dunes. It is not safe here. I tell you that I must go back."

Her companion only laughed a little wildly.

"There will be no going back tonight," she said. "You must

come with me. Set your feet down boldly. If you are afraid, take this."

She handed her a small electric torch.

"It's one of those new-fangled things for making light in the darkness," she remarked. "It's no use to me, for if I could not see I could feel. For us who live here, 'tis but an instinct to find our way, in darkness or in light, across the land where we were born. But if you are nervous, press the knob and you will see."

Jeanne took the torch with a little sigh of relief.

"Go on," she said. "I don't mind so much now I have this."

Nevertheless, as they moved along she found it sufficiently alarming. The top of the bank was but a few feet wide. The west wind, which came roaring down across the great open spaces, with nothing to check or divide its strength, was sometimes strong enough to blow them off their balance. On either side of the dyke was the water, black and silent. Here and there the torch light showed them a fishing-smack or a catboat, high and dry a few hours ago, now floating on the bosom of the full tide. They came to a stile, and Jeanne's courage once more failed her.

"I cannot climb over this," she said. "I shall fall directly I lift up my feet."

Kate turned round with a little laugh of contempt. Jeanne felt herself suddenly lifted in a pair of strong arms. Before she knew where she was she was on the other side. Breathless she followed her guide, who came to a full stop a few yards farther on.

"Turn on your light," Kate ordered. "Look down on the left. There should be a punt there."

Jeanne turned on the torch. A great flat-bottomed boat, shapeless and unwieldy, was just below. Kate stepped lightly down the steep bank, and with one foot on the side of the punt, held out her hand to Jeanne.

"Come," she said. "Step carefully."

"But what are we going to do?" Jeanne asked. "You are not going in that?"

"Why not?" Kate laughed. "It is a few strokes only. We are going to cross to the ridges."

Jeanne followed her. Somehow or other she found it hard to disobey her guide. None the less she was afraid. She stepped tremblingly down into the punt, and sat upon the broad wet seat. Kate, without a moment's hesitation, took up the great pole and began pushing her way across the creek. The tide was almost at its height, but even then the current was so strong that they went across almost sideways, and Jeanne heard her companion's breath grow shorter and shorter, as with powerful strokes she did her best to guide and propel the clumsy craft.

"We are going out toward the sea," Jeanne faltered. "It is getting wider and wider."

She flashed her torch across the dark waters. They could not see the bank which they had left or the ridges to which they were making.

"Don't be afraid," Kate answered. "After all, you know, we can only die once, and life isn't worth making such a tremendous fuss over."

"I do not want to die," Jeanne objected, "and I do not like this at all."

Kate laughed contemptuously.

"Sit still," she said, "and you are as safe as though you were in your own armchair. No current that ever ran could upset this clumsy raft. The only reason I am working so hard is that I do not want to be carried down past the ridges. If we get too low down we shall have to walk across the black mud."

Jeanne kept silence, listening only to the swirl of the water struck by the pole, and to the quick breathing of her companion. Once she asked whether she could not help.

"There is no need," Kate answered. "Shine your torch on the left. We are nearly across."

Almost as she spoke they struck the sandy bottom. Jeanne fell into the bottom of the boat. Kate, with a little laugh, sprang ashore and held out her hand.

"Come," she said, "we have crossed the worst part now."

"Where are we going?" Jeanne asked, a little relieved as she felt her feet land on the sodden turf.

"Towards the Hall," Kate answered. "Give me your hand, if you like, or use your torch. The way is simple enough, but we must twist and turn tonight. It has been a flood tide, and there are great pools left here and there, pools that you have never seen before."

"But how do you know?" Jeanne asked, in amazement. "I can see nothing."

Her guide laughed contemptuously.

"I can see and I can feel," she said. "It is an instinct with me to walk dry-footed here. To the right now — so."

"Stand still for a moment," Jeanne pleaded. "The wind takes my breath."

"You have too many clothes on," Kate said contemptuously. "One should not wear skirts and petticoats and laces here."

"If you would leave my clothes alone and tell me where you

are going," Jeanne declared, a little tartly, "it would be more reasonable."

The girl laughed. She thrust her arm through her companion's and drew her on.

"Don't be angry," she said. "It is quite easy now to find our way. There is room for us to walk like this. Can you hear what I say to you?"

"I can hear," Jeanne answered, raising her voice, "but it is getting more difficult all the time. Is that the sea?"

"Yes!" Kate answered. "Can't you feel the spray on your cheeks? The wind is blowing it high up above the beach. Let me go first again. There is an inlet here. Be careful."

They came to a full stop before a dark arm of salt water. They skirted the side and crossed round to the other side.

"Be careful, now," Kate said. "This way."

They turned inland. In a few minutes her guide stopped short.

"Turn on your torch," she said. "There ought to be a wall close here."

Jeanne did as she was bid, and gave a little stifled cry.

"Why, we are close to the Red Hall!" she said. Kate nodded.

"A little way farther up there is a gate," she said. "We are going in there."

"You are not going to the house?" Jeanne asked, in terror.

"No," Kate answered, "I am not going there! Follow me, and don't talk more than you can help. The wind is going down."

"But it is the middle of the night," Jeanne said. "No one will be astir."

"One cannot tell," Kate answered slowly. "It is in my mind that there have been strange doings here, and I know well that there is a man who watches this place by day and by night. He has discovered nothing, but it is because he has not known where to look."

"What do you mean?" Jeanne asked hoarsely.

"Wait!" her companion said.

They passed through the wooden gate. They were now in a little weedy plantation of undersized trees. The ground was full of rabbit holes, and Jeanne stumbled more than once.

"How much farther?" she asked. "We are getting toward the house."

"Not yet," Kate answered. "There are the gardens first, but we are not going there. Wait a moment."

She felt for one of the trees, and passed her hand carefully round its trunk. Then she took a few steps forward and stopped short.

"Wait!" she said.

She lay flat down upon the grass and was silent for several minutes. Then she whispered to Jeanne.

"Don't turn on your torch," she said. "Lie down here by my side, put your ear to the ground, and tell me whether you can hear anything."

Jeanne obeyed her breathlessly. At first she could hear nothing. Her own heart was beating fast, and the boughs of the trees above them were creaking and groaning in the wind. Presently, however, she gave a little cry. From somewhere underground it seemed to her that she could hear a faint hammering.

"What is it?" she asked.

Kate sat up.

"There is no animal," she said, "which makes a noise like that. It is somewhere there underground. It seems to me that it is some one who is trying to get out."

"Some one underground?" Jeanne repeated.

Kate leaned over and whispered in her ear.

"There is a passage underneath here," she said, "which goes from the Hall to the cliffs, and a room, or rather a vault."

"I know," Jeanne declared suddenly. "Mr. De la Borne showed it to us. It was the way the smugglers used to bring their goods up to the cellars of the Red Hall."

"We are just above the room here," Kate said slowly, "and I fancy that there is some one there."

A sudden light broke in upon Jeanne.

"You think that it is Lord Engleton!" she declared.

"Why not?" Kate answered. "Listen again, with your ear close to the ground. Last night I was almost sure that I heard him call for help."

Jeanne did as she was told, and her face grew white as death. Distinctly between the strokes she heard the sound of a man moaning!

CHAPTER XIV

Once more the two men sat over the remnants of their evening meal. This time the deterioration in their own appearance seemed to have spread itself to their surroundings. The table was ill-laid, there were no flowers, an empty bottle of wine and several decanters remained where they had been set. There was every indication that however little the two might have eaten, they had been drinking heavily. Yet they were both pale. Cecil's face even was ghastly, and the hand which played nervously with the table-cloth shook all the time.

"Forrest," he said abruptly, "it is a mistake to clear out all the servants like this. Not only have we had to eat a filthy dinner, but it's enough to make people suspicious, eh? Don't you think so? Don't you think afterwards that they may wonder why we did it?"

"No!" Forrest answered, with something that was almost like a snarl. "No, I don't! Shut up, and don't be such an infernal young fool! We couldn't have town servants spying and whispering about the place. I caught that London butler of yours hanging around the library this afternoon as though he were looking for something. They were a damned careless lot, anyhow, with no mistress or housekeeper to look after them, and they're better gone. Who is there left exactly now?"

"There's a kitchen-maid, who cooked this wretched mess," Cecil answered, "and another under her from the village, who seems half an idiot. There is no one else except Pawles, a man who comes in from the stables to do the rough work and pump the water up for the bath. We are practically alone in the house."

"Thank Heaven it's our last night," Forrest answered.

"You really mean, then," Cecil asked, in a hoarse whisper, "to finish this now?"

"I mean that we are going to," Forrest answered. "You know I'm half afraid of you. Sometimes you're such a rotten coward. If ever I thought you looked as though you were going back on me, I'd get even with you, mind that."

"Don't talk like a fool!" Cecil answered. "What we do, we do together, of course, only my nerves aren't strong, you know. I can't bear the thought of the end of it."

"Whatever happens to him," Forrest said, "he's asking for it. He has an easy chance to get back to his friends. It is brutal obstinacy if he makes us end it differently. You're only a boy, but I've lived a good many years, and I tell you that if you don't look out for yourself and make yourself safe, there are always plenty of people, especially those who call themselves your friends, who are ready and waiting to kick you down into Hell. I am going to have something more to drink. Nothing seems to make any difference to me tonight. I can't even get excited, although we must have drunk a bottle of wine each. We'll have some brandy. Here goes!"

He filled a wine-glass and passed the bottle to Cecil.

"You're about in the same state," he remarked, looking at him keenly. "Why the devil is it that when one doesn't require it, wine will go to the head too quickly, and when one wants to use it to borrow a little courage and a little forgetfulness, the stuff goes down like water. Drink, Cecil, a wine-glass of it. Drink it off, like this."

Forrest drained his wine-glass and set it down. Then he rose to his feet. His cheeks were still colourless, but there was an added glitter in his eyes.

"Come, young man," he said, "you have only to fancy that you are one of your own ancestors. I fancy those dark-looking ruffians, who scowl down on us from the walls there, would not have thought so much of flinging an enemy into the sea. It is a wise man who wrote that self-preservation was the first law of nature. Come, Cecil, remember that. It is the first law of nature that we are obeying. Ring the bell first, and see that there are no servants about the place."

Cecil obeyed, ringing the bell once or twice. No one came. They stepped out into the hall. The emptiness of the house seemed almost apparent. There was not a sound anywhere.

"The servants' wing is right over the stables, a long way off," Cecil remarked. "They could never hear a bell there that rang from any of the living-rooms."

Forrest nodded.

"So much the better," he said. "Come along to the library. I have everything ready there."

They crossed the hall and entered the room to which Forrest pointed. Their footsteps seemed to awake echoes upon the stone floor. The hall, too, was all unlit save for the lamp which Forrest was carrying. Cecil peered nervously about into the shadows.

"It's a ghostly house this of yours," Forrest said grumblingly, as they closed the door behind them. "I shall be thankful to get back to my rooms in town and walk down Piccadilly once more. What's that outside?"

"The wind," Cecil answered. "I thought it was going to be a rough night."

The window had been left open at the top, and the roar of the wind across the open places came into the room like muffled thunder. The lamp which Forrest carried was blown out, and the two men were left in darkness.

"Shut the window, for Heaven's sake, man!" Forrest ordered sharply. "Here!"

He took an electric torch from his pocket, and both men drew a little breath of relief as the light flashed out. Cecil climbed on to a chair and closed the window. Forrest glanced at the clock.

"It's quite late enough," he said. "It should be high tide in a quarter of an hour, and the sea in that little cove of yours is twenty feet deep. Come along and work this door."

"Have you got everything?" Cecil asked nervously.

"I have the chloroform," Forrest answered, touching a small bottle in his waistcoat pocket. "We don't need anything else. He hasn't the strength of a rabbit, and you and I can carry him down the passage. If he struggles there's no one to hear him."

Cecil pushed his way against the panels and opened the clumsy door. They groped their way down the passage.

"Faugh!" Forrest exclaimed. "What smells! Cecil," he added, "I suppose half the village know about this place, don't they?"

"They know that it has been here always," Cecil answered, "but they most of them think that it is blocked up now. We did try to, Andrew and I, but the masonry gave way. These lumps on the floor are the remains of our work. Keep your torch down. You'll fall over them."

Forrest stopped short. Curiously enough, it was he now who seemed the more terrified. The wind and the thunder of the sea together seemed to reach them through the walls of earth in a strange monotonous roar, sometimes shriller as the wind triumphed, sometimes deep and low so that the very ground beneath their feet vibrated as the sea came thundering up into the cove. Cecil, who was more used to such noises, heard them unmoved.

"If my people had left me such a dog's hole as this," Forrest declared viciously, "I'd have buried them in it and blown it up to the skies. It's only fit for ghosts."

The very weakening of the other man seemed for the moment to give Cecil added courage. He laughed hoarsely.

"There are worse things to fear," he muttered, "than this. Hold hard, Forrest. Here is the door. I'll undo the padlock. You stand by in case he makes a rush."

But there was no rush about Engleton. He was lying on his back, stretched on a rough mattress at the farther end of the room, moaning slightly. The two men exchanged quick glances.

"We are not going to have much trouble," Forrest muttered. "What a beastly atmosphere! No wonder he's knocked up."

Cecil, however, looked about suspiciously.

"Don't you notice," he whispered, "that we can hear the wind much plainer here than in the passage? I believe I can feel a current of fresh air, too. I wonder if he's been trying to cut his way through to the air-hole. It's only a few feet up."

He flashed his light upon the wall near where Engleton was lying. Then he turned significantly to Forrest.

"See," he said, "he has cut steps in the wall and tried to make an opening above. He must have guessed where the ventilating pipe was. I wonder what he did it with."

They crossed the room. The man on the couch opened his eyes and looked at them dully.

"So you've been improving the shining hour, eh?" Forrest remarked, pointing to the rough steps. "We shall have to find what you did it with. Hidden under the mattress, I suppose."

He stooped down, and Engleton flew at his throat with all the fury of a wild cat. Forrest was taken aback for a moment, but the effort was only a brief one. Engleton's strength seemed to pass away even before he had concluded his attack. He sank back and collapsed upon the floor at a touch.

"You brutes!" he muttered.

Cecil lifted the mattress. There was a large flat stone, sharp-edged and coated with mud, lying underneath.

"I thought so," he whispered. "Jove, he's gone a long way with it, too!" he muttered, looking upward. "Another foot or so and he would have been outside. I wonder the place didn't collapse."

Engleton dragged himself a little way back. He remained upon the floor, but there was support for his back now against the wall.

"Well," he said, "what is it this evening?"

"The end," Forrest answered shortly.

Engleton did not flinch. Of the three men, although his physical condition was the worst, he seemed the most at his ease.

"The end," he remarked. "Well, I don't believe it. I don't believe you have either of you the pluck to go through life with the fear of the rope round your neck every minute. But if I am indeed a condemned man. I ought to have my privileges. Give me a cigarette, one of you, for God's sake."

Forrest took out his gold case and threw him a couple of cigarettes. Then he struck a match and passed it over.

"Smoke, by all means," he said. "Listen! In five minutes we are going to throw you from the seaward end of this place, down into the cove or creek, or whatever they call it. It is high tide, and the sea there is twenty feet deep. As for swimming, you evidently haven't the strength of a cat, and there is no breathing man could swim against the current far enough to reach any place where he could climb out. But to avoid even that risk, we are going to give you a little chloroform first. It will make things easier for you, and we shall not be distressed by your shrieks."

"An amiable programme," Engleton muttered. "I am quite ready for it."

"Then I don't think we need waste words," Forrest said slowly. "You have made up your mind, I suppose, that you do not care about life. Remember that it is not we who are your executioners. You have an easy choice."

"If you mean," Engleton said, "will I purchase my liberty by letting you two blackguards off free, for this and for your dirty card-sharping, I say no! I will take my chances of life to the last second. Afterwards I shall know that I am revenged. Men don't go happily through life with the little black devil sitting on their shoulders."

"We'll take our risk," Forrest said thickly. "You have chosen, then? This is your last chance."

"Absolutely!" Engleton answered.

Forrest took out the phial from his pocket and held his handkerchief on the palm of his hand.

"Open the door, will you, Cecil," he said, "so that we can carry him out."

Cecil opened it, and came slowly back to where Forrest was counting the drops which fell from the bottle on to his handkerchief. Then he suddenly came to a standstill. Forrest, too, paused in his task and looked up. He gave a nervous start, and the bottle fell from his fingers.

"What in God's name was that?" he asked.

It came to them faintly down the long passage, but it was nevertheless alarming enough. The hoarse clanging of a bell, pulled by impetuous fingers. Cecil and Forrest stared at one another for a moment with dilated eyes.

"Can't you speak, you damned young fool?" Forrest asked. "What bell is that?"

"It is the front-door bell of the Red Hall," Cecil answered, in a voice which he scarcely recognized as his own. "There it goes again."

They stood perfectly silent and listened to it, listened until its echoes died away.

CHAPTER XV

For the fourth time the bell rang. The two men had now retraced their steps. Cecil, who had been standing in the hall within a few feet of the closed door, started away as though he had received some sort of shock. Forrest, who was lurking back in the shadows, cursed him for a timid fool.

"Open the door, man," he whispered. "Don't stand fumbling there. Remember you are angry at being disturbed. Send them away, whoever they are. Look sharp! They are going to ring again. Can't you hear that beastly bell-wire quivering?"

Cecil set his teeth, turned the huge key, and pulled back the heavy door. He gave a little gasp of astonishment. It was a woman who stood there. He held out his electric torch and stepped back with a sharp exclamation.

"Kate!" he cried. "What on earth are you doing here at this hour? What do you mean by ringing the bell like that?"

The girl stepped into the hall.

"Close the door," she said. "The wind will blow the pictures off the walls, and I can scarcely hear you speak."

Cecil obeyed at once.

"Light a lamp," she said. "It is not fair that you should have all the light. I want to see your face too."

"But Kate," Cecil interrupted, "why did you come like this? Why did you not — "

She interrupted.

"Never mind," she answered sternly. "Perhaps I did not come to see you at all. Light the lamp. There is something I have to say to you."

Forrest stepped forward from the obscurity and struck a match. The girl showed no signs of fear at his coming. As the lamp grew brighter she looked at him steadfastly.

"So this is the reason we are waked up in the middle of the night," Forrest remarked, with a smile which somehow or other seemed to lose its suggestiveness. "A little affair of this sort, eh, Mr. Cecil? Why don't you teach the young lady a simpler way of summoning you than by that infernal bell?"

Still Kate did not reply. She was standing with her back to the oak table in the centre of the hall, and the men, who were both watching her covertly, were conscious of a certain significance in her attitude. Her black hair was tossed all over her face; from its tangled web her eyes seemed to gleam with a steady inimical gaze. Her dress of dark red stuff was splashed in places with the salt water, and her feet were soaking. With her left hand she clasped the table; her right seemed hidden in the folds of her skirt.

"What do you want, Kate?" Cecil asked at last. "What do you mean by coming here like this? If you want to see me you know how, without arousing the whole household at this time of night."

"You are not fool enough," Kate said calmly, "to imagine that I came tonight to listen to your lies. I came to know whom it is that you are keeping hidden away in the smugglers' room."

Neither man answered. They looked at one another, and Cecil's face grew once more as pale as death.

"What do you mean?" he exclaimed. "What rubbish is this you are talking, Kate?" he added, in a sharper tone. "There is no one there that I know of."

"You lie," she answered calmly. "You lie, as you always do whenever it answers your purpose. Only an hour ago I lay upon the turf in the plantation there, and I heard a man moaning down in the store-room. Now tell me the truth, Cecil de la Borne. I do not wish to bring any harm upon you, although God knows you deserve it, but if you do not bring me the man whom you have down there, and set him free before my eyes at once, I'll bring half the village up to the mound there and dig him out."

Forrest stepped forward. His manner was suave and his tone was smooth, but there was a dangerous glitter in his eyes.

"This is rather absurd, Cecil," he said. "I do not know whom this young lady is, but I feel sure that she will listen to reason. There is no one down in the smugglers' store-room. If she heard anything, it was probably the rabbits."

"Lies!" Kate answered calmly. "You are another of the breed; I can see it in your face. I would not trust the word of either of you."

Forrest shrugged his shoulders. He glanced towards Cecil with a slight uplifting of the eyebrows.

"Your friend, my dear Cecil," he remarked, "is like most of her sex, a trifle unreasonable. However, since she says that she will believe no evidence save the evidence of her eyes, show her the smugglers' room. It would be a quaint excursion to take at this time of night, but I will go with you for the sake of the proprieties," he added, with a little laugh.

Cecil looked at him for a moment steadily, and then turned away. There was fear now upon his face, a new fear. What was this thing which Forrest could propose?

"She can come if she insists," he said slowly, "but the place has not been opened for a long time. The air is bad. It really is not fit for any human being."

The girl faced them both without shrinking.

"Perhaps you think that I should be afraid," she answered. "Perhaps you think that when I am there it would be very easy to dispose of me, so that I shall ask no more inconvenient questions. Never mind. I am not afraid. I will go with you."

Cecil shrugged his shoulders as he led the way across the hall.

"There is nothing to fear," he said, "except the bad air and the ghosts of smugglers, if you are superstitious enough to fear them. Only, when you are perfectly satisfied, and you are convinced that your errand here has been fruitless, perhaps I may have something to say."

The girl's lips parted. Curiously enough there was a note almost of real merriment in the laugh which followed.

"I am not very brave, my dear Cecil," she said, "but I am not afraid of you. I think that one does not fear the things that one understands too well, and you I do understand too well, much too well."

They reached the empty gun-room. Cecil threw open the hidden door.

"Will you go first or last?" he said to the girl. "Choose your own place."

The girl laughed.

"The door seemed to open easily," she remarked, "considering that it has not been used for so long."

"Never mind about that," Cecil said sharply. "Are you coming with us?"

"I am coming," Kate answered composedly, "and I will walk last."

"As you please," Cecil answered. "Come, Forrest, you may as well see this thing through with me."

As they stumbled along the narrow way, Cecil whispered in Forrest's ear.

"What are we going to do with her?"

"God knows!" Forrest answered. "Do you suppose that any one knows where she is? Who is she?"

"One of the village girls," Cecil answered, "an old sweetheart of mine. They are strange people, and have few friends. I doubt whether any one knows that she is out tonight."

Forrest passed on.

"If we are going to put our necks into the halter," he muttered, "a little extra trouble won't hurt us."

They paused before the door. The girl was looking at the padlock.

"A new padlock, I see," she remarked. "Listen!"

They all listened, and now there was no doubt about it. From inside the room they could hear the sound of a man, half singing, half moaning.

"Are those rabbits?" the girl asked, leaning forward, so that her eyes seemed to gleam like live coal through the darkness. "Cecil, you are being made a fool of by this man. I don't wish you any harm. Do the right thing now, and I'll stick by you. Let this man free, whoever he is. Don't listen to what he tells you," she added, pointing toward Forrest.

Cecil hesitated. Forrest, who was watching him closely, could not tell whether that hesitation was genuine or only a feint.

"It was only a joke, this, Kate," he muttered. "It was a joke which we have carried a little too far. Yes, you shall help me if you will. I have had enough of it. Go inside and see for yourself who is there."

Cecil threw open the door and Kate stepped boldly inside. Forrest entered last and remained near the threshold. Engleton started to his feet when he saw a third person.

"We have brought you a visitor," Forrest cried out. "You have complained of being lonely. You will not be lonely any longer."

Kate turned toward him.

"What do you mean?" she said. "We are going to leave here together, that man and myself, within the next few minutes."

"You lie!" Forrest answered fiercely. "You have thrust yourself into a matter which does not concern you, and you are going to take the consequences."

"And what might they be?" Kate asked slowly.

"They rest with him," Forrest answered, pointing toward Engleton. "There is a man there who was our friend until a few days ago. He dared to accuse us of cheating at cards, and if we let him go he will ruin us both. We are doing what any reasonable men must do. We are seeking to preserve ourselves. We have kept him here a prisoner, but he could have gained his freedom on any day by simply promising to hold his peace. He has declined, and the time has come when we can leave him no more. Tonight, if he is obstinate, we are going to throw him into the sea."

"And what about me?" Kate asked.

"You are going with him," Forrest answered. "If he is obstinate fool enough to chuck your life away and his, he must do it. Only he had better remember this," he added, looking across at Engleton, "it will mean two lives now, and not one."

Engleton rose to his feet slowly.

"Who is she?" he asked, pointing to the girl.

"I am Kate Caynsard, one of the village people here," she answered. "I heard you working tonight from outside. You heard me shout back?"

He nodded.

"Yes!" he said. "I know."

"I will tell the truth," the girl continued. "I was fool enough once to come here to meet that man" — she pointed to De la Borne — "that is all over. But one night I was restless, and I came wandering through the plantation here. It was then I saw from the other end that the place had been altered, and it struck me to listen there where the air-shaft is. I heard voices, and the next day they were all talking about the disappearance of Lord Ronald Engleton. You, I suppose," she added, "are Lord Ronald."

"I believe I was," he answered, with a little catch in his throat. "God knows who I am now! I give it up, De la Borne. If you are going to send the girl after me, I give it up. I'll sign anything you like. Only let me out of the damned place!"

A flash of triumph lit up Forrest's face, but it lasted only for a second. Kate had suddenly turned upon them, and was standing with her back to the wall. The hand which had been hidden in the folds of her dress so long, was suddenly outstretched. There was a roar which rang through the place like the rattle of artillery, the smell of gunpowder, and a little cloud of smoke. Through it they could see her face; her lips parted in a smile, the wild disorder of her hair, her sea-stained gown, her splendid pose, all seemed to make her the central figure of the little tableau.

"I have five more barrels," she said. "I fired that one to let you know that I was in earnest. Now if you do not let us go free, and without conditions, it will be you who will stay here instead of us, only you will stay here for ever!"

CHAPTER XVI

The smoke cleared slowly away. Engleton had risen to his feet, the light of a new hope blazing in his eyes. Forrest and Cecil de la Borne stood close together near the door, which still stood ajar. The girl, who stood with her back to the wall, saw their involuntary movement towards it, and her voice rang out sharp and clear.

"If you try it on I shoot!" she exclaimed. "You know what that means, Cecil. A pistol isn't a plaything with me."

Cecil looked no more toward the door. He came instead a little farther into the room.

"My dear Kate," he said, "we are willing to admit, Forrest and I, that we are beaten. You can do exactly what you like with us except leave us here. Our little joke with Engleton is at an end. Perhaps we carried it too far. If so, we must face the penalty. Take him away if you like. Personally I do not find this place attractive."

Kate lowered her revolver and turned to Engleton.

"Come over to my side," she said. "We are going to leave this place."

Engleton staggered towards her. He had always been thin, but he seemed to have lost more flesh in the last few days.

"For God's sake let's get out!" he said. "If I don't breathe some fresh air soon, it will be the end of me."

"In any order you please," Cecil de la Borne said smiling. "The only condition I make is that before you leave the place altogether, Kate, I have a few minutes' conversation with you. You can hold your pistol to my temple, if you like, while I talk, but there are a few things I must say."

"Afterwards, then," she answered. "We are going first out of the place. We shall turn seawards and wait for you. When you have come out, you will hand us your electric torches and go on in front."

"You are quite a strategist," Forrest remarked grimly. "Do as she says, Cecil. The sooner we are out of this, the better."

Kate passed her hand through Engleton's arm.

"Come along," she said. "Lean on me if you are not feeling well. Do not be afraid. They will not dare to touch us."

Engleton laughed weakly, but with the remains of the contempt with which he had always treated his jailers.

"Afraid of them!" he exclaimed contemptuously. "I fancy the boot has been on the other leg. Who you are, my dear young lady, I do not know, but upon my word you are the most welcome companion a man ever had."

The pair moved toward the doorway. Neither Forrest nor Cecil de la Borne made any effort to prevent their passing out. Kate turned a little to the right, and then stood with the revolver clasped in her hand.

"Please come out now," she said. "You will give your electric torch to him."

She indicated Engleton, who stretched out his hand. Cecil and Forrest obeyed her command to the letter. Engleton held the torch, and they all four made their way along the noisome passage. Forrest turned his head once cautiously toward his companion's, but Cecil shook his head.

"Wait," he whispered softly.

The thunder of the sea grew less and less distinct. Before them shone a faint glimmer of light. Soon they reached the three steps which led up into the gun-room. Cecil and Forrest climbed up. Kate and Engleton followed. Cecil carefully closed the door behind them.

"You see," he remarked, "we are reconciled to our defeat. Let us sit down for a moment and talk."

"Open the window and give me some brandy," Engleton said.

Kate felt him suddenly grow heavy upon her arm.

"Bring a chair quick," she ordered. "He is going to faint."

She bent over him, alarmed at the sudden change in his face. Her attention for one moment was relaxed. Then she felt her wrist seized in a grip of iron. The revolver, which she was still holding, fell to the ground, and Cecil calmly picked it up and thrust it into his pocket.

"You have played the game very well, Kate," he said. "Now I think it is our turn."

She looked at him indignantly, but without any trace of fear.

"You brute!" she exclaimed. "Can't you see that he has fainted? Do you want him to die here?"

"Not in the least," Cecil answered. "Here, Forrest, you take care of this," he added, passing the revolver over to him. "I'll look after Engleton."

He led him to an easy-chair close to the window. He opened it a few inches, and a current of strong fresh air came sweeping in. Then he poured some brandy into a glass and gave it to Kate.

"Let him sip this," he said. "Keep his head back. That's right. We will call a truce for a few moments. I am going to talk with my friend."

He turned away, and Kate, with a sudden movement, sprang toward the fireplace and pulled the bell. Cecil looked around and smiled contemptuously.

"It is well thought of," he remarked, "but unfortunately there is not a servant in the house. Go on ringing it, if you like. All that it can awake are the echoes."

Kate dropped the rope and turned back towards Engleton. The colour was coming slowly back to his cheeks. With an effort he kept from altogether losing consciousness.

"I am not going to faint," he said in a low tone. "I will not. Tell me, they have the pistol?"

"Yes," Kate answered, "but don't be afraid. I am not going back there again, nor shall they take you."

He pressed her hand.

"You are a plucky girl," he muttered. "Stick to me now and I'll never forget it. I've held out so long that I'm damned if I let them off their punishment now."

Cecil came slowly across the room.

"Feeling better, Engleton?" he asked.

Engleton turned his head.

"Yes," he answered, "I am well enough. What of it?"

"We'd better have an understanding," Cecil said.

"Have it, then, and be damned to you!" Engleton answered. "You won't get me alive down into that place again. If you are going to try, try."

"Come," Cecil said, "there is no need to talk like that. Why not pass your word to treat this little matter as a joke? It's the simplest way. Go up to your room, change your clothes and shave, have a drink with us, and take the morning train to town. It's not worth while risking your life for the sake of a little bit of revenge on us for having gone too far. I admit that we were wrong in keeping you here. You terrified us. Forrest has more enemies than friends and I am unknown in London. If you went to the club with your story, people would believe it. We shouldn't have a chance. That is why we were afraid to let you go back. Forget the last few days and cry quits."

"I'll see you damned first," Engleton answered.

Cecil's face changed a little.

"Well," he said, "I have made you a fair offer. If you refuse, I shall leave it to my friend Forrest to deal with you. You may not find him so easy, as I have been."

Kate stepped for a moment forward, and laid her hand on Cecil's shoulder.

"Mr. De la Borne," she said, "we don't want to have anything to say to your friend. We trust him less than you. Open the door and let us out."

"Where are you going to?" Cecil asked. "Engleton is not fit to walk anywhere."

"I am going to take him back home with me," Kate answered. "Oh, I can get him there all right. I am not afraid of that. He will have plenty of strength to walk away from this place."

"It is impossible, my dear Kate," Cecil answered. "Take my advice. Leave him to us. We will deal with him reasonably enough. Kate, listen."

He passed his arm through hers and drew her a little on one side.

"Kate," he said, "I'm afraid I haven't behaved exactly well to you. I got up in London amongst a lot of people who seemed to look at things so differently, and there were distractions, and I'm afraid that I forgot some of my promises. But I have never forgotten you. Why do you take the part of that miserable creature over there? He is just a young simpleton, who, because he was half drunk, dared to accuse us of cheating. We were obliged to keep him shut up until he took it back. Leave him to us. He shall come to no harm. I give you my word, and I will never forget it."

Kate looked at him a little curiously.

"Will you keep your promise?" she asked curiously.

Cecil hesitated, but only for a minute.

"Yes," he said, "I will even do that."

She withdrew her arm firmly, but without haste.

"Is that all you have to say?" she asked.

"I offer you my promise," he answered. "Isn't that worth something?"

"Something," she answered, "not much. I want no more to do with you, Mr. Cecil de la Borne. Don't think you can make terms with me for you can't. I only hope that you get punished for what you have done."

Cecil raised his hand as though about to strike her.

"You little cat!" he exclaimed. "We'll see the thing through, then. You are prisoners here just as much as though you were in the vault."

Forrest, who had spoken very little, came suddenly forward.

"We have talked too much," he said, "and wasted too much time. Let us have the issue before us in black and white. Engleton, are you well enough to understand what I say?"

"Perfectly," Engleton answered. "Go on."

"Will you sign a retraction of your charges against us, and pledge your word of honour never to repeat them, or to make any complaint, formal or otherwise, as to your detention here."

"I'm damned if I will!" Engleton answered.

"Consider what your refusal means first," Forrest said. "Open the passage door, Cecil."

Cecil pushed it back, and a little breath of the noxious odour stole into the room.

"You either make us that promise, Engleton," he said, "or as sure as I'm standing here, we'll drag you both down that passage, right to the end, and throw you into the sea."

"And hang for it afterwards," Engleton said, with a sneer.

"Not we," Forrest declared. "The currents down there are strange ones, and it would be many weeks before your bodies were recovered. Your character in London is pretty well known, and Kate here has been seen often enough on her way up to the Hall. People will soon put two and two together. There are a dozen places in the Spinney where one could slip off into the sea. Besides we shall have a little evidence to offer. Oh, there is nothing for us to fear, I can assure you. Now then. I can see it's no use arguing with you any longer."

"One moment," Kate said. "What about the young lady I left outside?"

Cecil turned upon her swiftly.

"Don't tell lies, Kate," he said. "It's a poor sort of tale that."

"At any rate it's no lie," Kate answered. "When I came to your front door, I left the young lady who was staying here only a few weeks ago, Miss Le Mesurier you called her, sitting in the barn waiting."

Cecil laughed scornfully.

"Did she drop from the clouds?" he asked.

"She has been staying at the farm," Kate answered, "for days. I brought her with me tonight because I thought that she might know something about Lord Ronald's disappearance. She is there waiting. If I do not return by daylight, she will go to the police."

"I think," Forrest remarked ironically, "that we will risk the young lady outside. Your story, my dear, is ingenious, but scarcely plausible. If you are ready, Cecil — "

The four of them were suddenly stupefied into a dead silence. Their eyes were riveted upon the door which led to the underground passage. Cecil's face was almost grotesque with the terrible writing of fear. Distinctly they could all hear footsteps stumbling along the uneven way. Forrest was first to recover the power of speech. He called out to Cecil from the other end of the room.

"Shut the door! Shut it, I say!"

Cecil took a quick step forward. Before he could reach the door, however, the girl had thrown her arms round his waist.

"You shall not close it," she cried.

"Who is it coming?" Cecil cried panting.

"God knows!" she answered. "They say the ghosts walk here."

He strove to loosen himself from her grasp, but he was powerless. Nevertheless he got a little nearer to the door. Forrest came swiftly across the room. Engleton struck at him with a chair, but the blow was harmless.

"Stand aside, Cecil," Forrest said. "I'll close it."

"I'm hanged if you will," was the sudden reply.

Andrew de la Borne stepped out of the darkness and stood upright, blinking and looking around in amazement.

CHAPTER XVII

Jeanne was sitting in the garden of the Caynsard farm. The excitement of the last twenty-four hours had left her languid. For once she lay and watched with idle, almost with indifferent eyes, the great stretch of marshes riven with the incoming sea. She saw the fishing boats that a few hours ago were dead inert things upon a bed of mud, come gliding up the tortuous water-ways. On the horizon was the sea bank, with its long line of poles, and the wires connecting the coastguard stations. They stood like silent sentinels, clean and distinct against the empty background. Jeanne sighed as she watched, and the thoughts came crowding into her head. It was a restful country this, a country of timeworn, mouldering grey churches, and of immemorial landmarks, a country where everything seemed fixed and restful, everything except the sea. A wave of self pity swept over her. After all she had lived a very little time to know so much unhappiness. Worse than all, this morning she was filled with apprehensions. She feared something. She scarcely knew what, or from what direction it might come. The song of the larks brought her no comfort. The familiar and beautiful places upon which she looked pleased her no more. She was glad when Kate Caynsard came out of the house and moved slowly towards her.

Kate, too, showed some of the signs of the recent excitement. There were black lines under her wonderful eyes, and she walked hesitatingly, without any of the firm splendid grace which made her movements a delight to watch. Jeanne was afraid at first that she was going to turn away, and called to her.

"Kate," she exclaimed, "I want you. Come here and talk to me."

Kate threw herself on to the ground by Jeanne's side.

"All the talking in the world," she murmured, "will not change the things that happened last night. They will not even smooth away the evil memories."

Jeanne was silent. There was a thought in her head which had been there twisting and biting its way in her brain through the silent hours of the night and again in her waking moments. She looked down towards her companion stretched at her feet.

"Kate," she said, "how did Mr. Andrew get the message that brought him to the Red Hall last night?"

"I sent it," Kate answered. "I sent him word that there were things going on at the Red Hall which I could not understand. I told him that I thought it would be well if he came."

"You knew his address?" Jeanne asked, a little coldly.

"Yes!" Kate answered.

"You have written him before, perhaps?" Jeanne asked.

"Yes!" the girl answered absently.

There was a short silence. Each of the two seemed occupied in her own thoughts. When Jeanne spoke again her manner was changed. The other girl noticed it, without being conscious of the reason.

"What has happened this morning, do you know?" Jeanne asked.

"They are all at the Red Hall still," Kate answered. "Major Forrest tried to leave this morning, but Mr. Andrew would not let him. He will not let either of them go away until Lord Ronald is well enough to say what shall be done."

"I wonder," Jeanne said, "what would have happened if Mr. Andrew had not arrived last night."

"God knows!" Kate answered. "He is a wily brute, the man Forrest. How was it that you," she added, "found Mr. Andrew?"

"I waited on the mound in the plantation," Jeanne said, "with my ear to the ground, and presently I heard a pistol shot and then a scuffle, and afterwards silence. I was frightened, and I made my way to the road and hurried along toward the village. Then I saw a cart and I stopped it, and inside was Mr. Andrew, on his way from Wells. I told him something of what was happening, and he put me in the cart and sent me back. Then he went on to the Red Hall."

Kate nodded slowly.

"I am glad that I sent for him," she said. "I am afraid that last night there would have been bloodshed if he had not come. When he was there there was not one who dared speak or move any more, except as he directed. He is very strong, and he was made, I think, to command men."

Jeanne's lips quivered for a moment. Her eyes were fixed upon the distant figure, motionless now, upon the raised sand-banks. Kate had turned her head toward the Red Hall, and was looking at one of the windows there as though her eyes would pierce the distance.

"Tell me," Jeanne asked. "I have seen you once with Mr. De la Borne. He is a great friend of yours?"

"He was," the girl at her feet whispered.

Jeanne found herself shaking. She stooped down.

"What do you mean?" she whispered.

Kate looked up from the ground. She raised herself a little. For a moment her eyes flashed.

"I mean," she said, "that before you came he was more than a friend. It was you who drove his thoughts of me away. You with your great fortune, and your childish, foreign ways. Oh, I talk like a fool, I know!" she said, springing up, "but I am not a fool. I do not hate you. I have never tried to do you any harm. It is not your fault. It is what one calls fate. Once," she cried, "we Caynsards lived along the coast there in a house greater than the Red Hall, and our lands were richer. Generation after generation of us have been pushed by fortune downwards and downwards. The men lose lands and money, and the women disgrace themselves, or creep into some corner to die with a broken heart. I talk to you as one of the villagers here. I know very well that I speak the dialect of the peasants, and that my words are ill-chosen. How can I help it? We are all paupers, every one of us. That is why sometimes I feel that I cannot breathe. That is why I do mad things, and people believe that I am indeed out of my mind."

She sprang to her feet. Jeanne tried to detain her.

"Let me talk to you for a little time, Kate," she begged. "You are none of the things you fancy, and I am very sure that Mr. De la Borne does not care for me, or for my fortune. Stay just for a minute."

But Kate was already gone. Jeanne could see her speeding down to the harbour, and a few minutes later gliding down the creek in her little catboat.

The Count de Brensault was angry, and he had not sufficient dignity to hide it. The Princess, in whose boudoir he was, regarded him from her sofa as one might look at some strange animal.

"My dear Count," she said, "it is not reasonable that you should be angry with me. Is it my fault that I am plagued with a stepdaughter of so extraordinary a temperament? She will return directly, or we shall find her. I am sure of it. The wedding can be arranged then as speedily as you wish. I give her to you. I consent to your marriage. What could woman do more?"

"That is all very well," the Count said, "all very well indeed, but I do not understand how it is that a young lady could disappear from her home like this, and that her guardian should know nothing about it. Where could she have gone to? You say that she had very little money. Why should she go? Who was unkind to her?"

"All that I did," the Princess answered, "was to tell her that she must marry you."

The Count twirled his moustache.

"Is it likely," he demanded, "that that should drive her away from her home? The idea of marriage, it may terrify these young misses at the first thought, but in their hearts they are very, very glad. Ah!" he added softly, "I have had some experience. I am not a boy."

The Princess looked at him. Whatever her thoughts may have been, her face remained inscrutable.

"No!" the Count continued, drawing his chair a little nearer to the Princess' couch, and leaning towards her, "I do not believe that it was the fear of marriage which drove little Jeanne to disappear."

"Then what do you believe, my dear Count?" the Princess asked.

His eyes seemed to narrow.

"Perhaps," he said significantly, "you may have thought that with her great fortune, and seeing me a little foolish for her, that you had not driven quite a good enough bargain, eh?"

"You insulting beast!" the Princess remarked.

The Count grinned. He was in no way annoyed.

"Ah!" he said. "I am a man whom it is not easy to deceive. I have seen very much of the world, and I know the ways of women. A woman who wants money, my dear Princess, is very, very clever, and not too honest."

"Your experiences, Count," the Princess said, "may be interesting, but I do not see how they concern me."

"But they might concern you," the Count said, "if I were to speak plainly; if, for instance, I were to double that little amount we spoke of."

"Do you mean to insinuate," the Princess remarked, "that I know where Jeanne is now? That it is I who have put her out of the way for a little time, in order to make a better bargain with you?"

The Count bowed his head.

"A very clever scheme," he declared, "a very clever scheme indeed."

The Princess drew a little breath. Then she looked at the Count and suddenly laughed. After all, it was not worth while to be angry with such a creature. Besides, if Jeanne should turn up, she might as well have the extra money.

"You give me credit, I fear," she said, "for being a cleverer woman than I am, but as a matter of curiosity, supposing I am able to hand you over Jeanne very shortly, would you agree to double the little amount we have spoken of?"

"I will double it," the Count declared solemnly. "You see when I wish for a thing I am generous. I can only hope," he added, with a peculiar smile, "Miss Jeanne may soon make her reappearance." There was a knock at the door. The Princess looked up, frowning. Her maid put her head cautiously in.

"I am sorry to disturb you, madam, against your orders," she said, "but Miss Jeanne has just arrived."

CHAPTER XVIII

The Count opened his mouth. It was his way of expressing supreme astonishment. The Princess sat bolt upright on her couch and gazed at Jeanne with wide-open and dilated eyes. Curiously enough it was the Count who first recovered himself.

"Is it a game, this?" he asked softly. "You press the button and the little girl appears. That means that I increase the stakes and the prize pops up."

The Princess rose to her feet. She crossed the room to meet Jeanne with outstretched arms.

"Shut up, you fool!" she said to the Count in passing. "Jeanne my child," she added, "is it really you?"

Jeanne accepted the proffered embrace, without enthusiasm. She recognized the Count, however, with a little wave of colour.

"Yes," she said quietly, "I have come back. I am sorry I went away. It was a mistake, a great mistake."

"You have driven us nearly wild with anxiety," the Princess declared. "Where have you been to?"

"Yes!" the Count echoed, fixing his eyes upon her, "where have you been to?"

Jeanne behaved with a composure which astonished them both. She calmly unbuttoned her gloves and seated herself in the easy-chair.

"I have been to Salthouse," she said.

"What! back to the Red Hall?" the Princess exclaimed.

Jeanne shook her head.

"No!" she said, "I have been in rooms at a farmhouse there, Caynsard's farm. I went away because I did not like the life here, and because my stepmother," she continued, turning toward the Count, "seemed determined that I should marry you. I thought that I would go away into the country, somewhere where I could think quietly. I went to Salthouse because it was the only place I knew."

"You are the maddest child!" the Princess exclaimed.

Jeanne smiled, a little wearily.

"If I have been mad," she said, "I have come to my senses again."

The Count leaned toward her eagerly.

"I trust," he said, "that that means that you are ready now to obey your stepmother, and to make me very, very happy."

Jeanne looked at him deliberately.

"It depends," she said, "upon circumstances."

"Tell me what they are quickly," the Count declared. "I am impatient. I cannot bear that you keep me waiting. Let me know of my happiness."

The Princess was suddenly uneasy. There was one weak point in her schemes, a weakness of her own creating. Ever since she had told Jeanne the truth about her lack of fortune, she had felt that it was a mistake. Suppose she should be idiot enough to give the thing away! The Princess felt her heart beat fast at the mere supposition. There was something about Jeanne's delicate oval face, her straight mouth and level eyebrows, which somehow suggested that gift which to the Princess was so incomprehensible in her sex, the gift of honesty. Suppose Jeanne were to tell the Count the truth!

"First of all, then," Jeanne said, "I must ask you whether my stepmother has told the truth about myself and my fortune."

The Princess knew then that the game was up. She sank back upon the sofa, and at that moment she would have declared that there was nothing in the world more terrible than an ungrateful and inconsiderate child.

"The truth?" the Count remarked, a little puzzled. "I know only what the world knows, that you are the daughter of Carl le Mesurier, and that he left you the residue of one of the greatest fortunes in Europe."

Jeanne drew a letter from her pocket.

"The Princess," she remarked, "must have forgotten to tell you. This great fortune that all the world has spoken of, and that seems to have made me so famous, has been all the time something of a myth. It has existed only in the imaginations of my kind friends. A few days ago my stepmother here told me of this. I wrote at once to Monsieur Laplanche, my trustee. She would not let me send the letter. When I was at Salthouse, however, I wrote again, and this time I had a reply. It is here. There is a statement," she continued, "which covers many pages, and which shows exactly how my father's fortune was exaggerated, how securities have dwindled, and how my stepmother's insisting upon a very large allowance during my school-days, has eaten up so much of the residue. There is left to me, it appears, a sum of fourteen thousand pounds. That is a very small fortune, is it not?" she asked calmly.

The Count was gazing at her as one might gaze upon a tragedy.

"It is not a fortune!" he exclaimed. "It is not even a dot! It is nothing at all, a year's income, a trifle."

"Nevertheless," Jeanne said calmly, "it is all that I possess. You see," she continued, "I have come back to my stepmother to tell her that if I am bound by law to do as she wishes until I am of age, I will be dutiful and marry the man whom she chooses for me, but I wish to tell you two things quite frankly. The first you have just heard. The second is that I do not care for you in the least, that in fact I rather dislike you."

The Princess buried her head in her hands. She was not anxious to look at any one just then, or to be looked at. The Count rose to his feet. There were drops of perspiration upon his forehead. He was distracted.

"Is this true, madam?" he asked of the Princess.

"It is true," she admitted.

He leaned towards her.

"What about my three thousand pounds?" he whispered. "Who will pay me back that? It is cheating. That money has been gained by what you call false pretences. There is punishment for that, eh?"

The Princess dabbed at her eyes with a little morsel of lace handkerchief.

"One must live," she murmured. "It was not I who talked about Jeanne's fortune. It was all the world who said how rich she was. Why should I contradict them? I wanted a place once more in the only Society in Europe which counts, English society. There was only one way and I took it. So long as people believed Jeanne to be the heiress of a great fortune, I was made welcome wherever I chose to go. That is the truth, my dear Count."

"It is all very well," the Count answered, "but the money I have advanced you?"

"You took your own risk," the Princess answered, coldly. "I was not to know that you were expecting to repay yourself out of Jeanne's fortune. It is not too late. You are not married to her."

"No," the Count said slowly, "I am not married to her."

The Princess watched him from the corners of her eyes. He was evidently very much distracted. He walked up and down the room. Every now and then he glanced at Jeanne. Jeanne was very pale, but she wore a hat with a small green quill which he had once admired. Certainly she had an air, she was distinguished. There was something vaguely provocative about her, a charm which he could not help but feel. He stopped short in the middle of his perambulations. It was the moment of his life. He felt himself a hero.

"Madam," he said, addressing the Princess, "I have been badly treated. There is no one who would not admit that. I have been deceived — a man less kind than I might say robbed. No matter. I forget it all. I forget my disappointment, I forget that this young lady whom you offer me for a wife has a dot so pitifully small that it counts for nothing. I take her. I accept her. Jeanne," he added, moving towards her, "you hear? It is because I love you so very, very much."

Jeanne shrank back in her chair.

"You mean," she cried, "that you are willing to take me now that you know everything, now that you know I have so little money? You mean that you want to marry me still?"

The Count assented graciously. Never in the course of his whole life, had he admired himself so much.

"I forget everything," he declared, with a little wave of the hand, "except that I love you, and that you are the one woman in the world whom I wish to make the Comtesse de Brensault. Mademoiselle permits me?"

He stooped and raised her cold hand to his lips. Jeanne looked at him with the fascinated despair of some stricken animal. The Princess rose to her feet. It was wonderful, this — a triumph beyond all thought.

"Jeanne, my child," she said, "you are the most fortunate girl I know, to have inspired a devotion so great. Count," she added, "you are wonderful. You deserve all the happiness which I am sure will come to you."

The Count looked as though he were perfectly convinced of it. All the same he whispered in her ear a moment later —

"You must pay me back that three thousand pounds!"

CHAPTER XIX

For the Princess it was a day full of excitements. The Count had only just reluctantly withdrawn, and Jeanne had gone to her room under the plea of fatigue, when Forrest was shown in. She started at the look in his drawn face.

"Nigel," she exclaimed hastily, "is everything all right?"

He threw himself into a chair.

"Everything," he answered, "is all wrong. Everything is over."

The Princess saw then that he had aged during the last few days, that this man whose care of himself had kept him comparatively youthful looking, notwithstanding the daily routine of an unwholesome life, was showing signs at last of breaking down. There were lines about his eyes, little baggy places underneath. He dragged his feet across the carpet as though he were tired. The Princess pushed up an easy-chair and went herself to the sideboard.

"Give me a little brandy," he said, "or rather a good deal of brandy. I need it."

The Princess felt her own hand shake. She brought him a tumbler and sat down by his side.

"You had to kill him?" she asked, in a whisper. "Is it that?"

Forrest set down his glass — empty.

"No!" he answered. "We were going to, when a mad woman who lives there got into the place and found us out. We had them safe, the two of them, when the worst thing happened which could have befallen us. Andrew de la Borne broke in upon us."

The Princess listened with set face.

"Go on," she said. "What happened?"

"The game was up so far as we were concerned," he answered. "Cecil crumpled up before his brother, and gave the whole show away. There was nothing left for me to do but to wait and hear what they had to say, before I decided whether or no to make my graceful exit from the stage."

"Go on," she commanded. "What happened exactly?"

"We were kept there," he continued, "until this morning, waiting until Engleton was well enough to make up his mind what to do. The end is simple enough. Considering that but for that girl's intervention Engleton would have been in the sea by now, and he knows it, I suppose it might have been worse. I have signed a paper undertaking to leave England within forty-eight hours, and never to show myself in this country again. Further, I am not to play cards at any time with any Englishman."

"Is that all?" the Princess asked.

"Yes!" Forrest answered. "I suppose you would say that they have let me off lightly. I wish I could feel so. If ever a man was sick of those dirty disreputable foreign places, where one holds on to life and respectability only with the tips of one's fingernails, I am. I think I shall chuck it, Ena. I am tired of those foreign crowds, suspicious, semi-disreputable. There's something wrong with every one of them. Even the few decent ones you know very well speak to you because you are in a foreign country, and would cut you in Pall Mall."

"It isn't so bad as that," the Princess said calmly. "There are some of the places worth living in. You must live a quieter life, spend less, and find distractions. You used to be so fond of shooting and golf."

He laughed hardly.

"How am I to live," he demanded, "away from the card-tables? What do you suppose my income is? A blank! It is worse than a blank, for I owe bills which I shall never pay. How am I going to live from day to day unless I go on the same infernal treadmill. I am an adventurer, I know," he went on, "but what is one to do who has the tastes and education of a gentleman, and not even money enough to buy a farm and work with one's hands for a living?"

The Princess moved to the window and back again.

"I, too, Nigel," she said, "have had shocks. Jeanne has come back. She has been at Salthouse all the time."

"It was probably she, then, who sent for De la Borne," Forrest said wearily.

"Perhaps so," the Princess assented, "but listen to this. It will surprise you. She came back and she told De Brensault in this room only a short while ago that her supposed fortune was a myth. De Brensault took it like a lamb. He wants to marry her still."

Forrest looked up in amazement.

"And will he?" he asked.

"Oh, I do not know!" the Princess answered. "Nigel, I am sick of life myself. There are times when everything you have been trying for seems not worth while, when even one's fundamental ideas come tottering down. Just now I feel as though every stone in the foundation of what has seemed to me to mean life, is rotten and insecure. I am tired of it. Shall I tell you what I feel like doing?"

"Yes!" he answered.

"I have a little house in Silesia, where I am still a great lady, half-a-dozen servants, perhaps, farms which bring in a trifle of money. I think I will go and live there. I think I will get up in the mornings as Jeanne does, and try to love my mountains, and go about amongst my people, and try to spell life with different letters. Come with me, Nigel. There is shooting and fishing there, and horses wild enough for even you to find pleasure in riding. We have tried many things in life. Let us make one last throw, and try the land of Arcady."

He looked at her, at first in amazement. Afterwards some change seemed to come into his face, called there, perhaps, by what he saw in hers.

"Ena," he said, "you mean it?"

"Absolutely," she answered. "Fortunately we are both free, and we can set our peasants an absolutely respectable example. You shall be farmer and I will be housewife. Nigel, it is an inspiration."

He bent over her fingers.

"I wonder," he murmured, "if there is good enough left in me to make it worth your while."

Late that afternoon another caller thundered at the door of the house in Berkeley Square. The Duke of Westerham desired to see Miss Le Mesurier. The butler was respectful but doubtful. Miss Le Mesurier had just arrived from a journey and was lying down. The Duke, however, was insistent. He waited twenty minutes in a small back morning-room and presently Jeanne came in to him.

He held out his hands.

"Little girl," he said, "you know what you promised. I am afraid that you have forgotten."

She smiled pitifully.

"No," she said, "I have not forgotten. I went away alone because I had to go, because I wanted to be quite alone and quite quiet. Now I have come home, and there is no one who can help me at all."

"Rubbish!" he answered. "There was never trouble in the world where a friend couldn't help. What is it now?"

She shook her head.

"I cannot tell you," she said, "only I am going to marry the Count de Brensault."

"I'm hanged if you are!" the Duke declared vigorously. "Look here, Miss Jeanne. This is your stepmother's doing. I know all about it. Don't you believe that in this country you are obliged to marry any one whom you don't want to."

"But I do want to," Jeanne answered, "or rather I don't mind whom I do marry, or whether I marry any one or no one."

The Duke was grave.

"I thought," he said, "that my friend Andrew had a chance."

Her face was suddenly burning.

"Mr. Andrew," she said, "does not want me; I mean that it is impossible. Oh, if you please," she added, bursting into tears, "won't you let me alone? I am going to marry the Count de Brensault. I have quite made up my mind. Perhaps you have not heard that it is all a mistake about my having a great fortune. The Count de Brensault is very kind, and he is going to marry me although I have no money."

The Duke stared at her for several moments. Then he rang the bell.

"Will you tell your mistress," he said to the servant, "that the Duke of Westerham would be exceedingly obliged if she would spare him five minutes here and now."

The man bowed and withdrew. The Princess came almost at once.

"Madam," the Duke said, "I trust that you will forgive my sending for you, but I am very much interested in the happiness of our little friend Miss Jeanne here. She tells me that she is going to marry the Count de Brensault, that she has lost her fortune and she is evidently very unhappy. Will you forgive me if I ask you whether this marriage is being forced upon her?"

The Princess hesitated.

"No," she said, "it is not that. Jeanne told him of her loss of fortune. She told him, too, without any prompting from me, that she would marry him if he still wished it. That is all that I know."

The Duke bowed. He moved a few steps across towards the Princess.

"Princess," he said, "will you make a friend? Will you let me take your little girl to my sister's for say one week? You shall have her back then, and you shall do as you will with her."

"Willingly," the Princess answered. "I am only anxious that she should be happy."

The Duke marvelled then at the sincerity in her tone. Nevertheless, for fear she should change her mind, he hurried Jeanne out of the house into his brougham.

CHAPTER XX

"So this," the Duke said, "is your wonderful land."

"Is there anything like it in the world?" Jeanne asked as she stood bareheaded on the grass-banked dyke with her face turned seaward.

Above their heads the larks were singing. To their right stretched the marshes and pasture land, as yet untouched by the sea, glorious with streaks of colour, fragrant with the perfume of wild lavender and mosses. To their left, through the opening in the sandbanks, came streaming the full tide, rushing up into the land, making silver water-ways of muddy places, bringing with it all the salt and freshness and joy of the sea. Over their heads the seagulls cried. Far away a heron lifted its head from a tuft of weeds, and sent his strange call travelling across the level distance.

"Oh, it is beautiful to be here again!" Jeanne said. "Even though it hurts," she added, in a lower tone, "it is beautiful."

A little boat came darting down the shallows. Kate Caynsard stood up and waved her hand. Jeanne waved back. A sudden flush of colour stained her cheeks. Her first impulse seemed to be to turn away. She conquered it, however, and beckoned to the girl, who ran her boat close to them.

"My last sail," the girl cried, as she stepped to land. "I am saying good-bye to all these wonderful places, Miss Le Mesurier," she added. "Tomorrow we are going to sail for Canada."

Jeanne looked at her in amazement.

"You are going to Canada?" she asked.

The girl, too, was surprised.

"Have you not heard?" she said. "I thought, perhaps, that Mr. Andrew might have told you. Cecil and I are sailing tomorrow, directly after we are married. He has bought a farm out there."

Jeanne felt for a moment that the beautiful world was spinning round her. She clutched at the Duke's arm.

"You are going to Canada with Cecil?" she exclaimed.

"Of course," Kate answered, a little shyly. "I thought, in fact I know that I told you about him. Won't you wish me joy?" she added, holding out her hand a little timidly.

Jeanne grasped it. To the girl's surprise Jeanne's eyes were full of tears.

"Oh, I am so foolish!" she declared. "I have been so mad. I thought — You said Mr. De la Borne."

"Hang it all!" the Duke exclaimed. "I believe you thought that she meant our friend Andrew. Don't you know that all the world here half the time calls Cecil, Mr. De la Borne, and Andrew, Mr. Andrew?"

Kate looked behind her, and touched the Duke on the sleeve.

"Wouldn't you like, sir," she asked, a little timidly, "to come for a sail with me?"

The Duke saw what she saw, and notwithstanding his years and his weight, he clambered into the little boat. Jeanne turned round and walked slowly towards the man who came so swiftly along the dyke. It was a dream! She felt that it must be a dream!

Andrew, with his gun over his shoulder, his rough tweed clothes splashed with black mud, gazed at her as though she were an apparition. Then he saw something in her face which told him so much that he forgot the little catboat, barely out of sight, he forgot the little red-roofed village barely a mile away, he forgot the lone figures of the shrimpers, standing like sentinels far away in the salt pools. He took Jeanne into his arms, and he felt her lips melt upon his.

"The Duke was right, then," he murmured a moment later, as he stood back for a moment, his face transformed with the new thing that had come into his life.

"Dear man!" Jeanne murmured.

They watched the boat gliding away in the distance.

"I believe," he declared, "that they went away on purpose."

She laughed as they scrambled down on to the marsh, and turned toward the place where he had first met her.

"I believe they did," she answered.

THE END